Village Secrets

TALES FROM TURNHAM MALPAS

Rebecca Shaw

An Orion paperback

First published in Great Britain in 1998
by Orion
This paperback edition published in 1999
by Orion Books,
an imprint of The Orion Publishing Group Ltd,
Orion House, 5 Upper St Martin's Lane,
London WC2H 9EA

An Hachette UK company

11 13 15 17 19 20 18 16 14 12

Reissued 2010

A CIP catalogue record for this book is available
from the British Library.

ISBN 978-0-7528-1762-0

Printed and bound in Great Britain by
Clays Ltd, St Ives plc

The Orion Publishing Group's policy is to use papers that
are natural, renewable and recyclable products and
made from wood grown in sustainable forests. The logging
and manufacturing processes are expected to conform to
the environmental regulations of the country of origin.

www.orionbooks.co.uk

INHABITANTS OF TURNHAM MALPAS

Sadie Beauchamp	Retired widow and mother of Harriet Charter-Plackett.
Willie Biggs	Verger at St Thomas à Becket.
Sylvia Biggs	His wife and housekeeper at the rectory.
Sir Ronald Bissett	Retired trades union leader.
Lady Sheila Bissett	His wife.
Louise Bissett	Their daughter and Secretary at Turnham House.
James (Jimbo) Charter-Plackett	Owner of the Village Store.
Harriet Charter-Plackett	His wife.
Fergus, Finlay, Flick and Fran	Their children.
Alan Crimble	Barman at The Royal Oak.
Linda Crimble	Runs the post office at the Village Store.
Pat Duckett	Village school caretaker.
Dean and Michelle	Her children.
Bryn Fields	Licensee of The Royal Oak.
Georgie Fields	His wife.
Craddock Fitch	Owner of Turnham House.
Jimmy Glover	Taxi driver.
Revd. Peter Harris MA (Oxon)	Rector of the parish.
Dr Caroline Harris	His wife.
Alex and Beth	Their children.
Barry Jones	Estate carpenter.
Mrs Jones	His mother.
Jeremy Mayer	Manager at Turnham House.
Venetia Mayer	His wife.
Liz Neal	Playgroup leader.
Kate Pascoe	New head teacher.
Sergeant	Village policeman.
Ellie	His wife.
Greenwood Stubbs	Head gardener at Turnham House.
Sir Ralph Templeton	Retired from the diplomatic service.
Lady Muriel Templeton	His wife.
Dicky Tutt	Scout leader.
Bel Tutt	Assistant in the village store.
Vera Wright	Cleaner at the nursing home in Penny Fawcett.
Don Wright	Her husband.
Rhett Wright	Their grandson.

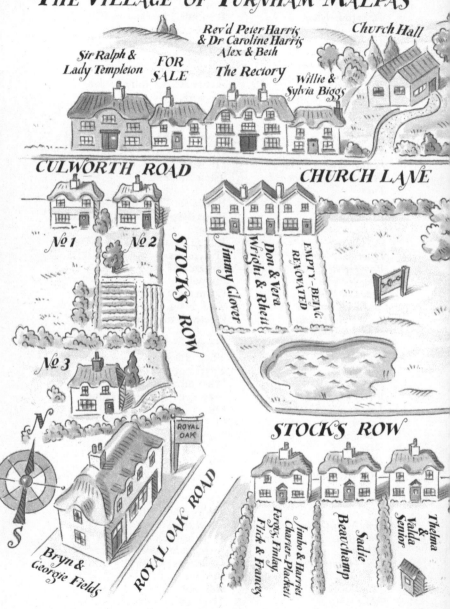

THE VILLAGE OF TURNHAM MALPAS

Rev'd Peter Harris
& Dr Caroline Harris
Alex & Beth

Church Hall

Sir Ralph &
Lady Templeton

FOR
SALE

The Rectory

Willie &
Sylvia Biggs

CULWORTH ROAD

CHURCH LANE

No 1

No 2

STOCKS ROW

Jimmy Glover

Don & Vera
Wright & Rhett

EMPTY – BEING
RENOVATED

No 3

ROYAL
OAK

STOCKS ROW

N

S

ROYAL OAK ROAD

Bryn &
Georgie Fields

Jimbo & Harriet
Charter-Plackett
Fergy, Finlay,
Flick & Fran

Sadie
Beauchamp

Thelma &
Valda
Senior

Chapter 1

'She's here, Jimbo – Miss Pascoe! We've seen her car. It's just pulled up outside the school-house. She's got here earlier than we expected. Where's that box of stuff? Hurry up, we're waiting!'

Jimbo was at the till taking money. He broke off to pick up a cardboard box from behind the counter. 'Give her my regards. Here it is. Put the carrier bag in the drinks fridge in with it, will you? There's milk and butter and things in there, didn't want it going off.'

Pat Duckett eagerly took charge of the box and the carrier bag and Hetty Hardaker held open the door while she squeezed through.

'You know, Pat, Jimbo really is very generous. I just hope she appreciates it. Here, let me take the carrier bag.'

'Right, thanks. Well, you'll have her to deal with more than me, being a teacher – I'm only the caretaker. I don't mind telling you it'll be a breath of fresh air, it will. Nothing wrong with old Mr Palmer, but he did need a kick in the pants as you might say didn't he? A shaking-up like.'

'He did, but he was still a good teacher. I shall miss him.'

'Too right, so shall I.' Across the road, Pat saw a young woman dressed in black struggling to get a huge cat basket out of the boot of her car. 'There she is! Good morning, Miss Pascoe! Welcome to the school.'

Hetty Hardaker's greeting was rather more reserved than Pat's but just as sincere. 'Welcome, Miss Pascoe.'

Kate put the basket down beside the car and held out her hand. 'Kate, if you please, and it's Ms Pascoe to the children. Nice to see you again, Hetty. Looking forward to working with you. You've been here such a long time, I shall look to you for advice.' She turned to Pat. 'And you must be the caretaker. You were away when I visited the school.'

'Not away, no such luck, but blinking ill with one of them bugs you get nowadays.'

'Oh, that's right. I remember the rector telling me.'

Hetty indicated the box Pat was carrying. 'This is a "welcome to Turnham Malpas gift" from Jimbo Charter-Plackett at the Store. There's bread and tins and things, and in here' – she held up the carrier bag – 'is some milk and butter and cheese too, just to help you along.'

'The fridge is switched on, I did that yesterday,' Pat said eagerly.

'That's very kind. You wouldn't get that in a city school, would you?'

Hetty agreed. 'I don't think you would. Look, we'll put these inside for you and leave you to get settled in.'

Pat hitched the box a little higher, for it was beginning to slip from her grasp. 'The door's open, I left the keys on the windowsill in case I wasn't here in time.'

She followed Ms Pascoe inside. Somehow, despite having given the house a good clean, Pat felt the house wasn't 'right' for Ms Pascoe. Didn't suit her personality. Too faded, too masculine. Still, that was up to her. She was a modern young thing – well, not that young – thirty perhaps. She'd make some changes and not half. Time would tell. Pat hoped she wouldn't make too many changes too soon. New broom and all that.

'I don't think you could have chosen a colder day. Still no snow yet, thank goodness. I hear you've been teaching in Africa. Bit of a change, coming here in winter.'

'Well, I've been back in England for six months now, so I'm getting acclimatised, thanks. You've been more than kind. I won't hold you up.'

Seeing it as a dismissal Hetty began to leave followed by Pat, who in reality would have loved to stay for a chat. She made a stab at prolonging the conversation. 'Hope you get settled in all right, *Ms* Pascoe. If you've any problems, give me a bell. The phone's connected like you asked and I've put my number by it – just in case.'

'Why, thank you, that's very kind. Thank you too, Hetty, for taking the time to welcome me. See you soon. Bye bye.'

The two of them walked across the school playground without speaking. They turned to wave and Kate waved back.

When they were well out of earshot in Jacks Lane, Pat said, 'Dad'll be home for lunch soon, I must be off. She seems OK.'

'She does, although I'll reserve my judgement yet awhile. Bye Pat, thanks for coming, I'm sure she appreciated it.'

Kate Pascoe dumped the heavy basket beside the schoolhouse door and, full of anticipation, looked up at the stone lintel above her head. A.D. *1855*. Like Pat had said, the keys had been left for her inside on the windowsill. Huge old keys – good grief, they could belong to a prison! Now, alone, she could take time to savour the place. There came a faint musty smell to her nostrils. She let Cat out of her basket and watched her step swiftly down the narrow passage to the first room. Kate followed more slowly.

The room had windows looking out to the side of the playground, curious old arched windows giving a kind of churchified feeling to the place – to remind the head teacher that this was a Church of England school and that he or she must act accordingly? Kate mused.

The walls were a boring beige – a typical old-fashioned bachelor choice. The fireplace was a kind of 1930s tiled affair, a neat fan of newspaper concealing the grate. When she pushed open the kitchen door she had the distinct feeling that it really *was* 1855. A huge butler sink, bleached a scorching white, with a wooden draining board stood in one corner, the brass taps above the sink burnished bright. Beside what had been a fireplace, but which was now covered by a sheet of plywood, was a large cupboard, majestic in its proportions. Everywhere was clean but that was the nicest thing one could say about it. Someone had made an effort. The kitchen was large enough to have a table in, she'd do that. There was, thank heavens, plumbing for a washing machine and an outlet for a dryer, and several power points. Next to the sink stood an old and stately cooker. It worked! The gas flame flared busily blue when she turned it on. It had been cleaned, too. How many teachers had cooked a lonely supper on it? Kate wondered.

She emptied the carrier bag Jimbo had sent and was storing the contents away in the fridge, though she wouldn't be able to eat most of it, when there came a knock at the front door.

Standing outside, well-wrapped up against the cold, was a well-dressed lady holding a plastic cake box.

'Good day to you, Miss Pascoe. Welcome to Turnham Malpas and to the school. My name's Muriel Templeton.'

'Good day to you too, Miss Templeton. Do come in. It's too cold to stand outside.'

'I'm not staying, not when you're so busy. I've just called with a cake for you. Home-made – chocolate. Mr Palmer had a sweet tooth; I thought perhaps you might have, too.'

Kate studied her visitor's delicate features and white hair. There was a shy quality about her but at the same time a kind of strength. The light-blue eyes looked kind.

'Well, Miss Templeton, you really are nice. You're my second lot of visitors and I haven't been here more than about fifteen minutes!'

Muriel beamed with pleasure. 'Oh well, you see, we're a very friendly village and we're so glad to have fresh blood in the school. I do hope you like living here, though I don't know how you possibly couldn't. It's so lovely hereabouts. My husband suggested I called . . .'

'Oh, I beg your pardon, you're *Mrs* Templeton.'

'Truth to tell, I'm Lady Templeton though I'm still not used to it myself.'

'I see. Well, Lady Templeton, thank you so much for the cake. It sounds absolutely delicious.'

'Has the rector called yet?'

'No, not yet, but he promised he would.'

'Well, he will then. He always keeps his word. Right, I'll leave you to get on. We live along Church Lane – come to call anytime if you're in need of help. Keep the church on your right and we're the fourth house along.'

'Thank you. I'll remember if I'm in need of help.'

'Bye bye then. See you in church!' Muriel waved as she left the school playground.

Kate put the cake box on the kitchen worktop and

carried on with her familiarisation tour of the house. The bathroom was downstairs. Brass taps, high-sided cast-iron bath, a washbasin large enough to bath a baby in, and a lavatory boasting a high cistern and chain for flushing. Upstairs, the one huge bedroom was again masculine in taste, with bare stained boards, a single curtain rail at each of the two windows. There were no clean patches on the wall to show where pictures had hung. Whoever had cleaned it for her had done a thorough job. It might be old-fashioned, but it was scrupulously clean.

Cat had investigated the entire house by now and given her approval by sitting down in front of the empty grate and washing her face. There was an hour to go before the van arrived with their furniture. Kate went out to the car again, and began lugging in boxes and bags – some for the bedroom, some for the kitchen, some for the living room. It had character, had this place, oh yes – a feeling of years long gone and plenty of atmosphere. Cat liked it and that was good. Never lived in England before and yet she'd taken to it as if she'd lived there all her life.

When she'd emptied the car, Kate went to take a look at the school from the outside. The windows were high and only by standing on tiptoes could she see anything at all. There were four classrooms: one for the playgroup, one for the Infants and two for the Juniors. She could just manage to see into the kitchen, which appeared clean and quite modern. A spotless roller towel awaited the beginning of term. The windows to the hall were even higher and she couldn't see anything at all.

Back at the house she wandered around the ground floor, then explored the upstairs again. It would take her one day to get straight, she decided, and then she'd decorate room by room. Rich dark colours, bright curtains, and that awkward corner in the bedroom where the ceiling sloped and one couldn't quite stand would be just right for . . . The sound of voices brought her back to earth.

'Hello, any one at 'ome?'

Kate made the removal men a mug of tea each and supervised where she wanted her furniture placing. Her books would have to stay in their cardboard boxes till she bought some bookshelves. Some, her special ones, would go upstairs in that awkward corner.

Cat observed all the activity from her position on the living-room windowsill. After their experience with the animal when they'd been loading the van, the men walked by her with respect. The excuse for her attacking them was that Cat was nervous, having just come out of quarantine, but the scratch on Bert's leg was deep enough, nervous or not. His trouser leg kept sticking to the blood as he walked. He quite fancied going to the hospital for a tetanus; you never could tell nowadays, specially when the damn creature had been in Africa. Yes, he decided: he'd finish this job and off he'd go.

There came a knock at the door. 'Hello, it's Peter Harris.'

One of the men called upstairs, 'Vicar's 'ere, Miss!'

Kate went downstairs to welcome him. 'How nice to see you again, Rector. Do come in.'

'I won't if you don't mind, just called to see if you found everything all right?'

'Oh yes, thank you. Bit hectic moving in, but everything's fine.'

'Here are flowers for you from my wife. She thought they might help to make the school-house more welcoming.'

'That is lovely of her – please give her my heartfelt thanks. They smell wonderful.'

'Good, glad you like them. Pat Duckett said she would clean the house for you, open a few windows and such for a while. It's been nearly six months since

Michael Palmer left, so we felt it needed an airing despite the cold.'

'Couldn't be cleaner.'

'Heating working OK?'

'I haven't noticed!'

'Let me know if there's anything we can do for you, won't you? The rectory's two doors beyond the church.'

'Of course. Thanks for calling.' Kate stood at the door and watched him go. Well over six feet tall, broad-shouldered, good-looking, reddish-blond hair . . . he didn't look anything like the kind of rector she'd come to expect from books and films. It was his intense, all-seeing blue eyes of which she would have to be wary. She felt he could see deep inside her, and that would never do.

Kate stepped out of the door to look at the small patch of ground that was the school-house garden. Winter made it difficult to tell what grew there; she'd have to wait till the spring to find out. Of course, there were her special plants in plastic bags in the kitchen which she would have to get in quickly before they died.

For Cat's sake, she managed to get a cosy fire going in the living-room grate. She'd found wood neatly chopped and a supply of kindling in the small shed at the side of the back door, a large box of matches by the cooker. Someone wanted to make her welcome. She left Cat and, taking her set of keys, wandered slowly across in the dark to the main door of the school.

It was the largest key that opened it. The narrow passage which served as a cloakroom for some of the children's coats – obviously the infants for the pegs had nursery animal pictures beside each of them – gave off the usual school smell – a mixture of polish, disinfectant and that other, mysterious ingredient of which all English schools smelled. It excited her. What an opportunity to bring stimulus and excitement into the lives of these pliable young children. The sophistication of town children didn't lend itself to her kind of teaching. She needed fresh open young minds, untainted by city streets and scepticism. Innocence – that was it.

Kate had seen the head teacher's office when she'd visited the school, but she'd forgotten how small it was – scarcely more than a cupboard. There was a smaller key on the ring and she found it opened the filing cabinet squeezed between the washbasin and the hanging space the staff used for their coats.

The records were neatly written, indeed fastidiously written, with wry comments such as: '*just like his father*' or '*lazy like her two sisters*'. That must be satisfying, to have such a stable community. They'd said at the interview that Michael Palmer had been at the school for years and years. She could understand now she was here, why he'd taken so long to leave.

It felt cold in the school and Kate wished she'd put on her coat. She locked the main door with the huge key; it was a solid, heavy wooden door – obviously the original one. What vibes there'd be in this building! She could feel them already – the spirits of children long gone into the world. Kate wondered what kind of a success or otherwise they'd all made of their lives.

Back in the house she made herself a drink while Cat went out for a stroll. She knew Cat would be back. There was no running away, ever, for her. The two of them were kindred spirits.

Upstairs in the bedroom she had made a temporary altar in the awkward corner where she couldn't stand up. She sat before it, legs crossed, the backs of her hands resting on her thighs. The scent of the incense crept into every nook and cranny of the room. She lit a candle and meditated. Oh yes, this ancient village was just the right place for her.

Chapter 2

'Mummy! Mummy!'

'Flick? I'm in the kitchen.' Harriet turned to look as her daughter raced in from the hall.

'Mummy! Ms Pascoe's got the most enormous cat!'

'What's she like?'

'She's black, black all over. She's got the greenest eyes you've ever seen — just the colour of your engagement ring. Green as green. And she comes to school, Ms Pascoe says, every day.'

'I should hope she does if she's a teacher.'

'Oh Mummy, I'm not talking about her, I'm talking about her *cat*.'

'Oh, I see.' Harriet chuckled. 'I really meant Miss Pascoe. What's she like?'

'It isn't Miss it's *Ms* Pascoe. Well, she's just like her cat. She's dressed all in black with the greenest eyes you've ever seen too. She's so slender!'

'Is that the cat or Miss Pascoe?'

'Oh Mummy, grow up! I liked Mr Palmer, but Ms Pascoe, she's going to be gorgeous. Daddy will love her.'

'Will he, indeed. There's your drink. Biscuit?'

'Yes, please.' Flick perched on a kitchen chair and

blew a kiss to little Fran who had emptied the cupboard where Harriet kept her baking tins, and was sitting surrounded by them. She had a wooden spoon and was making a lot of noise pretending to mix a cake in the largest of the tins. 'I'm glad I'm in the top class, because I've got Ms Pascoe all the time. Her cat hasn't got a name.'

'Why not?' Harriet helped herself to a biscuit and sat down to talk with Flick, who tossed her long brown plaits over her shoulders out of her way and took a drink of her milk before answering.

'She says it's because she, that is Ms Pascoe, doesn't know what the cat's name is and she doesn't want to upset it by calling it a name which isn't it, if you see what I mean. So she just calls it Cat.'

'Oh, I see. What about your Hartley and Chivers then?'

'I hadn't thought of that!' Flick looked worried. 'Oh dear! Do you think I've been upsetting them all this time, calling them a name they aren't?'

'I doubt it. They know when they're on to a good thing. My guess is they've kept quiet about their names because they don't want to cause any upset. They seem quite happy, don't they?'

'I wouldn't want to give them split personalities. Just think if I'd called Hartley "Tiger" instead, when all the time he's a quiet cat and wouldn't say boo to a goose!' She finished the rest of her milk. 'Ms Pascoe's cat sleeps on the classroom windowsill. We're not supposed to touch her. She's an untouchable cat, says Ms Pascoe. Touching is *verboten*. But it's quite difficult because, as you know, I like cats. I have an affinity with them, Ms Pascoe says. Ms Pascoe says that cats *allow* us to look after *them*. We don't own them like ordinary people think we do. Ms Pascoe's cat is very intelligent, she says. I think I shall devise intelligence tests for my two and see how they score.'

'Apart from the cat, was school all right – first day back and all that?'

'Oh yes! Ms Pascoe says we're going to have a wonderful time at school, now she's come. I'm glad I'm not in Mrs Hardaker's class – she looks a bit grim. So does Mrs Duckett. She was quite snappy with me when I went to the kitchen to get a clean saucer for the cat's water – said she was the school caretaker and not a zoo-keeper. The twins started in the playgroup today. Beth cried, and cried. Come to think of it, she cried all morning.'

'Oh dear. Poor Beth.'

'Well, she is only just three.'

'I know, but she's always been the confident one.'

'Well, she isn't now. We could hear her all over the school. The rector came, because Mrs Neal couldn't do a thing with her. Her face was all blotchy when he took her home. He had to carry her under his arm because she wouldn't walk, and her legs were kicking and she was screaming. Good thing he's big and strong, isn't it?'

'Oh dear. Still, it won't last long – she'll soon get used to it.' Harriet asked Flick to play with little Fran for a while. 'She's missed you, and so have I, you being away all day, first day of term.'

'OK. Come on, Fran, we'll play with the doll's house,' and Fran trotted off after Flick. Harriet tidied the tins away, and began to make the evening meal.

She glanced at the clock. Four o'clock. Jimbo would be back soon. Harriet looked out of the kitchen window. She never liked the garden in winter. No snow yet though, thank goodness. It was already almost dark. This was Jimbo's worst time of the year. Somehow the dark months didn't suit his personality; besides which,

December and January were his busiest time of the year for catering. By the time Christmas and the New Year were over he was exhausted.

The door banged. 'It's me. Boys home yet?'

'No, not yet.'

'Darling!' Wrapping his arms around her waist, Jimbo kissed the back of Harriet's neck and said, 'Mmmmmm. My darling. Where are the girls?'

'Playing with the doll's house.'

'Flick OK?'

'She's fallen in love.'

'Good God! Not yet, surely. She's only ten.'

'No, stupid. With her new teacher and the teacher's cat.'

'Ah! So how is this Miss What's-er-name?'

'*Ms* Pascoe, if you please. Well, Flick says you'll love her.'

'Will I, indeed. My word.' Looking in the kitchen mirror, he stroked his bald head, straightened his bow tie, and grinned at himself.

'Jimbo!'

'Only joking. She's Ms then?'

'She is. Busy day?'

'Very busy. Truth to tell, Harriet, the Store's turning into a gold mine. I envisaged it as a front for our other activities and never really expected to do more than break even, but not any more. It stands in its own right now – so does the mail order. Your mother is in her seventh heaven; she was positively skipping round the mail-order office this afternoon. Christmas, with the new mincemeat and the new chutney and your idea of a hamper-for-one, broke all previous records. "Sadie," I said, "you're a pearl without price!" I've invited her for supper tonight. All right?'

'Yes, that's fine.'

'We'll have wine, I think. Do the old girl good.'

'Not so much of the old. She was only eighteen when I was born, you know.'

Jimbo laughed. 'We'll be able to run her a good long while yet, then.'

'Ruthless you are! Completely ruthless.'

'I've decided, this year, come hell or high water, the whole family is going to have a holiday together. You, me, the children . . .' He heard the front door open. 'That's the boys home. Feed the brutes, quick.'

Harriet put a plate of biscuits and glasses of Coke on the table. 'Come and get it!' Fergus and Finlay strolled in. The two of them, though not twins, were the same height. Fergus had inherited his father's heavy build, while Finlay was slightly built like Harriet and with his mother's dark hair; they had Jimbo's round head and face, with determined chins like their father's.

They sat down. 'Where's the girls?'

'Playing with the doll's house.'

'Thank God! Give us a bit of peace.'

'Yes, your mother *has* had a busy day and hello to you both.'

'Sorry, Dad. First day back and that.' Fergus helped himself to a second biscuit. 'I worked out today I've got five more years and two terms, counting this one, to do at school. I don't think I shall last that long.'

'Pity you can't come running with me in the morning. Gets the old adrenalin flowing, makes a good start to the day.' Jimbo threw a mock punch or two at Fergus' head.

'Thanks, but I much prefer slumping on the old school-bus, Dad. It's a drag back and forth to Culworth, day in day out.' Finlay stretched his legs out and by mistake kicked the table. Coke splashed everywhere. 'God, what a mess!'

'Calm down, calm down.' Harriet mopped up the sticky pool.

'What's the new Head like? Can't believe old Palmer's gone for ever.'

'*Mr* Palmer to you.' Harriet chuckled. 'She's called Ms Pascoe, and Flick says Daddy will love her.'

'Watch out, Mum. I can see the headlines now: *Turnham Malpas entrepreneur disappears with delectable new headmistress.*'

Jimbo aimed another playful cuff at Fergus' head. 'Grandmother is coming to supper tonight, so please, homework done, pronto pronto, then you can entertain her.'

'Oh good, she's teaching us poker. Have you any money, Finlay? You know she likes to play for high stakes.'

'Harriet! Your mother is teaching your sons bad ways. Gambling at their age indeed!'

'Funny how they're *my* sons when they're up to no good. Clear off, boys, and get your work done.' Harriet was chopping carrots furiously. 'Poor little Beth screamed the school down this morning apparently. Liz Neal sent for Peter and he had to take her home.'

'Poor little mite. She's usually so bouncy. How can we possibly know what terrors they are experiencing?'

'True. I'm wondering if it's Caroline going back to doctoring that's caused it.'

'Ah, hadn't thought of that. She can scream when she wants to, that child. I bet they could hear her all over the school.'

They could hear her all over the school on Wednesday, too. Peter took her and Alex in good time to give Beth a chance to settle before the others arrived. He stayed for half an hour and then tried creeping out while she was busy, but as he reached the door Beth realised what he was doing and began screaming again.

Liz Neal took hold of her and told Peter to go, so he did, but Beth would not be pacified. There was a knock at the door and in came Ms Pascoe. She shouted above the din Beth was making: 'This won't do, you know. We can hear her even with the doors shut. What's her name?'

'Beth Harris. She's the rector's little girl.'

'Spoilt only child, is she?'

'Oh no. Her twin's here too. That's him over there playing in the sand – the one with the reddish hair. Beth, darling, hush hush.'

'I would have thought the rector would have brought them up better than this. Send for him or her mother. Where's she?'

'Dr Harris is taking a surgery this morning.'

'I see. Well, we can't go on like this. Either someone stays with her or she goes home. You'll have them all crying if this continues. She didn't cry yesterday, did she?'

'She wasn't here; she only comes Monday, Wednesday and Friday.'

'I see. Well, that's more than enough – but do something, *please*. OK?' Ms Pascoe patted Beth's leg but Beth tried to kick her and Ms Pascoe had to jump aside. 'My word. What a hellcat she is.'

'She is not. This behaviour is most unlike her.' Liz struggled to contain Beth, who was trying to kick Ms Pascoe again. 'She's normally a very social being.'

'Well, you must sort it out somehow. I'm teaching my class to meditate and this isn't helping.'

Meditate? thought Liz. 'Can I borrow your phone, please?' she said aloud.

'Of course. Gladly.' And Kate Pascoe swept back to

her class. There were twenty of them aged nine to eleven. Nine boys, eleven girls. Eager. Bright. Perfectly splendid material.

From her window where Cat lay sleeping, she saw the rector carrying Beth Harris home. She was still scream-ing and her sturdy little legs were still kicking out. Peter Harris' face was briefly visible as he turned to check for traffic before crossing the road. His expression was a strange mixture of anger and distress.

Chapter 3

Jimbo was in the Store on Friday busy serving his customers. His boater, short-sleeved white shirt and red bow tie, combined with the red-and-white striped butcher's apron he wore, gave him a certain panache. This morning he sported a brilliant scarlet and acid yellow ribbon around his beloved boater. Jimbo's particular brand of repartee delighted his customers, and there was plenty of it today; he was feeling particularly bouncy, having completed the year-end figures and found them so very satisfactory. He raised his boater in greeting to Pat Duckett.

'Good morning, Mrs Duckett. How's school this term?'

'Mrs Duckett?'

'Well, Pat then.'

'Bring back Mr Palmer, is all I can say. The sooner the better.'

'Oh dear – like that, is it? I was told your new Head was gorgeous.'

'I don't know who told you that, but from where I'm standing I wouldn't 'ave said so. Still, early days yet. Things might settle down – new broom and all that.'

Jimbo leant forward and whispered in her ear, 'If things are really bad, why not give your notice in and work for me permanently?'

Pat gave him a surprised look. 'Really?'

'Well, you'll soon be married, so you won't need the daily grind, will you, not to quite the same extent? And you proved yourself at the Show. Organised the refreshment marquee like a dream, you did.'

'Did I?'

'You know you did. I could find lots of work for you. I've so many requests coming in for catering that I shan't be serving in the shop before long.'

'You mustn't give that up. You're the reason people come in. They like your style – does 'em good. Oh dearie me, look, you have a visitor.'

Jimbo turned to see where Pat was pointing. Sitting on the chair by the customers' coffee machine was Beth Harris. Her sturdy little legs were swinging back and forth, her thumb was in her mouth and her face was streaked by dried tears. She'd taken out of her pocket the piece of old cot blanket she called her 'lover' and was rubbing it intently back and forth across the end of her nose.

'Heavens above.' Jimbo strode gently across to Beth. 'Good morning, my love. Come to see your Uncle Bimbo?' Beth nodded. 'Well, that's lovely. Your Uncle Bimbo is pleased to see you. Come with me and we'll find Flick's Grandma Sadie and we'll see what she's got for you.' He held out his hand. She slipped off the chair and confidently put her hand in his. They disappeared into the back of the Store to find Sadie in her mail-order office. She was packing some jars of Country Cousin Marmalade into one of Jimbo's fancy boxes.

Jimbo caught Sadie's eye and winked. 'Now, Grandma Sadie, have you got something a hungry little girl could eat while her Uncle Bimbo makes a phone call?'

'Of course. Sit here with me, darling, and we'll find something for you.' Jimbo slipped away to use the phone in his office.

Beth took the little box of Smarties Sadie gave her and said, 'Thank you.' Then: 'I want my mummy.' Tears began to trickle down her face.

Sadie looked at Beth's lovely rounded cheeks, her startlingly bright blue eyes, the soft ash-blonde hair, and her heart went out to her. What a sweet dear beautiful child she was. Each and every tear was painful to watch. 'Beth, Mummy's not far away and she'll be back for lunch, you know.'

'I want my mummy.' The words were blurred by her constricted throat and the tears which began coming too fast to count.

Sadie bent down to put her arms around her. 'I know, dear, I know. But you're getting a big girl now and big girls do some things by themselves, don't they? Alex does, doesn't he? Alex is being a big boy. You've to be a big girl. Is Alex still at school?'

Beth nodded.

'Shall your Grandma Sadie take you back to him then?'

'NO! I want my mummy!' The wails began to grow louder. The box of Smarties was dropped on the floor and she wept.

Sadie felt quite unable to cope with Beth's overwhelming sadness and longed to be rescued.

The rescue came in the form of Peter.

He ducked his head as he came into Sadie's office. 'Beth, my darling child. Come here.' He bent down and picked her up off the chair and held her close.

'I want my mummy.'

'I know, darling, I know. But see here, Beth, Mummy has not gone away for ever. Mummy will be back for her lunch and that isn't very long, is it? Now, Daddy's going to take you back to school. Mrs Neal will be worried, so we'll go and tell her where you are. Right now – OK?'

'NO! I'm not going back there! I'm not! I'm not!'

'I shall be with you, promise.'

'All the time.'

'All the time, I promise. Thank you, Sadie. Thank you.'

'All part of a day's work! Any time. Bye bye, darling. Chin up!'

Beth wouldn't smile. She merely looked down at her over Peter's shoulder and allowed herself to be carried away.

Pat watched the two of them leave the Store.

'Poor little mite. She's got a good pair of lungs, I'll give 'er that. I'll think over what you said about . . .' Pat nodded significantly to Jimbo because they couldn't exchange confidences as the Store had filled up again with customers, '. . . yer know, and talk it over with my intended.'

Jimbo nodded from behind the till and gave her the thumbs–up. 'Don't be too long about it.'

School playtime was just beginning when Peter crossed Jacks Lane and took Beth back to school. Kate Pascoe was in the hall.

'Good morning, Rector. Hello, Beth. All right now?'

'Good morning, Ms Pascoe. Sorry about all this trouble we're having. It must be very upsetting. I'll take her through to the playgroup and see Liz Neal and then I'll have a quick word, if I may.'

'Of course. See you in a moment. We're just having coffee. Like one?'

'Yes, please.'

The staff drank their morning coffee in the hall because the Head's room was too small to accommodate them. Hetty Hardaker and Margaret Booth, a pretty, energetic, fair-haired girl whom the whole of the infant class adored on sight, were sitting in the hall with Kate Pascoe when Peter returned with Beth in his arms. Hetty had worked at the school for ten years, and had hoped for the headship. Margaret had replaced 'poor' Toria Clark, as everyone always called her. They were both eyeing Kate Pascoe warily. The atmosphere was less than cordial.

Peter stood Beth down on the floor and she stood, quietly sobbing, gripping his cassock. 'Good morning, Hetty, Margaret. Sorry this daughter of mine is causing so much trouble. It's really very unlike her. She's the one with all the bounce and confidence. This has come as a great surprise.' He turned to Kate. 'I'm sorry she ran away, but concerned that no one had realised.'

'Oh, but we did, and we'd been searching for her. Jimbo rang just as we were about to phone you to see if she'd gone home.'

'I beg your pardon. I think I'll take her home for the rest of the morning.'

'Taking her home will solve nothing. You'll have to be firm. She's got to learn.'

Hetty Hardaker intervened. 'She'll learn nothing by being left to cry herself to exhaustion, *Miss* Pascoe. The rector's quite right to take her home. There's something very disturbing for Beth here, I don't know what, but there is.' She placed her coffee mug on the top of the piano and glared at Kate.

Kate ignored her. 'Well, Rector. Either she stops crying or she stays at home – the choice is yours. It's too disrupting for the other children. Our meditation time was quite ruined again today.'

'I'll take Beth back home for now. I'll phone you later, Ms Pascoe, if I may.'

'Kate, please.'

'Kate, then. Sorry again about all this.'

'So, Caroline, I've asked Kate Pascoe over for coffee tonight. Firstly as an apology about Beth's behaviour and secondly to find out more about her.'

'You sound as though you suspect her of something quite dreadful.'

'No, not dreadful – but meditation? For ten-year-olds?'

'I see what you mean. I shall look forward to this – it could be a very interesting evening.' She didn't notice Peter looking at her, surprised at her apparent lack of concern about Beth. 'If you've finished lunch, we'll clear away. Sylvia's got plans for turning out the children's room this afternoon. She'll be back any minute.'

They heard the front door open and in a moment Sylvia came into the kitchen. 'I've had a thought,' she told them both. 'Shall I stay with Beth at playgroup on Monday? It might help.'

Peter said he and Ms Pascoe were going to discuss it this evening and he'd let her know. When she got shut out like Peter had shut her out just now, Sylvia knew there was trouble brewing. Sighing, she snapped open the dishwasher. Please God not more trouble. They'd had enough last year for a lifetime and then some.

Peter was on the telephone so it was Caroline who opened the door to Kate.

'Good evening, Kate. Do come in. I'm Caroline, the rector's wife. How do you do?'

Kate shook hands and approved of Caroline. She appreciated her businesslike approach and she was so up-to-speed for a rector's wife. 'Not a very nice night, is it?'

'No, it isn't, but at least it isn't snowing. This time last year we had thick snow for weeks. Most unusual. We're in the sitting room – do go through and take a pew, the coffee's almost ready.'

As she carried the tray from the kitchen across the hall Peter came out of his study. 'That was Dicky Tutt, giving me the date for the Scout jumble sale – March the twentieth. Make a note and then we can have a clear-out. Kate here?' He pushed the sitting-room door open a little wider to accommodate Caroline's tray. 'Good evening, Kate. I don't need to introduce my wife, do I? Obviously you've already met. Firstly, I'm so sorry about Beth. She's gone from being a perfectly happy sociable little being to this hysterical monster, and we're not sure how to tackle it. My inclination is to take her each morning and stay with her for say ten minutes, then bring her home. Gradually lengthen the time she stays.'

Kate listened to his proposition. She noticed Caroline was saying nothing. She was the child's mother, for God's sake.

'How do you feel, Caroline?'

'Coffee? Milk? Sugar?'

'Black, please. No sugar.'

Caroline sat down beside Peter and took a sip of her coffee. 'Frankly, I'm completely at a loss. Although they are twins I prefer to treat them as completely separate individuals.' Kate nodded in agreement. 'If Alex is fine then he goes all morning. If Beth is finding it difficult then we adapt things to suit her. I think Peter's idea is a good one. Sylvia could always stay with her if he is busy.'

'Sylvia is employed as housekeeper, darling, primarily.'

'You have a housekeeper?'

24

Caroline raised an eyebrow. 'Yes, do you have a problem with that?'

'No, no. I'm just surprised, that's all. I'm all for throwing them in at the deep end. It's surprising how resilient small children can be when once they see you mean business. However, basically it's not for me to say, is it? Liz Neal is the one who takes the brunt of it. What I deplore is the disturbance it causes to the children whose school it actually is. Meditation is impossible with all that racket.'

Peter said, 'I wondered about that.'

'The disturbance?'

'No, the meditation.'

'It's the modern equivalent to assembly.'

'I see. It always was called prayers, or assembly.'

'I dare say, but nowadays we have to cater for all religions, not just Christianity.'

'May I point out that all the children are white and Christian.'

'Just because they are white, it does not mean they are Christian.'

'At Turnham Malpas School they all are. All, except the two Paradise children, go to our Junior Church or the Methodist Church in Little Derehams. The school is a C. of E. foundation and the parents expect prayers and religious teaching. You took the post on that understanding.'

'I did. But are you saying there is no room for silence and private thought?'

'No, certainly not. Of course there's room for it, but there must be the other side too. In Michael Palmer's time we had Friday-morning prayers in the church. Hetty and Margaret were quite happy to go along with that. If you prefer, I could take prayers on Fridays in the school instead, but I should be disappointed.'

Kate looked to Caroline for support but got none. 'Then I shall have to adapt, shall I not? If Hetty Hardaker is willing to take prayers then she can. I shall conduct the silent thinking, afterwards.'

Caroline held up the coffee pot. 'More coffee?'

'Yes, please.' Kate saw two of Caroline's cats standing in the doorway. 'Oh, what lovely creatures! Come, puss, puss, puss.' Tonga and Chang fluffed their tails and arched their backs; Tonga spat and then they fled.

To cover his embarrassment at the weird attitude of their normally attention-seeking cats, Peter plunged in with, 'Then we shall for the moment compromise, but it must be clearly understood, Miss . . . *Ms* Pascoe, that there must be religious teaching even if you don't do it yourself. It is your responsibility to attend to that, however much you prefer not to. Hetty Hardaker did it all last term whilst we had no head teacher, so I'm sure she and Margaret will be quite happy to continue. We'll review the situation at half-term.'

'Very well. I shall do as you say, Rector.'

Caroline wanted to know more about Kate herself. 'Settling in at the school-house, Kate?'

'Yes, thanks. It's terribly dowdy, though. I'm brightening it up. When it's done, will you come for supper one evening? Or perhaps you won't have a babysitter.'

'Sylvia does it for us, so yes, we'd love to come. In fact, I've never been inside the school-house and we've lived here almost four years, so it will be interesting for us, won't it, Peter?'

'Yes, it will.' He looked at Kate. 'Now – about May the first.'

'Yes?'

'On that day, Michael always had Maypole dancing on the Green. All the parents are invited, there are cups of tea and a May Queen. Do you do Maypole dancing?'

'Ye olde phallic symbol? Village maidens dancing round in homage – rites of spring and all that jazz. Of course! Delighted to take part. Must go, want to do some more decorating before bed. Thanks for the coffee. Hope Beth settles down soon. Won't be long before you get my invitation. I'm a tigress once I get started.'

Caroline saw her out and went back into the sitting room to find Peter had gone. He was in his study, searching along his bookshelves.

'What are you looking for?'

'Maypole dancing. An innocent colourful pursuit, I thought, until tonight. I'd no idea that was what it represented. Phallic symbol, indeed! Is nothing sacred any more?'

Caroline laughed. 'Oh, Peter! She makes a change from strait–laced Michael Palmer anyway. He was a bit too solemn, wasn't he?'

'It's no laughing matter, my darling girl. We've got problems there and no mistake. I dread to think what will happen next.'

Chapter 4

Jimbo met Kate the following morning. She came into the Store carrying a large shopping bag. He raised his boater to her and said, 'You must be Kate Pascoe from the school. Good morning to you!'

She put down her bag and reached out to shake hands with him. 'Indeed I am. And you must be Flick's father. She said you owned the Store. She was going to launch herself into a long story about how well you were doing, end-of-year accounts and that kind of thing, but I cut that short! But I do see what she means. It certainly is a wonderland. And I thought all village stores were on their last legs.' She looked appreciatively around the Store. 'I think perhaps I haven't thanked you for sending me that starter pack for my pantry? I really did appreciate your kindness. I've got to stock up my cupboards now.'

'We'll deliver for you if you wish.'

'No, that won't be necessary, thank you. There's only one of me. Soya milk?'

'Ah! We do have some but I don't get a great call for it — just one other customer who has a daughter allergic to cow's milk. Check the dairy cabinet, I think you'll find some.'

Kate wandered away, leaving Jimbo to carry on replenishing the fresh fruit display. The doorbell jangled and Kate heard Jimbo welcoming another customer. 'Ralph, this is a pleasure! Don't often see you in here.'

'Hello, Jimbo. Milk is what we need for the moment. We used the last drop at breakfast-time and Muriel's wanting her coffee.'

'Indeed and why not. I'll get it for you.'

'No, no, don't trouble yourself, I can get it. I'm going up tomorrow to see old Fitch about the cricket pitch. Care to come with me?'

'Much as I would like to, I'm afraid business calls. I'm quite sure you can manage without me!'

'Got to get it on a business footing, you see. No loose ends. Knowing his propensity for deviousness I want things quite clear-cut. Any more news about team members?'

'Indeed. Ah, Ms Pascoe. May I introduce our new head teacher, Sir Ralph? Kate Pascoe, this is Sir Ralph Templeton. He and his wife Lady Muriel Templeton live in the village.' Ralph extended a welcoming hand. Kate shook it with a half-smile on her face. He was certainly distinguished-looking – thin, tanned, with thick white hair, an aristocratic beaked nose, and the wearer of an extremely expensive overcoat.

'How do you do, young lady. Very pleased to meet you. My wife's already made your acquaintance; she said how charming you were and she was right. We needed new blood in the school. May I wish you every success?'

'Thank you, Ralph.' Kate didn't notice Jimbo flinch when she omitted Ralph's title. 'That's very kind of you. Did I hear you mentioning a cricket team?'

'You did. We've spent last summer and this winter resurrecting the old cricket pitch. It's a vast improvement on what it was but still not as good as Lord's – not yet.'

'I played cricket with my brothers when I was at home. Fabulous game.' Ralph raised an eyebrow at the use of the word 'fabulous'. 'I wouldn't expect to play in the team, but I'm a good hand at cricket teas. Would I be of any use? Or maybe you've got all that side of it organised already.'

Jimbo declared they hadn't and he'd be glad of help. 'I'm having nothing to do with the catering side. It's all voluntary, you see, so I'm sure Muriel and Caroline – you've met Caroline – ' Kate nodded ' – would be delighted by your offer.'

'I'm certain they would. Thank you very much.' Ralph smiled at her and went to collect the fresh milk.

'I've found some soya milk, Jimbo. I'm a vegan – I don't suppose you have many of those in the village.'

'Ah! First time I've met one in the flesh, so to speak. Is there anything at all which you specially favour? If so, I'll make sure we get it in. Can't have you starving to death!' Jimbo couldn't help remembering all the food he'd sent her. Privately he wondered where it had all gone.

Kate heaved her overflowing basket onto the shelf by the till. 'Today I'm OK. Thanks though, I'll let you know. Don't forget about the cricket teas, will you? I really mean what I say.'

'Certainly shan't. I shall pass on your offer to the appropriate quarter. There's your change – thank you very much.'

'What superb carrier bags! Much too nice for recycling as pedal-bin bags!' Kate grinned at him and went out.

'Well, Ralph, there's one thing for certain – I shan't be able to retire on what Kate spends in here. A vegan – God help us! Hope she doesn't start a new trend!'

'About the team . . .'

'Oh yes. I've got a list. Here it is.' He removed a piece of paper from a clipboard, and handed it to Ralph who put on his reading glasses and stood to one side while Jimbo continued dealing with customers.

Ralph read the list out in an undertone. 'Dicky Tutt . . . he should be good behind a bat but can he run, that's the question. Jimbo . . . Gilbert – oh that's a surprise. Surely Little Derehams will have something to say about us poaching one of their star players?'

'Well, it's Gilbert's decision. He asked me, not the other way round. Apparently he's sick of having to kowtow to their Captain who's high-handed and not the slightest bit democratic, and Gilbert says he's not a child and won't be treated like one.'

'Oh well, then, we'll have him! If I remember rightly he's an excellent batsman.'

'He is. Score average last season twenty-one.'

'Excellent!' Ralph returned silently to considering the list. Barry Jones . . . yes, Peter . . . yes, Neville . . . the slimy toad, Malcolm . . . the milkman, the Sergeant . . . Dean Duckett . . . Kenny and Terry Jones and Rhett Wright. An odd collection but some good may come of them; we've got to start somewhere. He flicked the list with the back of his hand and said aloud: 'Well, Jimbo, I must say you've done well. A good start. Right, I'll be off. Here's the money for the milk. I'll let you know how I get on. Strange girl, that Kate.'

'Rather gorgeous, I thought! Those green eyes . . . Nice of her to help with the teas.'

'Hmm.' Ralph shut the door and went off home looking forward to his coffee just as Muriel was. As he walked round the village green, Ralph admired the houses and the church. Home, Turnham Malpas, that was where he really belonged. His heart was here, where he'd spent his first years. It didn't matter a damn that he

31

wasn't in the Big House any more. He could cheerfully leave that to old Fitch, because he, Ralph, had what Fitch hadn't – a loving passionate wife. Never mind all that hooey that passion belonged only to the young; he and Muriel had proved them wrong. As Ralph crossed Church Lane he said to himself, I just hope my damned ticker holds out and we have many years of fun before us.

'Muriel, my dear, here's the milk. I've just been introduced to Ms Pascoe from the school. Curious sort of girl – well, woman. Just hope she doesn't let the village down with newfangled ideas.'

Muriel opened the carton of milk and poured some into the tiny china jug on the tray. She checked that she had everything – Ralph's sweeteners, the coffee, teaspoons, cups, saucers. She was using the ones she'd brought from her own house when they'd married. She was so glad she had someone to share her nice china with. Dear Ralph!

'There we are, I've got everything. Come and tell me what you think of her.'

'All black – she's dressed in black. One thing in her favour, though, she's willing to lend a hand with the cricket teas.'

'Oh excellent! She can't be all bad then.'

'No, she can't, can she?' Ralph chuckled. 'I've that appointment with Fitch tomorrow. They'll be starting on the pavilion as soon as the weather improves – won't that be grand? We've fifty years of neglect to put right. I can just remember seeing my father batting. It was a hot summer day. My sunhat made my forehead sticky so I pushed it off; Mama wiped my face with cologne and put it back on again. That's something I remember about her – she always smelt beautifully. God! I'm sounding like a very sentimental old trout. Got to stop.'

'There's nothing the matter with memories, Ralph, nothing at all. Especially lovely ones.'

'No, you're right. Thank you for the coffee, my dear. I'm going to my study to open the post and to plan my meeting with Fitch. He'll be handing out money like there's no tomorrow, so long as it bolsters his campaign.'

'Campaign?'

'He's wanting to be president of the club.'

'But a Templeton is always president!' Muriel was scandalised. 'It'll have to be you.'

'I rather hope it might. Tradition and all that . . . but times have changed and money speaks loudest now.'

'I shall tell him,' Muriel said fiercely. 'If you have any trouble with him, let me know and I shall go up there and put him straight. President of the cricket club . . . Whatever next!'

Ralph smiled at her. 'I do believe you would.'

As he pulled up on the gravel at the front of the Big House the following day, Ralph couldn't help his heart lurching slightly. The place always had that effect on him. It really was time he let the past rest in peace.

To his surprise, Craddock Fitch's secretary Louise was working.

'Good afternoon, Louise. I hadn't expected to find you here on a Saturday.'

'Good afternoon, Sir Ralph. I've been having a few days holiday while Mr Fitch was away so I thought I would catch up while the House was quiet.'

'Did you go anywhere exciting?'

'To Paris.'

'Oh, wonderful! What a coincidence,' Ralph said suddenly, struck. 'Gilbert Johns has just been to Paris, too. Did you bump into him, by any chance? We had a chat about a recital he was going to in Notre Dame. He was so looking forward to it. Don't suppose you went, too?'

Ralph noticed that Louise was blushing. 'We didn't bump into each other. Mr Fitch is ready for you.'

'Thank you.' Ralph headed towards the library.

'Er . . . excuse me, Sir Ralph, Mr Fitch isn't in his office, he's in his private flat. Do you know where that is?'

'Oh yes, I do.' This was the hardest bit, walking up the stairs and along the corridors. Memories flooded his mind, but he mustn't let himself be disarmed by them; he needed to be on his mettle. The thought entered his head that old Fitch had decided to have the meeting in the flat deliberately, to disconcert him.

The door of the flat was open so Ralph tapped with his signet ring on one of the carved panels and called out, 'Craddock? Ralph Templeton.'

He heard quick positive footsteps. 'Ralph! Do come in.' Ralph wryly noted that Mr Fitch's country tweeds were so entirely co-ordinated that he looked as though he'd stepped straight out of the window of a Savile Row tailor, then grimly recollected the man himself was no tailor's dummy.

'Craddock! Good afternoon.'

'I've had tea organised for us. Is that satisfactory, or would you prefer something stronger?'

'Tea will be fine.' Ralph seated himself in a huge armchair, a patriarchal kind of chair; its twin was the other side of the fireplace and Mr Fitch went to sit in it.

Sadie Beauchamp carried in the tea tray. Ralph and, belatedly, Mr Fitch, stood up.

'Good afternoon, Sadie. How nice to see you.'

'Hello, Ralph. You're back. Had a good holiday? I'll catch up on your news with Muriel next week. Must dash. Everything's there, Craddock, I'll be off now.' She put down the tray on the big round coffee table standing in front of the fire between their chairs, and beamed at them both. She and Mr Fitch kissed each other's cheeks and she left.

Mr Fitch explained she'd been having lunch with him and had volunteered to make the tea before she left. Ralph replied, 'I see. Lovely woman, Sadie. Sharp mind, even sharper tongue!' Mr Fitch smiled his agreement.

They talked idly about this and that, and in particular about the international situation, and each in their turn prophesied the outcome, and then Mr Fitch put down his cup, dabbed his mouth with his napkin, and fired his opening shot.

'If I'm putting money into this cricket team I shall expect to be president.'

'Ah! I see. I thought perhaps you might.'

'Oh yes. There's no point in beating about the bush. I'm allowing the use of Rector's Meadow, paying for the renovations – or more accurately, the complete rebuilding of the pavilion – buying and supplying the equipment, too, and that's what I want in return.'

'It's completely against tradition.'

'Is it?'

'Templetons have been presidents since the cricket club was first started by my great-great-grandfather.'

'Well, it's more than fifty years since the last Templeton, your late lamented father, was president, plus no cricket team for fifty years, so I think we could safely say there's been a break with tradition, don't you?'

'The village won't like it.'

'Come off it, Ralph. God! There's hardly a soul living who remembers all that stuff. No, move with the times, I say. Money counts. Where else would you get it from if not from me?'

Bitingly Ralph replied, 'It would be pleasant if you could be a little more gracious about it.'

'*Gracious*? What's there to be gracious about? Facts are facts.'

'The village won't like it,' Ralph said again.

'They'll have to take a deep breath and swallow hard then.'

'Don't forget you've come up against their wrath once before.'

Mr Fitch gave Ralph a piercing look. 'About the church silver, you mean?' He flicked some ash from his cigar into the flames and paused for a moment. 'It was only the effigy they made, hanging from the tree.'

'And all the things going wrong here. The heating being off for three days in the dead of winter, your tyres let down, the strike of the kitchen staff and the—'

'You mean all that was engineered?'

'Of course. Hadn't you realised that?'

Unwilling to admit in front of Ralph that it had never occurred to him that the opposition from the village could be so vicious, he paused before replying. 'Well, it had crossed my mind, naturally; it all did seem rather odd, but I didn't take it seriously.' He sat silently watching the flames leaping up his chimney. The devil they did.

Ralph said, 'You'd have to be here fifty years at least before they accepted you, and unfortunately you've not got that much time left.'

Mr Fitch's head came up with a jerk. 'Neither have you.'

'True, true, but then I'm one step ahead. I'm already accepted and have been for centuries.'

'So they'll take my money but not me?'

'In a nutshell.'

'Damn them!!'

'That's just it.'

'What is?'

'Your attitude.'

Craddock Fitch strode about the room, puffing furiously on his cigar, his brown gleaming shoes rapping sharply on the polished floor. He came to a halt on the huge round rug in front of the fire. As he stubbed out his cigar in the ash-tray on the coffee table he said, 'You're saying if I insist on being president I shall lose what little kudos I might have already gained?'

'Something like that.'

'Who are these people who think they can dictate to me?'

'It is their village, their cricket team, not yours, not mine.'

'At this rate there'll be no progress.'

'Not much.'

'Well, I'm damned.' Mr Fitch stabbed his well manicured hand in Ralph's direction. 'All right then, you be president, but my name goes above the pavilion door. *The Henry Craddock Fitch Pavilion* – that'll sort 'em. No doubt who's paid for it then, eh? And my company logo on the gear I buy – you know, "sponsored by et cetera". Right?'

'Done!' They shook hands on the deal. Ralph glanced up at Mr Fitch, taking care to veil the twinkle in his eyes. 'And you can donate a cup, if you like.'

'Two! One to the batsman with the highest score in the season, and one to the bowler with the best average.'

'Done! I'll have another cup of tea, if I may. Now let's get down to business. Finance first. Shall you want rent for the pavilion? I rather hope not, for the first year at least.'

Mr Fitch raised his eyebrows at Ralph's outspokenness. 'I don't know how you got so high in the Diplomatic Service. There's not much diplomacy about your dealings!'

Chapter 5

'Kiss, kiss, my darling children. Mummy's off to make poorly people better, isn't she? Now Beth, Mummy won't be long. Sylvia's going to take you and stay for a while aren't you, Sylvia?'

'Of course. Will you show me where the sand is, Beth? I love playing in the sand.'

Alex said, 'Me will, Sylvie, me will. Me knows where the sand is. Beth doesn't.'

Beth stamped her foot. 'Beth does.'

'Beth doesn't 'cos you won't play.'

'I will.'

'You won't.'

'That will do, children. *Please*. Now I'm going. Be good, and Mummy will have a present for you when she comes back.'

'Beth not going.' She sat down on the hall floor.

'Sylvia! I really must go or I shall be late.' Caroline kissed the two of them on the tops of their heads, and fled with her medical bag to her car.

Sylvia cheerfully went to get the children's coats from the hall cupboard. 'Now Alex, aren't you going to have a lovely time in playgroup today? I wonder if they'll have the sand out today for your Sylvie to play in. Or shall I play with the water? Do they have water to play with, Beth?'

Beth ignored her. She looked up when she saw her father's feet appear beside her. He bent down and stood her up. 'Coat on, Beth.' She allowed him to dress her, then she took hold of Sylvia's hand and set off without another word. Sylvia was greatly relieved. But the relief was short-lived. Within five minutes of arriving, Beth had disappeared. The playgroup door had been open for only a moment as another of the children arrived and Beth had slipped out. The moment she realised what had happened, Sylvia ran out of school but there was no sign of Beth.

Jimbo found her sitting on the same chair, sucking her thumb and rubbing her nose with her lover, but this time there were no tears, only deep sadness.

'Well now, Beth. Hello. Come to see Uncle Bimbo again? You left your Smarties last time. Shall we go get them?' Beth ignored him. 'Come with Uncle Bimbo, eh?' It was as if he hadn't spoken. He looked round the Store and asked a customer to keep an eye on her while he phoned Peter and the school.

Peter took her back to the classroom. Sylvia was out searching the playground, Liz Neal was distraught and Kate Pascoe was seething.

'Really, Rector, again!'

'Yes – again. I might add that my daughter is here under your protection. I can hardly be pleased with the way you're carrying out your duties.'

'I didn't qualify in containing Houdinis – what teacher has? The only way to keep Beth in is to lock all the doors – which I resolutely refuse to do. This is *not* a prison. In any case, the playgroup is not strictly under my authority. Although I do everything I can to help, the actual responsibility is Mrs Neal's. But the responsibility for your daughter's personal safety is getting too much.'

Liz apologised. 'I'm terribly sorry, Peter. I've never had this before. How about if we give her a break? Perhaps Alex going home and saying how much he enjoys himself might have a beneficial effect on her attitude. Or else it is that she's just not quite ready. Not all children take to it as easily as Alex has.'

'I think maybe you could be right. We'll keep her at home this week and try to find out what the problem is. Thank you. I'm sorry for all the trouble.'

'That's all right. We can't expect to run a playgroup without some hiccoughs.'

Kate returned to her class. Peter and Sylvia took Beth home. She ran through the door shouting, 'Mummy! Mummy!' When she couldn't find Caroline she went to Sylvia, clutched hold of her skirt and never left her side all morning.

'Beth is staying at home for the rest of the week.'

Caroline swallowed her last drop of coffee and said, 'You've decided to keep her at home this week? Without consulting me?'

'Yes.'

'Peter!'

'Her heart – her tender, loving heart is broken.'

'She'll soon get over it. Children can be like that – they don't like change.'

'I said her heart is broken.'

'I heard.'

'The pain is unbearable for her.'

'Nonsense.'

'I won't have my decision altered. She is not going on either Wednesday or Friday.'

'Just a moment. We are both of us her parents; decisions are joint ones.'

'In this case, I'm sorry, but my decision is final. I

cannot remember when I felt the need to assert my authority so positively, but that is what I'm doing now. She is not going this week. She is putting her life at risk to tell us she is unhappy. Do you realise that? *Her life at risk*. She has twice crossed Jacks Lane *on her own*, when she is far too young and far too distraught to have any road sense. It only needs Barry Jones to come hurtling round the corner like he frequently does and . . . and it will all be too late.'

'This is arrogant interference in my domain.'

'Broken hearts *are* my business.'

'You're being very dramatic.'

'You didn't see her face when she couldn't find you when we got home.'

'This is ridiculous. She loves Sylvia, she'll be all right with her.'

'It was I who made her go this morning, and I shouldn't have done so. Look, Caroline, I don't wish to discuss it any further. I shall be in my study if I'm needed.' Peter stood up and pushed his chair under the table.

'That's right, hide in your study – you've had your say, trespassed where you shouldn't, so off you go to avoid any further discussion.' Peter looked down at her. It was her eyes which eventually avoided his. He turned on his heel and left the dining room.

Caroline began clearing the table. She caught the sound of Beth screaming as she crossed the hall. By the time she'd reached the bedroom, Beth was hysterical. Caroline hugged her tight, talking to her and trying to calm her fears. 'Have you had a nasty dream? Never mind then, Mummy's here, hush, hush, darling. There, there.' Caroline rocked her back and forth, back and forth and gradually the cries subsided. When she'd wiped her tears away for her, Caroline asked what the matter was. 'Can you tell Mummy what frightened you? Tell me, darling, please?'

'Mrs Neal, it was Mrs Neal.'

'She's a lovely lady, a friend of Mummy's.'

'Mrs Neal gave me a present.'

'Oh, how nice! That was a lovely dream, not a nasty one, surely.'

'She gave me lots of . . .' Beth sobbed. 'She gave me lots of worms, wiggly worms, all wiggly in my ha-a-n-n-nd.'

'Oh darling, I'm so sorry. But it was only a dream, you know. There aren't any worms here really, are there? Look, see, open your eyes. No worms. Just a dream. Mummy will lie down on the bed and wait till you go back to sleep. How's that?' Beth clutched hold of her and closed her eyes. 'No worms, Mummy?'

'No worms, darling.' It was ten minutes before Beth relaxed enough to go back to sleep.

Peter left Caroline with all the dishes to clear and stack, an activity which, if he hadn't got an evening meeting, they usually did together. When she'd finished, she went in the sitting room to watch television. It was more than an hour before she heard Peter come out of the study. He didn't come immediately into the sitting room but went to the kitchen. She could hear him putting on the kettle and getting out cups. This was his way, she knew, of making amends for his outburst. Well, he wasn't going to get around her that way. Other women had careers and children! Why on earth shouldn't she? She'd make it work. Beth would just have to get used to the idea that her mother had other things in her life besides children. Much as she loved her, she loved general practice too. She'd had to give it up when she and Peter got married and he'd moved parish; hospital work had been the easier option at the time.

Though she'd liked the hospital, it wasn't quite her métier. She was really enjoying general practice and *nothing* was going to stop her. Why shouldn't she have two lives? They could well afford Sylvia . . .

'Coffee, darling?'

'Yes, please.'

Peter put down the tray in front of her, and sat a moment in silence before he poured it. 'Instant, couldn't be bothered with the other. You don't mind?'

'No, not at all.'

'Ralph tells me he's been up to the Big House and persuaded Mr Fitch not to be president of the cricket club. But he's giving two cups and his name's going above the pavilion.'

'Oh, good – Mr Fitch will love that. Says something for Ralph's expertise in diplomacy, don't you think?'

'Exactly. I'm looking forward to the summer. I always liked cricket. Here's your coffee – is that all right?'

'Yes, thank you. You'll have to get back into your stride; you haven't played a stroke since we've known each other.'

'You're right – I shall have to get my eye in again. My best score was forty-five against Magdalen way back in . . . Can't remember.'

'It's no good, Peter.'

'What isn't?'

'Trying to talk as though nothing has happened. It has, and I'm very annoyed.'

Peter put his cup back on the coffee table and, fidgeting with his wedding ring, sat waiting for her to speak again.

'Why can't I have the best of both worlds? Other women do. Other women are back at work after six weeks at home with a new baby. They have nannies organised or au pairs organised, and everything goes with a swing.'

'Does it?'

'Oh yes.'

'On what do you base your assumption? Someone you know?'

Caroline sipped her coffee. 'Well, no one specific but you do hear about them.'

'In newspaper articles on the women's page?'

'Don't sneer, Peter, it's beneath you.'

'You putting the needs of your child second is beneath you.'

'So I'm to give up, am I? Let people down? Stay at home, play the role of Mummy ad infinitum? When shall I be allowed my life? When she's gone to university?'

'Now you're being ridiculous.'

'Ah! You're not?'

'No. Next time she makes it out of school, she may not go to Jimbo's.'

'Well, they'll have to take proper care of her, won't they? I'll have a word with Liz Neal. She'll sort it for me.'

'You are her anchor, you see. She loves you dearly; she relies on you for her security. Not Sylvia, not me. *You.*'

'Well, this job is only for six months.'

'I know.'

'You've put your sad expression on.'

'I haven't put it on. I look sad because I *am* sad. But there we are. I would marry an intelligent, highly motivated, passionate woman . . .'

'I married that kind of a man too.'

'You did, indeed. My own way this week?'

Caroline hesitated and then gave in. 'Very well.'

★

44

At five minutes to nine the following Monday, Hetty Hardaker rang the school-bell to call the children in. Margaret Booth came out to collect her infants.

'Rector's coming this morning – look.'

'So he is. Let's hope he has better success than he had last Monday, or else Madam will be fuming again.'

'You don't like her, Hetty, do you?'

'Kate Pascoe is a totally different ball-game from Michael Palmer and I don't . . . That will do, boys. In line, if you please. Flick, your shoelace is undone. That's lovely, Stacey – I'll look properly when we get inside. Brian, you've dropped your reading book. Pick it up quickly before it gets trodden on. Come along then, children, in we go.'

Peter waited until the main rush of children had gone in. He held Beth's hand tightly. Alex ran in without even a backward glance. Beth had her lover in her other hand, and under her arm her old rabbit from her baby days. With one ear missing it didn't look the least bit respectable, but she didn't care. Peter took her into the playgroup room and tried to make himself as inconspicuous as possible. Beth stood beside him, thumb in mouth. Nothing could tempt her to join in. Kate Pascoe popped her head round the door at playtime.

'Still here, Rector? All's quiet this morning. Coffee?'

'Yes, please.' Beth consented to having her drink and biscuit seated beside Alex at a little table, so Peter left her and went into the hall to join the three teachers.

'I've decided I don't want to continue having prayers in the church,' Kate began. 'I'd much rather have it in here, in school. Takes less time, for one thing . . .'

Hetty Hardaker indignantly interrupted. 'You have not consulted me about that, nor Margaret. I think it should be decided between us, don't you, Margaret?'

'Well, I enjoyed going into church. The rector does such good services for children; they all loved it and I think—'

Kate held up her hand for silence. 'Well, I think the rector could do just as good services here too. What do you think, Peter?'

'I prefer the church but then the school is yours so we must do as you wish.'

'Thank you. We'll see you Friday then, in here at nine o'clock.'

Hetty objected. 'It seems to me that, bit by bit, you are abdicating your responsibility for the religious teaching in this school. I'm to take prayers, you take meditation; whatever it is children of this age have to meditate on, I don't know – possibly who won the FA Cup or who's got the most Cub badges or something, or praying Dad will win the lottery this week and what they'll do with the money. Now we're told we can't go into church which we all know the rector prefers.'

'Hetty, may I remind you that I am Head here.' Kate's voice was hard.

'I don't need you to remind me. I *know*, only too well. I don't agree to this move at all, I'm sorry.'

Peter intervened. 'It isn't as if the children are not getting any religious instruction, Hetty, is it?'

'No, Rector, but it's being diluted.'

'I'm sure Kate doesn't—'

Kate interrupted Peter with a brusque, 'We have to move with the times.'

Hetty's face flushed with anger. 'That is the classic excuse for not keeping up standards. Mr Palmer would never have agreed . . .'

'Mr Palmer isn't Head here, *I am*. And I shall run the school as I see fit.'

Hetty Hardaker stood up, her voice heavy with

sarcasm as she said, 'Time for the bell. May I ring it, or shall you as it is *your* school?'

Before Kate could answer, Liz Neal rushed into the hall. 'Anyone seen Beth come this way? She's disappeared again.'

Beth had missed Peter and gone to look for him. She'd tried the rectory door but couldn't reach the bell, and Sylvia, who was upstairs, hadn't heard her knocking. So now she had nobody, nobody at all. Finding Muriel's door open, she went in.

Ralph found her in his study, sitting on a chair in the window rocking backwards and forwards sucking her thumb, sobbing.

He shut the front door and locked it to keep her safe while he went in search of Muriel. She was on her knees in front of her china cabinet, giving it a good clear-out.

'Muriel, my dear, we have a problem.'

'What's that?'

'Beth is sitting in my study, crying.'

'Oh dear. Ring the school, they'll be looking for her.' She got up from her knees and headed for the study. Over her shoulder she said, 'Ring the rectory, too. On the upstairs phone, then she won't hear. I'll sit with her.'

Muriel's heart bled when she recognised the utter desolation Beth was feeling. 'Oh, my dear. Will you let Moo sit you on her knee?'

'Moo, Moo, where's my mummy?'

When Muriel had got her safely seated on her lap she answered, 'Well, Beth, before your mummy got you, she was a doctor, you know.'

'I know.'

'And she was a very good doctor, too. Everybody loved her.'

'Mummy love me?'

'She does, darling, yes, she does. Very much. You and Alex.'

'And Daddy?'

'Oh yes, and Daddy too. Well, now your mummy has the chance to help poorly people again. You'd like that, wouldn't you, for Mummy to help poorly people?'

'Little girls too, Moo Moo?'

'Oh yes. She gives medicine to little girls and little boys to make them better. So that's good, isn't it?'

'I need medicine. I've got a tummy ache.'

'Oh dear.'

'A really truly bad tummy ache.'

Ralph, meanwhile, had heard the bell and opened the door to Peter. 'She's in my study with Muriel,' he said, reassuringly.

'Very sorry about this. Thank you so much for taking her in.'

'She came in by herself. I'd left the door open for a moment and in she popped.'

'Thanks anyway. It's terribly worrying.'

'Daddy, got a truly bad tummy ache, need Mummy's medicine.'

'Well, I've got some at home.'

'All right then.'

She slipped down from Muriel's knee and, taking Peter's hand, pulled him towards the door.

'Aren't you going to say something to Muriel?'

'Thank you, Moo Moo. Come on, Daddy. Go home.'

Peter half-smiled a goodbye to Muriel, but his eyes were grim with both temper and despair.

Chapter 6

Muriel called on Caroline that same afternoon. She was anxious and had decided to take the bull by the horns. She would tackle Caroline – something she was not accustomed to doing, but she was so moved by Beth's distress that she felt compelled to interfere. No, not interfere, just *talk*. She'd been worried by the thin line of Peter's lips as he'd left the house, and she knew by instinct that things were not well at the rectory.

'Muriel, how lovely! Do come in.'

'Are you free to talk for a moment?'

'Yes, of course.'

'Is Peter in?'

'No – why? Is it him you've come to see?'

'No, it's you actually.'

'Thank you very much indeed for taking pity on Beth this morning. I really do not know what we're going to do about her. I thought she'd be so happy to go to playgroup.'

'Well, she isn't, is she?'

Caroline's shoulders slumped. 'No, you're right there. Come in the sitting room, please. Do sit down. Sylvia's just taken the twins to see Harriet and Fran so we've got a while before they'll be back. You're quite right, of course. I just don't know what to do next.'

'You must be very worried.'

'I am. Peter is angry but of course he won't say it's because I'm working – yet I know that's what he thinks it is. I can see that it might be true, but I don't know how to solve it. Beth pretended to have a bad tummy and said she couldn't eat anything, but as soon as I got home she ate an enormous lunch. The two things don't add up.'

'I can remember when I was a little girl first starting school, I got tummy ache too, and my mother had to come all the way from the Garden House to collect me. Within five minutes of getting home I was playing with my dolls as happy as a lark. I remember the stomach ache felt very genuine.'

'You were fretting?'

'Of course. It took a couple of weeks for my father to see through this and then he put his foot down and made me stay at school. In those days, you see, they weren't quite so understanding as we are nowadays. But at least I knew my mother was at hand if I needed her.'

'So what are you telling me?'

'I think Beth is feeling deserted. All of a sudden she is expected to go to playgroup and settle down, while at the same time her mother has apparently begun disappearing. And where has she gone? You know – I know – Peter knows – but *Beth doesn't*. For all she can tell, you could have gone to the moon, and might never be coming back.'

'Would it be better if I gave it up?'

'Not yet. You've a brain, Caroline, and I can quite see you need to use it.'

'I do. I've loved being at home all this time, but suddenly it isn't quite enough. Solve it for me, Muriel.'

'I've been thinking, how about taking her to see

where you work? You could go to the surgery and show her your desk and such-like. Perhaps if she has a picture of where you are in her mind, she will settle better.'

'Oh, Muriel!' Caroline stood up and grasping Muriel's shoulders, gave her a kiss on each cheek. 'Where would I be without you? Of course, it's worth a try. And, yes, you're quite right. I've done too much at all once – I see that now. But the chance came up and I took it without thinking of the consequences; it all seemed to fit in so nicely. It was asking too much of her, wasn't it?'

'I think perhaps so. Alex, you see, has taken it in his stride, but not all children are the same, are they? I must go. Ralph is wanting me to view the improvement in the cricket pitch – since yesterday, would you believe! I'm glad you and I are doing the cricket teas, and we've got Kate Pascoe to help too. Isn't that lovely?'

'It is indeed. Though I'm not in her good books, I'm afraid, because of Beth.'

'Never mind, we'll solve it.' Muriel turned back to add, 'You see, you can't let Peter take sole responsibility for her; he's got his own job to do. If he was off into Culworth every day to an office you couldn't rely on him, could you?'

'Certainly not. Thank you, Muriel, for helping me to see daylight.'

'Peter is very upset.'

'I know, and I haven't helped.'

'He's a dear, wonderful man. He's achieved so much since he came here. We hadn't – well, *I* hadn't – realised just how bad things had become; we needed him to revitalise us. In this day and age he has mountains to move in his work, you know; there's so much apathy towards the church. Well, I'd best be off. Bye bye, my dear. It will all work out, you'll see.'

*

'Tomorrow morning I'm taking the children to the surgery in Culworth.'

'Are you concerned about Beth's stomach? Is she worse?' Peter looked up from his book. He shut it with a snap as he waited for Caroline's reply.

'No, not at all. I'm taking them both to see where I go to work. Then they've got a picture of where I am when I disappear.'

'Ah, I see! That your idea?'

'Well, truth to tell it was Muriel's.'

'Muriel's?'

'Yes, she came round to see me. She'd pointed out I've done too much all at once and that's why Beth is so upset. It might work. We'll see.'

'If it does, I shall be relieved. She could be right.'

'I think she could. I owe you a thank you, Peter, for not pointing out to me that you never wanted me to work in the first place, and that it was all my fault.'

'You're right, I didn't want you to work. But at the same time I can see why you want to.'

'Are we friends again then?'

'Never been anything else but friends. It was just something we disagreed about. I love you, you see.'

'I love you, too. I'm sorry about all this.' Caroline ran her fingers through her hair.

'If it doesn't come right?'

'Ah! Well, I made a promise to you that if the children were upset then I would stop and I shall. But can I give it one more chance?'

'Of course. Take a toy or something of Beth's and put it on your desk – let her choose it. Then she'll feel there's something of her with you and you give her something to put in her pocket that belongs to you.'

'Peter, you are an angel! Of course, what a good idea.' She placed her hand on his cheek and bent to kiss him.

His understanding of her and his willingness not to blame her for Beth's problem brought to the fore all her passionate love for him. Caroline knelt down in front of him between his knees. Peter put down his book and gathered her to him. He hugged her close, enjoying the scent of her, the lovely familiar feel of her warmth against his. He began moving his hands over her body, appreciating the slimness of her, the roundness of her hips, and then he took her head in his hands and kissed her lips. With his fingers he began smoothing her hair, tracing the curve of her ears, his eyes feasting on the shape of her face, her jaw, her eyebrows. Then taking her head between his hands again, he looked into her eyes. 'When shall I ever stop finding you so inviting?'

'Never, I hope, because I find *you* overwhelmingly exciting. We shall probably be still at it in our nineties!'

'Darling! You'll be such a gracious old lady.'

'Thanks very much! I don't feel like an old lady at the moment, but I am getting cramp in my foot. Ouch!' She slipped from his grasp and sat down to rub her foot. Peter pulled off her shoe and massaged her foot.

'Oh, that's better. Thanks.'

'Let's go to bed.'

'Let's. It's only half-past nine, but let's. I was going to do some jobs ready for tomorrow.'

'Let tomorrow take care of itself. Come on.' Peter pulled her to her feet and with his arm round her waist set off towards the stairs.

'We haven't locked up! I'll check the back door and the cat flap. You do the front bolts.'

Chang and Tonga were already in bed. 'Peter! Mimi's not in yet.'

'Never mind, she's always the last in, and it is early.'

'I shall worry.'

'Don't, she'll be all right. Hurry up!'

Chapter 7

Before he pinned it up, Jimbo read the postcard Sylvia had brought for his Village Voice noticeboard.

'Mimi gone missing? Caroline will be upset.'

'She is. We waited all day yesterday for her to come home but she hasn't, and Dr Harris is very upset. Mimi was the first cat she had, you see, and she's quite old now — for a cat, that is.'

'Poor old thing.'

'I think she'll be back. She's the one who brings all the mice home and one day a young rat, heaven help us!'

'Oh God! Where did she put it?'

'Well, we caught her trying to struggle through the cat flap with it in her mouth, but she couldn't quite make it through and had to leave it outside.'

'Thank God for that!'

'Exactly.'

'I assume it was dead?'

'Oh no, she brings them home alive and gives them to Dr Harris.'

'What a delightful habit.'

'As you can imagine I'm not best friends with Mimi but I don't like to think of her as being missing. We're conducting a hunt in Rector's Meadow this afternoon – that's her favourite hunting ground, you see.'

'I'll put the card up right now. I'll mention it around, see if anyone's spotted her.'

'Thank you.'

'How's Beth this morning?'

'Well, she's gone to playgroup with one of Dr Harris' scarves tied round her neck and an old handbag of hers with some treasures in it, and Dr Harris has taken BooBoo, an old toy rabbit of Beth's, with her. Fingers crossed, it seems to have worked. I've been playing with her for nearly an hour and suddenly she said I could go. So I went. But I'm going back to sneak a look in school before I go home. Dr Harris took them both to see the surgery yesterday and Beth seems more resigned now. If you find her on your chair again, please ring me, won't you?'

'Of course I shall. Straight away. Damned worrying, her floating about the village like that. Damned worrying.'

'I'll get my shopping done then. Thank you, Mr Charter-Plackett.'

'Hope the dreaded Mimi turns up.'

When Sylvia went back to the school at a quarter to twelve to collect the children she walked into a full-scale row.

Pat Duckett was standing in the hall, floormop in one hand, mop bucket by her side indignantly protesting to Kate Pascoe that the floor was clean by anyone's standards and she—

'I'm sorry Pat, but it isn't. The children laid down to do their floor exercises and every one of them was dusty and grimy when they stood up.'

'They'll 'ave to dust themselves off then, won't they? Stands to reason when the floor's been walked on all morning and it raining too! Every time someone steps outside a classroom they 'as to walk on the hall floor. Small wonder the floor gets dusty, at the very least, by the end of the morning.'

'It simply won't do – and then to eat their food in here with all that dust.'

'Well, I'm sorry *Ms* Pascoe but it isn't on my list of things to do, mopping the floor before I gets the tables out. There isn't time.'

'Time there will have to be. I can't think what the office would say if they came and saw the floor in this state.'

'And while we're putting our cards on the table, what about that cat?'

'What about it?'

'I don't never remember anyone bringing a cat to school, 'cept those days when Mr Palmer had an animal day and everybody brought something. A cat reg'lar isn't the thing in a school. Heaven knows what germs it might be bringing. Oh hello, Sylvia. What do *you* think about a cat in school?'

'To be honest, I don't know. Is there something in the regulations or anywhere?'

Kate Pascoe pointed to the floor. 'I've my class to get back to. Please see that this floor is clean before the tables are put out.' She turned on her heel and went back to her class.

Pat screwed the mop dry and began mopping. Then she leant on the mop handle and said, 'You don't want a job as school-caretaker, do yer, Sylvia?'

'No, thanks.'

'I thought not. I'm about at the end of my tether with her. And that cat. It spits if yer get too close. It 'as claws like a tiger's. I reckon it's related to a panther. Black as night, evil it is. It's got all-seeing eyes. Does my nerves no good at all.'

'You'd better leave.'

'I've half a mind to. I reckon it can put the evil eye on yer − yer know, like yer read in books. If cats start disappearing it'll be 'er that's spiriting 'em away.'

Mindful of Mimi, Sylvia went off to collect Alex and Beth, thinking over what Pat had said. It was all ridiculous of course but . . . 'There you are, come along then, you two. Had a nice morning?' Beth held up a picture for her to see.

'Oh Beth, that *is* lovely, Mummy will be pleased. What have you made, Alex? A car. That's splendid. Let's get home. We've got everything, I think. Come along then. Bye bye, Mrs Neal.' Beth's thumb was in her mouth, her lover tickling her nose, the scarf still round her neck, her handbag hanging from her arm. Alex skipped blithely along, his sister walked quietly, as though weighed down by care. Sylvia glanced down at her; at least she hadn't run off. Thank goodness.

Caroline put the children's boots on and then her own. 'Come along, children. Ready, Sylvia?'

'I am. Have you seen my gloves?'

'Here they are on the table.'

'Oh, right, so they are.'

They crossed Pipe and Nook Lane and climbed over the wall into Rector's Meadow. The children ran along in front kicking a ball while Caroline and Sylvia walked behind looking in the grass as they went and calling. The wind was keen and Caroline pulled her scarf more closely round her neck.

'Mimi! Mimi! Really, I suppose it's pointless calling. If she sees us she'll come, won't she?'

'Yes. Have you seen Kate Pascoe's cat?'

'No, but we shall tonight. That's where we're going when you sit in.'

'Oh, I hadn't realised. Pat says it's related to a panther. She doesn't like its eyes.'

'Oh, honestly!'

'That's what I thought.'

'We could try the old barn, couldn't we?' Caroline pointed to the stone barn alongside the wall adjoining the Big House estate. 'She might have got in there and can't find her way out.'

'That's an idea. Yes, we'll do that.'

They wandered all the way round the edge of the field calling for Mimi and looking in the long grass, but there was no sign of her. When they reached the barn Sylvia said, 'The door isn't locked. Never is. And look – there are places at the bottom of the door where she could have got in. It's rotting away.' She took hold of the bracket where the padlock once was and pulled the door open. It opened about a foot and then jammed and they all squeezed in.

Once a barn for holding winter-feedstuff for cattle, it still had bale upon bale of hay stacked against the walls. The thick stone walls had withstood a couple of centuries of weather and were still as strong as the day it was built. The roof, a sturdy construction of timber and tiles, was intact; the only light came from two square openings high up at the apex of the opposite shorter walls. The hay was dry and old and long past its usefulness.

Caroline called, 'Mimi! Mimi!' but there was no answering mew, only a scuffling amongst the bales. 'This place is huge. It would make a fantastic house, wouldn't it?'

Sylvia said, 'I heard something then.'

'Did you? I didn't. Do you think it's Mimi?' Alex and Beth were climbing onto a bale and jumping off with great shrieks of delight. 'Mind! Careful, you two.'

Sylvia's eyes widened when she heard the rustling noises again. She mouthed rather than said, 'Rats?' Caroline looked at her in silent horror.

'I've always had a dread of . . .'

'So have I.'

'Come along, children, Mimi's not here. Let's go home. Mummy's feeling cold. A hot drink, I think, when we get back. Time to go, darlings, come along. We're wasting our time. I'd rather find her dead than not *know*. That's the hardest part, not knowing.' Despairingly she called again: 'Mimi! Mimi! No, it's no good. Let's go. Don't forget your ball, Alex. I wonder if she's gone into Sykes Wood? I'll try there tomorrow perhaps, as a last resort.'

'Peter, I've just had a thought. If Kate is a vegan, what on earth shall we have to eat?'

'I'd forgotten that. I can see I shall be having a bacon sandwich when I get home to fill me up.'

'I can't think what vegans make for a dinner, can you?'

'You'll soon find out.'

'Ready?'

The lights were on at every window in the school-house when they got there. Caroline was full of anticipation. She loved seeing other people's houses; it gave one such a brilliant clue as to what made them tick.

Peter rang the bell and they heard footsteps approaching the door. 'Do come in. Isn't it cold tonight?' Kate was in black, a kind of evening dress with long sleeves and bugle bead decoration on the bodice. Caroline had come in a smart winter dress and felt she'd made an error of judgement, but it was too late now. Kate's long black hair was plaited and the end of the plait fastened up on top of her head with a wide velvet ribbon. It left her long thin neck quite bare; around her throat was a selection of thin silver necklaces with pendants of one kind or another hanging from each one.

Tonight she wore make-up – a magenta lipstick with magenta eyeshadow between her eyebrow and eyelashes and a black line all around her eye. Peter found her rather alarming; Caroline was amused. What kind of statement was she making here? She was like something out of a nightmare. Her long pointed nails – the kind which made Caroline wonder however the owner managed to achieve even the simplest task without the nails getting in the way, were painted to match her lipstick. Somehow Caroline didn't fancy food prepared by hands which looked like that. But then she shrugged her shoulders; she was being quite ridiculous. What on earth had long nails to do with the food she ate?

What really took her breath away was the decoration of the narrow entrance hall. Where she, Caroline, would have used light colours to give the passage width, Kate had used dark navy. The ceiling was light blue with silver stars of different sizes stuck to the ceiling. The same treatment had been given to the tiny sitting room – dark walls and a light blue ceiling, but this time golden suns with rays coming from them were stuck all over the ceiling. God! If Michael Palmer could see this!

Peter said, 'I love your decorations – they are so unusual. You must have worked awfully hard to get all this done in such a short time.'

'I have. At the weekend I stayed up all night to get finished. I'm glad you like it. I know it's not to everyone's taste, but I've tired of magnolia and all that dratted stippling effect and stencilling everyone's been doing for years. Thought I'd have a change.'

Caroline seated herself on a sofa draped with Indian throw-overs. She sank almost to the floor, the sofa was so soft. Peter sat in a chair more suited to a tiny elderly aunt than a man of six feet five. He dwarfed it and it looked in serious danger of collapsing under his weight.

'A drink?' Kate suggested. 'The meal's almost ready.' They both nodded. 'I have orange juice or elderflower wine. Or dandelion if you prefer.'

'Well, I've never tried either so I'll plump for the elderflower, thanks.'

'So will I.' Peter raised an eyebrow as Kate left to get the glasses. He mouthed 'Help' and went to sit on the sofa beside Caroline. She kept her face straight and looked round the room. The pictures were of wild stark landscapes and one was of sea crashing onto dark, forbidding rocks. There was a kind of threatening effect to the pictures which quite unnerved Caroline. How could Kate be so pleasant and yet like – actually choose to buy – such forbidding prints?

'This elderflower is very refreshing, Kate, very pleasant.' Caroline lifted her glass in a toast to Kate.

'It is, isn't it? The dandelion is very potent, so you can try some before you go home. At least you don't have to drive!'

'Do you make the wines yourself?'

'I do but not this one; a friend gave me this.'

'Can I help with the dinner at all?'

'Oh no. Well, you could carry things in. I'll just check the potatoes and then I'll give you a shout.'

Peter sipped his elderflower wine and silently gazed at the decor and the furnishings. It really was quite amazing. He felt something brush his leg and he jumped. He looked down to see what had touched him, and found himself staring into a pair of the greenest eyes he had ever seen. 'Good grief, it's a massive cat.'

'Shush!' Caroline looked towards the kitchen door, and hoped Kate hadn't heard him.

'It's a monster! I thought Tonga was big but this is

ridiculous. Hello, puss.' Cat spat and Peter hastily pulled back his hand.

Kate called from the kitchen, 'Ready, Caroline!'

'I'm coming.'

Between them they carried in a huge selection of salads. The protein was provided by what looked like meatloaf. There were thick slices of French bread and a dish with what looked like butter in it, but couldn't be. She brought in hot new potatoes in a covered dish and invited them to sit down.

Peter admitted that out of ignorance he thought vegans lived on the odd lettuce leaf and a bowl of rice. 'Obviously I'm very wrong. This looks like a feast fit for a king!'

Kate nodded her head in acknowledgement. 'Certainly not, Rector, that really does show abysmal ignorance.'

'I do beg your pardon.' He bent his head to say a silent grace.

'This is a nutloaf I made myself to an old Turkish recipe. The salads are self explanatory. The spread is not butter but made from soya beans.'

They began to help themselves and Kate whilst filling her plate said, 'Beth seems to have had a better morning, Caroline.'

'Yes, she does. I'm hoping we've turned a corner. It just needed a bit of careful thought and we think we've found the solution.'

Peter helped himself to a pile of new potatoes and said, 'Tell me, Kate, are you settling in OK?'

'Oh yes, thank you. Bit of a blip this afternoon, though, I'm afraid.'

'Oh? Anything I can help you with?'

'Pat Duckett has given in her notice.'

'I'm sorry to hear that. She's been at the school a long time.'

Kate rolled her eyes heavenwards. 'So she frequently tells me.'

'Does she give a reason?'

'Yes – me.'

'You?'

'Yes. I won't have things slipshod, you know. It won't do. She's got very lax.'

'I see. I'm surprised. Then we shall have to find someone quick. Still, we have a whole month, don't we? She'll have given a month's notice.'

'Well, no, she hasn't. She's leaving on Friday. Says she's not bothered about her pay.'

'Oh? That's most unlike Pat. She's been so reliable. The office will want an explanation of such a hurried departure.'

'I know. I wondered if there were any mothers who come to mind who might be interested.'

Caroline was enjoying the food beyond her wildest expectations. It was so spicy and aromatic, she had to give credit where it was due. 'This food is delicious,' she enthused. 'I'd love to try a few of your recipes. How about Bel Tutt?'

Kate looked puzzled. 'I don't know that dish. Is it good?'

'No, it's not a recipe! It's a person. She might be interested in the job.'

'Oh, I see.'

'Dicky Tutt is the Scout Leader and Bel helps. Any nonsense and Bel wades in. They've all learned to respect her!'

'If you'll give me her number, I'll give her a ring.'

Peter offered his help. 'Better still, I've some paper-work for Dicky which I'm dropping into his house tomorrow. I'll have a word with Bel myself if you like. Explain the situation.'

'Thank you, Rector, please do that. If she's interested I'll see her any time out of school hours.'

Next morning, Peter had a real hangover. 'This must be the result of that second glass of dandelion wine. I feel terrible, what about you?'

'Ghastly! I'm so glad I haven't got surgery today. I've a dreadful pain in my head.'

'Same here. Quite weird, actually. I keep thinking ridiculous thoughts.'

'She did warn us it was potent. I shall stick to water if we go again.'

'So shall I. I'm not going running this morning – I just can't. I'll dash off and say my prayers and then come home. Jimbo will laugh. He always declares he's much fitter than me, and boasts he could do double the distance if he had the time. The children are still asleep.'

'They're tired from playgroup.'

'You stay in bed till they wake up.'

'I shall. I wonder if Mimi will come home today? I'm going walking in Sykes Wood this morning, see if I can find her.'

'Not by yourself?'

'No, Sylvia said she would come too. Even though she has never liked Mimi.'

'I'm not surprised.'

'Peter!' He grinned. Caroline snuggled down; he went to the bathroom and groaned when he saw his reflection in the mirror. He looked appalling and felt it.

Peter was in his study when he heard the doorbell ring. Shortly afterwards, Sylvia tapped on his door.

'Rector, have you time for a word with Pat Duckett?'

'Of course. Come in, Pat.'

'Thank you, Rector.'

'Here, sit down, make yourself comfortable. Is it too early for coffee, Sylvia?'

'Seeing as it's you sir, no, it's not. Milk and sugar, Pat?'

'Just milk, please.'

When she'd left the room, Peter turned to his visitor. 'Now, Pat, what can I do for you?'

Pat peered closely at him. 'Aren't you well, Rector?'

'I'm fine, thank you.'

'Oh, but you don't look it. Anyways, Rector, I've come to tell you that I've made a right mess of things. Given in my notice.'

'Kate Pascoe told me so last night when we went to her house for dinner.' Pat tut-tutted at this. 'I'm very sorry indeed. You've always done such a good job, come hail or shine. Seven, eight years is it now?'

'Thereabouts. I got on really well with Mr Palmer. We 'ad our ups and downs but it was mostly ups. But . . . well, I can't see eye to eye with *Ms* Pascoe. I'm not saying she's in the wrong, it's just that we're not on the same wavelength, if you get me. We had a flaming row. She wanted this doing and that doing, all extras and some quite unnecessary, I think, and it's sending me timings all wrong and I'm nearly dizzy with it. Anyway, when I got home and cooled down I thought, You fool, Pat Duckett, giving yer notice in just when yer need the money. So I 'aven't actually written it, only *said* it – so do you think you could put in a good word for me and get me job back? I wouldn't ask but we all know how persuasive you can be.' Head on one side she grinned at him. 'Would you?'

'I very likely could, if that's what you want. I mean, why can't you get on with her?'

'I don't really know – can't put me finger on it. It's just that I'm worried, like – don't know whether I'm coming or going. Barry says I'm imagining it. Anyway, I've decided I'm being daft and I'd like to carry on and I shall try to adapt.'

Sylvia came in with the coffee. They chatted for a while as they drank it but Peter came no nearer to finding a clue as to why Pat was upset with school. It was as she said: she just didn't feel right.

'Not long now, Pat.'

Pat raised her eyebrows. 'I don't know what you mean. Oh, the wedding! Our Michelle's that excited.'

'Aren't you?'

'He's a lovely man, is Barry. Honest, hardworking, good at his job – and he really likes the children and they like him.'

'That isn't what I asked.'

Pat put down her empty mug. 'I can't quite believe it's happening to me, you see, Rector. I've had years of struggle, and never expected to be happy again. Truth to tell, I wasn't that happy with me first. Now and then I get a glimmer of how happy I'm going to be, but I'm not going to get too excited.' Pat fidgeted with her beads. 'You never know, I might be making a big mistake.'

'Well, you *are* going to be happy again – I'm sure you are. I've had a long chat with Barry and I'm positive everything will be fine. Believe me. You deserve it. Barry's a great chap.'

'He's wicked, he is.' She grinned at him. 'I won't take any more of your time, I'll be off. When that Ms Pascoe said she'd be glad for me to leave, she meant it, she really did. You could have a difficult job on your hands. If you don't succeed don't worry, it *is* my fault. After all, it might make me take the plunge and do more jobs with Jimbo. I don't quite believe in myself enough you see, to do that.'

'Jimbo's a very astute businessman. He wouldn't be asking you if he didn't believe in your capabilities.' Peter stood up and saw her to the door. 'I'll give you a ring when I've seen her. I'll do my best. Good morning, Pat. God bless you.'

'Thank you, Rector, thank you.'

Chapter 8

Beth watched her mother getting her boots out from the hall cupboard, then Alex's and then her own. 'Mummy, no playgroup morning?'

'No, darling. We're going for a walk in Sykes Wood to see if we can spot Mimi.'

'Sylvie coming?'

'She is.'

'Don't like playgroup. Don't like Pascoe.'

'*Ms* Pascoe, Beth. Why?'

'Funny.'

'Oh, come on, she's nice. Here, lift your foot. That's it. You can do the other one yourself, can't you? Show Mummy.'

'Can't.'

'You can.'

'Can't.'

'*Won't*, more like. I'll do it then. Here's your coat, put it on.'

'Can't. Mummy do it.'

'Alex has got himself ready except for his buttons.'

'Beth can't.' She stuck her thumb in her mouth and took her lover from her pocket. Caroline kissed her and

68

dressed her herself. If dressing Beth was what it took to make her happy then she'd dress her.

'Not going to playgroup 'morrow.'

'We'll see. Ready, Sylvia?'

'Coming.'

The four of them left the rectory and walked along Church Lane. The world and his wife seemed to be out and they exchanged greetings with two of the week-enders who were spending a holiday week redecorating and were off to get food at the Store, then with the gardener sweeping the drive of Glebe House. When they passed the gate to the Big House, they read its smartly painted notice telling them it was TURNHAM HOUSE and in small letters underneath *Fitch plc London and Brussels*. They climbed the stile into Sykes Wood and followed the well-worn path which led right through the middle of the woods. Alex rushed along ahead of them with Beth following slowly in his wake.

'Jimmy Glover buried his dog Sykes here, do you remember?'

'I certainly do, Dr Harris.'

'Along with all his snares; he said he buried them really deep so the foxes couldn't dig them up. Mimi! Mimi! Shout for Mimi, darlings.'

Alex and Beth shouted until they were hoarse, but Mimi didn't appear. They came to a clearing and Alex pounced on a burnt stick. Right in the middle of the clearing was a large circle of ashes and burnt branches and twigs.

'Look, Mummy, bonfire.'

'So there is.' She felt the ash. 'It's cold. Fancy having a fire in the woods in the middle of winter.'

Sylvia looked down at the ash, and poked it about with her boot. 'Could have been in the summer. It's difficult to tell when it was.'

Alex rushed to Caroline. 'There's a glove – look, Mummy. Man lost a glove.' It was a large, thick black-woollen glove with a big hole in the thumb, a kind of burnt hole as though the owner had been wearing it while tending the fire. But it wasn't wet or dirty or going rotten. It had been left quite recently.

'Throw it down, Alex, there's a good boy. How odd!' Caroline shivered with the cold.

Sylvia persuaded herself she knew the answer. 'It'll be the Scouts on one of their midnight hikes. Cooking sausages and things, you know what they're like.'

'Of course, you're quite right. It will have been them. Beth, what have you found? What is it?'

'A stick, a big stick.' She dragged the stick along the ground. The end was burnt as though it had been used for poking the fire. As she dragged it along, some rags from just under the surface of the ground became entangled with it. There'd been a half-hearted attempt to bury them.

'Curiouser and curiouser!' Caroline bent down to look at the rags, which turned out to consist of an old shirt and a woman's blouse, dirty and wet.

Sylvia, still poking about with her boot in the soft loamy soil close to the ashes, suddenly glanced at Caroline to make sure she wasn't looking, and bent down to pick up something and put it in her pocket. She said, 'Let's go. It's nothing to do with us. Come on, Dr Harris, let's leave it be. I don't like it here. We shouldn't go any further. Let's turn back.'

'Very well. Come along, children, we'll go home. Mummy's cold and I'm sure you must be too. We'll have to forget looking for Mimi today.'

Sylvia was shuddering. 'There's something unpleasant here and no mistake. Hurry up, children, please. Come on, Dr Harris, let's get away from this place!'

'Why, you're shaking!'

'I am. There's things here not for the likes of us.'

'You mean it wasn't the Scouts?'

'I hope not. Baden Powell will be spinning in his grave if it was.'

'Are you psychic or something?'

'No, but there's a funny feeling here I don't like.'

'Now I'm frightened. Two grown women getting the wind up, this is ridiculous.' Nevertheless Caroline took the hands of Alex and Beth and hastened them along. Both she and Sylvia breathed a sigh of relief when they had climbed the stile and were standing out in the road. Then, they both burst out laughing.

'We are stupid, really we are!' Caroline kept tight hold of the children as Barry Jones hurtled by in his van. He waved, slammed on his brakes, came to a screeching halt, and then reversed dangerously up to them.

'Morning! What's up?'

'Oh, nothing. We just talked ourselves into being frightened in the wood back there. Sylvia reckons there's something there not for the likes of us. We're searching for my cat Mimi – she's been missing for three days now, and she's the smallest of my Siamese, so I'm worried. Don't suppose you've seen her on your travels?'

'Sorry, no I haven't. I'll keep a look out for her though. Bye, Dr Harris, keep smiling. Bye, Sylvia, bye kids!'

'There's no two ways about it. I'm going to have to accept that my Mimi is gone for ever. It's one whole week today since I last saw her.'

Jimbo offered his sympathy. 'I'm really sorry. It's downright awful not knowing, isn't it?'

'It is. Leave the card on the Village Voice noticeboard a little longer will you, Jimbo, please? Just in case. I've been round Rector's Meadow twice and once into Sykes Wood but no luck. You never know, someone might have found her though and given her a home. They might even see the card.'

'She was quite old?'

'Twelve – no, thirteen. However, there we are. No Mimi.'

'Shall you get another?'

'No, I shan't. Your two cats are all right, are they?'

'Yes, why do you ask?'

'Just wondered if we had a phantom cat-stealer, that's all. Silly of me really, but you do wonder.'

Jimbo began adding up Caroline's purchases. 'Beth's getting better at playgroup?'

'Yes, thank you – a little. Alex is perfectly all right, that's what's so odd. You'd think they'd react the same, wouldn't you?'

'That'll be ten pounds ninety-seven pence, please.'

'Thanks. Flick liking her new teacher?'

'Oh yes. Thinks she's lovely.'

'Good, I'm glad. I'll be off then.'

Caroline carried home the shopping, put it away in the fridge and the cupboards. Having decided that Mimi was a closed chapter in her life she was feeling in need of sympathy, and Peter being the only one who could satisfy her need, she went to find him. But he'd left a note on his desk to say he'd *gone to Penny Fawcett, back for lunch*.

Caroline sat down in the easy chair in his study and thought about her cat. She'd been sweet and gentle in the house, but a holy terror where hunting was concerned. Chang and Tonga had always accepted that she was the senior cat and, if she so chose, they allowed her to push them aside and finish off their food. Now, as if in answer to her thoughts, the two of them stalked into the study.

'Come on then, come up.' She patted her knee and they both jumped up onto her lap. She stroked them each in turn, enjoying their companionship. She thought about Mimi when she'd first got her, a small creamy-coloured tiny thing, soft and warm. The tears began to fall and she had to fumble in her pocket for her handkerchief. Sylvia came in.

'There's a letter come through the door for the rector. I'll— Why, whatever's the matter?'

Caroline sniffed. 'I'm being silly. I'm thinking about Mimi and how I shall miss her. But she's only a cat. I've got to keep things in perspective, haven't I?'

'Yes, but I can understand.'

'She was my first cat before I met Peter, you see, and it was lovely to come home to my flat and find Mimi waiting; it made all the difference. It's not knowing the end that's the worst. I *know* she wouldn't have gone off to live with someone else. Anyway, at least I've got these two.'

'Indeed you have.'

The children came bursting in through the door.

'And these two!!'

'Mummy, play tiddlywinks. Come on.'

Caroline pushed the cats onto the floor and stood up. 'I certainly shall. What else are mummies for? Come on.' She grinned through her tears at Sylvia and said, 'Sorry for being such a fool.'

'Not at all. I can quite understand.'

Chapter 9

'Far be it from me, Ms Pascoe, to criticise your methods. Taking the children here there and everywhere is lovely, but when the end result is that it shortens the time the children spend on the three Rs, then it is *not* at all beneficial. In fact, I think it's a retrograde step.'

'Hetty! There's more to life for children of this age than pen and paper. What on earth can they find to write about if their experiences are so narrow? If they lived in a city they'd be doing all sorts of exciting things, but country children's horizons are so limited.'

'But think of the money. I know it's lovely to walk on the walls in Culworth and learn about the Romans first-hand as you might say, but that will be the second outing your children have had this term.'

'So, what's wrong with that? You can take *your* children whenever you like.'

'I know that, but you see a lot of the children round here are not very well off. Two outings in the first half of the term is a lot for their parents.'

'Nonsense! No parent minds providing money when it's to the children's advantage.'

'What if they're unemployed like the Watsons? They've got two in your class.'

'Then we shall use school funds if they can't afford it.'

'We only used to have an outing in the summer term when Mr Palmer was here.'

'Mr Palmer *isn't* here, is he? I am. And I shall be obliged if you don't keep telling me about what *used* to happen, Hetty! Now is now.'

Hetty turned to Margaret. 'What do you think, Margaret?'

'Well, I . . .'

But Hetty interrupted her. 'This business of the children coming straight into school the moment they arrive in the mornings. We've never allowed it before.'

Kate grew impatient. 'There you go again, Hetty. In the past. It won't do.'

'I'm thinking about our responsibilities. I was here at quarter past eight on Tuesday morning and there were already three children in the school. It's not right.'

'Pat Duckett is here.'

'She is not legally responsible, as well you know.'

'Oh really! What harm can come to them?'

'Once the parents realise that the children can come straight into school they'll be sending them at some ungodly hour, just to get them out of the way so they can get off to work. Speaking of ungodly, I took real exception to you talking about Hinduism in that manner yesterday. None of us are Hindu and the children must be very puzzled. They never see a coloured person from one week to the next.'

'All the more reason why they should learn about them then.'

'I disagree. What do you think, Margaret?'

'Well, I . . .'

'The rector won't be at all pleased.'

Kate smiled. 'Don't tell him then. It *is* my school.'

Hetty encouraged Margaret to support her. 'Say something, Margaret.'

'I think—'

'I have been employed as Head, and as far as I can, within the bounds of the national curriculum, I shall teach as I see fit, and if going on an expedition helps them to understand the world better, then on an expedition we shall go.'

'My children will be complaining. It makes me look mean.'

'You arrange an outing for them, then. Broaden their outlook, encompass the world if you can. Isn't that so, Margaret?'

'Oh! Yes, I supp—'

Realising she was fighting a losing battle, Hetty asked Margaret: 'Whose side are you on?'

'I don't—'

Kate got up to go. 'Time I was off. Got people coming for a meal. I'll love you and leave you.'

Hetty Hardaker waited till she was out of earshot then said bitterly, 'Well, some support I got from you, I must say.'

'You didn't give me a chance to speak.'

'I asked your opinion.'

'I know, but you interrupted or Kate did.'

'It's not right. I *know* it's not right.'

'Where shall you take your class then?'

'Heaven alone knows; I'll have to think of some-where. I hate school outings, it's the worry of losing someone.'

Margaret gathered her things together. 'I'm off. She's only trying to do her best and she does have a point.'

'About what?'

'About the children's limited experiences.'

'You could be right.'

'I am. She's like a breath of fresh air.'

'Hmm.'

'Mr Palmer was not at all flexible, you know.'

'Yes, but the children were well-taught. We shan't be getting anyone into Prince Henry's or Lady Wortley's if we do as she says. We've three children sitting the entrance exams next week; there's not a word about that, is there?'

'There's more to life than academic success.'

'You try telling the parents that!'

'Harriet? Kate Pascoe here. Hello. Would it be possible to pop into school to see me this week? Round about four when the children have gone?'

'Why, yes, of course. Is there a problem with Flick?'

'Nothing serious, just wanted a chat.'

'I'll come today then. About four?'

'Lovely, thanks. Be seeing you!'

Harriet replaced the receiver and stood watching Fran who was glued to the children's TV. What on earth did Kate want to see her about? Flick hadn't said anything.

She dialled Jimbo's mobile phone number. 'Hello, Jimbo? Could you come home early today? Well, Kate Pascoe from the school has rung and wants me to go and see her this afternoon about four. I don't know what for, but she does. You don't have a clue, do you? No, I haven't either. Be home just before four, darling? OK, bye.'

When Flick got home Harriet asked her if she'd done anything naughty at school.

'No, of course not, Mummy. As if I would.'

'Well, no, of course I know you wouldn't, but do you have any idea why Miss Pascoe wants to see me?'

'Ms Pascoe? No, I haven't. It's my entrance exam next week – maybe it's something to do with that.'

'Oh, yes. That'll be it. Of course.'

Harriet left Jimbo with instructions about Fran and wended her way to the school.

Kate offered her a coffee but Harriet declined. 'You have one if you wish. Don't let me stop you.'

'I will, if that's all right. Hard work, teaching.'

'I'm sure it is. Do we have a problem? Is that why you've asked to see me?'

'Not a problem as such.' She stirred her coffee while she found the right words. 'I do worry about Flick, do you?'

'Not particularly.'

'I see. She's very uptight, isn't she?'

'I wouldn't have said so.'

'That's how she comes across in school. Always a bundle of energy, first with her hand up, eager to please. Very competitive.'

'She comes from a competitive family.'

Kate smiled. 'Of course. But I think she needs to relax a little and let the world go by, don't you know.'

'She does, at home. Reads books by the score, laid on her bed.'

'That's it, you see. Reading . . . not very relaxing, is it?'

'What do you suggest?'

'My suggestion is,' Kate paused and eyed Harriet carefully as though debating the wisdom of what she was going to say next, 'she doesn't go ahead with the entrance exam.'

Harriet was startled. 'Not go ahead! What can you possibly mean?'

'I mean she should go to a school where, unlike Lady Wortley's, there will be less pressure to succeed. I'm pretty sure she'll find the stress of a high-flying school too much and she could have serious problems.'

'Just a moment. You are basing your opinions on, what is it, three weeks experience of her? You know she's very bright, and Lady Wortley's is where she needs to be to reach her potential.'

'Harriet, there are other ways of reaching one's potential without stretching oneself to breaking point.'

Harriet frowned. 'Breaking point? What on earth are you talking about? Are you having this same conversation with the other parents?'

'Oh yes, I am. I think it's terribly important that the children have an all-round experience in school, and I honestly think Prince Henry's and Lady Wortley's are very one-sided.'

'Well, Kate Pascoe, I'm afraid Flick will have to put up with a one-sided life if she gets in, and let's hope she does, because *she* can't wait to get there. I'm sorry, but we have no intention of withdrawing her from the exam, and I should imagine you will find the same attitude with the other parents. I'm amazed, I truly am.'

'You'd rather put your prestige before the well-being of your daughter?'

'My prestige?' Harriet suddenly began to feel very angry.

'You know – "Oh, my daughter is at Lady Wortley's. She'll meet all the right people . . ." et cetera, et cetera.'

'I think you've overstepped the mark, Kate. Your opinions about class have no place here. You can take it from me that my daughter is sitting the exam, full stop. I'll leave you now, the boys will be home shortly – from Prince Henry's I might add – and they're in need of TLC when they get in.'

'There you are, you see. It's the pressure.'

'Pressure, my foot!'

'Please don't be upset with me, I'm only thinking of Flick's welfare.'

'I'm sorry. Yes, of course you are. Thanks for talking with me anyway. I'll speak to Jimbo about what you've said, but I already know his answer.'

'Thanks for coming. I'm just sorry I haven't persuaded you.'

'You won't, I'm afraid. Good afternoon.'

'Bye.'

'So what do you think? Are we being too pushy? I was so wild I gave her a real mouthful, I'm afraid. I could have bitten my tongue out afterwards.'

Jimbo shifted his arm from under Harriet's shoulder and rubbed the pins and needles away. 'My dear Harriet, I love Kate Pascoe. She fills the eye every time she comes in the Store, but – and I mean but – she has odd ideas and I think this must be her oddest.'

'But what if she's right? I mean, look at Alex. Goes to playgroup as happy as Larry, yet Beth can hardly bear to walk through the door. Two children from the same mould and their reactions so different. Perhaps like they say an onlooker sees most of the game. Maybe Flick isn't like the boys; maybe she couldn't stand the pressure. She did have that fearful accident.'

'I know she did, but she's got guts. Even the specialist Archie what's-his-name said so. No, I think we're doing the right thing. She's got to be given her chance just like the boys. If she doesn't get in, then all well and good – it's meant to be.' He paused. 'But she will!'

'Jimbo! No wonder she's so competitive.' Harriet turned on her side and looked into his eyes from three inches away. 'Do you really find Kate attractive?'

'Of course, what man wouldn't?'

'Really. I can't see it, you see.'

'Well, you're a woman.'

'I can see Simone Paradise is attractive.'

'God, that woman and Kate make a pair. Rice this and nut that, soya milk and pasta that. How they survive I don't know.'

'They were talking outside the Store the other day. Simone's children were running wild as usual and she took not a blind bit of notice of them. They were very engrossed. Maybe they were swopping recipes!'

'There is a kind of recognisable affinity between them, isn't there?'

'They don't dress alike though, and they've got totally different lifestyles.'

'I know, but there is some indefinable something or other. However, give me a solid well-fed woman like yourself any day.'

'I know I've put weight on since I had Fran, but really.'

'Come here to your Jimbo. God, I love you.'

'I'm glad. Will you talk to Flick or shall I?'

'I shall. I shall tell her we'll love her just the same whatever happens. Too competitive indeed!'

Chapter 10

Ralph received a letter from Mr Fitch outlining the financial arrangements for the cricket club. He was halfway through reading it when he broke off to admire the headed notepaper, which had *Turnham Malpas Cricket Club* at the top. The words were printed in old-fashioned type, a little like the Ye Olde Teashoppe signs painted above so many pretentious cafés. In smaller type below it said *President: H. Craddock Fitch.*

'H. Craddock Fitch? Muriel?'

'Coming.' She appeared in the doorway dressed for going out.

'Muriel! That man up there – is there no end to his conniving? He's put his name on the cricket club notepaper as president.'

'Ralph! No, he can't have done. He promised.'

'I know, but he damn well has, after he agreed. Right, that's it. The knives are out.'

'What shall you do?'

'I'm not sure. Confrontation? He'll only laugh.'

'Is he at the Big House at the moment?'

'Possibly – he has signed the letter personally. But his terms are very, very reasonable. No rent to pay on the pavilion for two years – which is far longer than I had hoped. We shall be on a sound financial footing by then. He's providing all the equipment, we can't grumble at that, though how we can take ourselves seriously with *Fitch plc* emblazoned across our chests I don't know.'

Muriel sat down and began to laugh. 'Oh really, you do take this cricket business far too much to heart. It's only a game.'

'Only a game!' Ralph was appalled. 'My dear, I have played cricket all over the world. It is not a game to be treated lightly. A piece of home, no matter the temperature or the altitude, a game which cuts a swathe through race, creed and colour. I remember once in Venezuela . . .'

'Ralph, I have no time for cricket stories. I have to be off – Celia Prior will be here any moment now. We're having lunch together, I told you yesterday.'

'In Culworth?'

'Yes, she's taking me in her car. I've left you some lunch out in the kitchen.'

'Thank you, my dear. You enjoy yourself. She's very nice.'

'She is.'

'Arthur is going to be our official score-keeper.'

'Oh, how lovely. There's Celia's car. Bye bye, dear.' She kissed his cheek, and left in a flurry of lost gloves and a handbag she'd put down somewhere but couldn't remember where.

Ralph stood watching Muriel get into Celia's little Rover. Well, he'd better find out if old Fitch was in residence, and if he was, he'd have to sort him out. The damned fellow didn't behave according to the rules of a gentleman. He could deal with him if he did. He and old Fitch didn't . . . what was it Muriel said the other day? Oh, that was it: he and old Fitch 'didn't sing from the same hymn-sheet'.

'I changed my mind.' Craddock Fitch tapped the ash from his cigar into the cut-glass ash-tray on his desk.

'Changed your mind?'

'Yes. I thought, damn it, I'm rebuilding the pavilion, I'm providing all the gear – why *shouldn't* I be president?'

'I thought we'd agreed.'

'We had.'

'This is a bit infra dig.'

'Don't quote your Latin tags at me, Ralph Templeton, just to impress me with your education. Take it or leave it – Craddock Fitch is President. Now, I have another meeting in five minutes. Is there anything else?'

'No, nothing else. But you disappoint me.'

Mr Fitch said he was sorry, but the tone of his voice implied he didn't care a fig about disappointing anyone.

'Good morning.' Ralph stood and left the library seething.

Needing to let off steam to someone who understood his mood he went to the Store.

'Morning, Jimbo. Got a minute?'

'For you, yes.' He called to his assistant to attend the till and then invited Ralph into the storeroom at the back.

He took off his boater and laid it on a shelf and invited Ralph to sit on his stool.

'Well? I can see you're very annoyed.'

'I am. Fitch has changed his mind.'

'About the pavilion?'

'Oh no, not about that. He loves the idea of his name above the door too much. No, it's not that.' Ralph paused, then: 'He's decided to be president.'

'The devil he has! I thought you said he'd agreed for it to be you?'

'He did.'

'Everyone's going to be very upset,' Jimbo predicted. 'He'll poke his interfering nose into everything we do. He won't be a president in name only, you can bet your life on that.'

'Exactly. But you be careful, Jimbo. I know how much you have at stake with him businesswise, so don't do anything silly, will you? You see, not being a gentleman he doesn't play by the same rules as you and me.'

'There's no way we can find the money to rebuild the pavilion on our own. Look at the first estimate we got – what was it, thirty-five thousand pounds? You'd think we were repairing Buckingham Palace!'

'Much as I should like to step in and pay for it, I really can't. Got to see Muriel's well provided for.' Ralph paused for a moment. 'And, of course, I've sunk a great deal of money into the houses in Hipkin Gardens.'

'But what a gesture. You've brought eight families into Turnham Malpas who wouldn't have had a cat in hell's chance of being here otherwise. It's going to make such a difference to the school. That's worth something by anyone's standards.'

Ralph stood up. 'Thank you. I've taken up enough of your time, so I'll be off. I shall take this blow like a true gentleman, and say not another thing to him about it!' Ralph smiled wryly at Jimbo, shook hands and left.

The bar in The Royal Oak simmered with the news of Mr Fitch deciding to be president.

'Who told you, Willie?' Jimmy asked.

'Malcolm, when he left the milk.'

'How does he know?'

'How does he know anything? He hears all his news from all the housewives he chats up on his round.'

Jimmy drained the last of his ale, slapped his tankard down on the table and said, 'Well, I for one feel right upset. We all know it should be Ralph. But then old Fitch is paying for the pavilion and that. I bet the bats will be the best money can buy.'

'Yes, and then you know what?'

'What?'

'He'll expect the team to be top every season.'

'That's his trouble yer see, always 'as to be best.' Jimmy scowled. 'Nothing about the game. Now Ralph would see it as how good a game yer played and that, but not his nibs, oh no. I don't know for certain but I bet he's giving a cup.'

'Two!'

Jimmy laughed joyously, and thumped the table with his fist. 'I knew it! I knew it!'

The other drinkers glanced up and smiled.

'Tell us the joke, Jimmy,' someone shouted.

'Old Fitch is giving two cups for the cricket.'

They all laughed uproariously.

'Typical.'

'Show-off.'

'He's like a great big kid.'

'Thinks he can buy his way in – well, he can't.'

'Not likely. The laugh is he doesn't realise we know what he's up to. Thinks we're daft.'

'Still, we can take the benefits and laugh like drains when we gets home.'

'Yer right there! What else can we screw out of him, eh?'

'Nice smart chairs for us to sit on instead of lolling about on the grass?'

'China cups for us tea!'

'Waitress service!'

'Champagne when we win!'

'The list is endless!'

They all fantasised a while longer about Mr Fitch and his generosity and then one group in particular put their heads together and became conspiratorial.

Jimmy nodded his head in their direction. 'Wonder what they're up to? No good, by the looks of it.'

Willie twirled his glass round on its little mat, and then casually remarked: 'Heard anything odd about Sykes Wood lately?'

'No. Why?'

'My Sylvia and Dr Harris found an old bonfire in there in that clearing where the old charcoal-burners used to be. Remember?'

'Bit before my time.'

Willie was annoyed by his flippancy. 'You know what I mean. I'm serious. 'Ave yer?'

'No. Nothing funny about 'aving a bonfire, is there?'

'No, but Sylvia got really frightened. They'd gone to look for Dr Harris' cat. It's gone missing, yer know. Mimi, it's called. Well, she . . .'

'Yes?'

'If I tell you something, can I have yer absolute promise not to tell anyone?'

'Hope to die.' Jimmy drew his finger across his throat and bent his head closer.

'Sylvia found something.'

'What? Like a skellington or something?'

'No.' Willie drew closer. 'She found Mimi's collar.'

'No!'

'Right close by the bonfire – not in it but near it.'

'What did Dr Harris say?'

'Sylvia never told her. Bent down and popped it in 'er pocket and didn't let on.'

'Collar, yer say?'

'Yes.'

'Funny, that.'

'Exactly. Then Sylvia got this strange feeling and begged Dr Harris to go home. She felt all shaky. Unfastened it was, the collar, and the buckle quite stiff, so it weren't no accident it came off. It hadn't got pulled off while Mimi was climbing a tree or anything; it had been *taken* off. Found the collar but not the cat.'

'Strange. But 'ow did she know it was Mimi's collar?'

'Her collar's brown to match the markings on her face, and it 'as a little identification thing on it. So she knows.'

'But she hasn't told Dr Harris?'

'Well, she was going to later, like, but she didn't know how she was going to tell her and she kept putting it off and then one day she found her crying about the cat, and didn't like to say anything, in case she made matters worse. So I've said she's to tell the rector and see what he thinks.'

'That's best. I'll 'ave a wander round there, see if I find anything. I knows them woods like the back of my 'and.'

'Thanks, Jimmy. I 'oped yer would. If anyone should know them woods it'll be you, considering 'ow much poaching yer did in there. But not a word. Dr Harris mustn't find out from anyone except the rector.' Willie tapped the side of his nose and Jimmy winked in agreement.

Sykes Wood, eh? He knew just where Willie meant. The charcoal-burners' cottages had long since disappeared, most of the stones carted away for building other houses years and years ago, but the clearing was still there. Odd that. He'd have a look tomorrow before he went to work.

Chapter 11

'Mummy! Mummy!' Flick slammed the front door and raced through to the kitchen. 'Mummy, we've been on a walk.'

'Where to?'

'Sykes Wood. We've been communing with nature.'

Harriet folded up the ironing board and went to the fridge to get Flick her drink. 'What does one do to commune with nature?'

'Well, one of the things we did was to hug a tree.'

'Hug a tree? Whatever next.'

'It's all to do with listening to what the tree says to you.'

'And what did yours say to you? Here's the biscuit tin. Want one?'

Flick chose a Bourbon and bit a huge piece off it so her mouth was too full to answer. Harriet said, 'I would have thought that with your exam tomorrow, a bit of hard work would have been more appropriate.'

Flick sipped her milk and then began, 'Well, Kate said that—'

'"Kate said"? Ms Pascoe, surely.'

'She says that as we are in our last year we can call her Kate.'

'Well, I don't approve at all.'

'Get up to speed, Mummy. You're so old-fashioned. Though Mrs Hardaker did say *she* didn't like us calling Ms Pascoe Kate, and *she* thought we should be working but Ms Pascoe said "Nonsense" and Mrs Hardaker's lips went all straight like they do when she gets cross. She said, "Miss Pascoe, I really think——" But Ms Pascoe just tossed her head and said, "Come along, Class Three, away from these four walls out into the world, for another brilliant experience" so we did.'

'So what did you hear when you hugged your tree?'

'Well, I didn't hear anything actually, because there were creepy-crawlies all in the cracks in the bark and I couldn't concentrate in case they got in my hair.'

'So you didn't have a brilliant experience.'

'No, it was a bit disappointing. Kate says trees scream when they get a branch chopped off or get cut down. She says when the world was young we would have been able to hear them but not now. That's dreadful, isn't it? I never thought they could feel hurt. I shall worry now. Shall I go and rest ready for tomorrow?'

Harriet laughed. 'That's your way of saying you'll go and join Fran watching television, is it?'

'Yes.'

'Well, it's not for long. She's getting square eyes, absolutely hypnotised she is and doesn't understand one tenth of what she watches, so you must get her to play in a while.'

'OK.'

Flick came back from the day of examinations exhausted. Harriet had collected her in the car at three o'clock and when she saw how weary Flick looked she began to have reservations about her angry retort to Kate.

'How did it go? Everything all right?'

'Mummy, I'm so tired. It was quite exciting though. Two girls burst into tears, another one fainted, and one went out to be sick. The lunch was lovely, and the teachers! They were so kind.'

'And the exam?'

'Oh, that. Quite easy, actually.'

Harriet's heart sank. Quite easy? Oh dear. That could mean she hadn't understood what was required of her. 'Well, I'm glad. We'll just have to wait and see. You won't have to be too disappointed if you don't get in. Daddy and I, Grandma Sadie and the boys and Fran will all love you just the same, you know.'

'I know. Daddy's already told me that about five times.'

'Sorry, but it's true.'

'I know.' Flick looked out of the car window. Parents! She knew she would get in. It was where she was destined to be and she couldn't wait to play lacrosse – such a distinguished game. She'd seen some of the girls going out to the playing-fields from the window of the examination room, and longed to join them. The uniform! Oh, roll on, September! 'When I get home I shall give Fran a big hug and tell her all about it,' she declared, 'then she'll know for when it's her turn, and I shall want a cup of tea and a piece of cake.'

'OK, fine. You can go in the Store and choose a fancy cream one if you like.'

'Great! Shall I have to pay? I've no money on me.'

'You know Daddy's rules.'

'Yes.' Flick sighed.

Harriet dropped her off outside the Store with a pound coin in her hand.

'Don't be long. I'll put the kettle on.'

Flick decided to wander around the Store for a moment; it seemed a long time since she'd been in there and it was only right she should know what was going on. She'd have to tell Daddy that the greetings card shelves were not quite as full as they could be, and that his new assistant was spending too much time chatting instead of taking the money quickly when there was a queue. People hated waiting. Ms Pascoe came in.

'Hello, Kate! I had a lovely time at the exam, I've just got back. Did you miss me?'

'Of course I did. Everything all right?'

'Oh yes, thanks. It's lovely, I hope I get in.'

'If that's what you want, so do I.'

'I do. I'm buying a cream cake for a treat.'

'Some fresh fruit would do you more good.'

Flick laughed and tossed her head. 'But I'm having a cream cake, sorry!'

She lingered by the video-lending shelf and pondered whether or not to ask Mummy if she could borrow one. Being short she couldn't be seen over the top of the stand and quite by mistake she overheard two women talking. One of them was Kate Pascoe. 'Ten o'clock. Tonight.'

The other voice said 'Righteo. We'll be there.' Flick slipped quietly to the end of the shelving and peeped round the corner. It was Simone Paradise who had answered.

She bought her cream cake and went home, and told Fran all about the exam, and watched television and fell asleep for a short while dreaming of playing lacrosse wearing that wonderful purple sweater she'd seen on the girls that very afternoon.

'Harriet! This damned tie won't behave itself. Help! Rescue me, please, I'm running late.'

'You never have been able to do these ties. Why don't you buy one of those made-up ones?'

'I have bowed to modern technology in all corners of my life but I will not bow to a made-up tie. That is definitely sartorially *verboten*.'

'OK, OK. There we are. You look good. Much better in that suit now you've lost weight.'

'Thank you – I do, don't I? More youthful, don't you know.'

'Hurry up!'

Flick was reading Fran a bedtime story and she shouted through the bedroom door. 'Why isn't Mummy going?'

'It's all men tonight, my dear child.'

'I thought Ms Pascoe and Mrs Paradise were going.'

'Certainly not, though I mightn't mind Ms Pascoe, she's a cracker.'

Harriet, standing in the doorway, said, 'Why did you think they were going?'

'I heard them saying they were meeting at ten o'clock. So I thought they must be going where Daddy's going.'

'Ten o'clock? You must have misheard. They would have said seven o'clock.'

'I'm not daft, Mummy.'

Harriet shrugged her shoulders and went in to kiss Fran good night. 'Good night, my sweetheart.'

Fran lay on her side, snuggled up to the cuddliest teddy bear her grandmother had been able to find. Her long dark lashes fluttered as she began dropping asleep, one hand tucked under a rosy cheek. 'Ni', ni'.'

'Time for your bath, Flick, you must be tired. Thanks for reading the story.'

Jimbo shrugged on his overcoat and gave Harriet a hug. She straightened his silk scarf and kissed his cheek.

'Have a good time.'

'I will. Be all right?'

'Of course. I won't wait up.'

Harriet stood at the door watching him start up the car and waved as he turned up Stocks Row. As she locked the door the thought crossed her mind, what on earth had Simone Paradise and Kate Pascoe got in common? Not a blind thing as far as she could see.

Harriet had decided to spend the evening while Jimbo was out, going over the accounts on the computer in the study. She'd just switched on and was checking through in her mind which aspect she would take a look at first when she heard the front door being unlocked.

'Jimbo? Is that you? Hello-o-o?'

'Only me, darling.'

'Mother!' Harriet went into the hall. 'I didn't expect you tonight.'

'Thought I'd keep you company. Where are the boys?'

'Scouts. Coffee or something stronger?'

'Stronger. You'd better get one for yourself. You might need it.'

'Why, what's the matter?'

'I need your advice.'

'*My* advice – since when?'

'Since last night. I'll sit down.'

'Of course. Whisky?'

'And water.'

They sat in the study, Harriet patiently waiting to hear what she was supposed to be advising about.

Sadie swirled the whisky glass round and round in her hand. She was elegantly dressed as always, her long slim legs in fine nylon tights and smart high-heeled shoes, her outfit a straight black skirt, silver-grey long-sleeved silk shirt, and a scarf loosely tied around her throat. Harriet admired her as she sat deep in thought sipping her whisky. 'Well, I'm waiting?'

'I'm thinking of getting married.'

'I beg your pardon?'

'Like I said, I'm thinking of getting married.'

'To whom?'

'Craddock Fitch.'

Harriet was stunned. She couldn't believe she'd heard correctly. 'You? Marriage to Craddock Fitch? Are you pulling my leg?'

'As if I would. He's asked me and I'm almost ready to say yes.'

'I see. Well, you did know him when he was a strip of a lad. I was aware you were seeing a lot of him, but *marriage* . . . Are you sure?'

'Are you asking that as a fully mature adult or as a child of mine?'

'Ah! At times like this the two are very mixed. It's difficult to know which I am at the moment.'

'Exactly. I don't know which I am, either. Am I a grown woman and a grandmother – heaven help us! – or have I gone back to being a seventeen-year-old like I was when I first refused him. Maybe I've taken leave of my senses.'

'Why *did* you refuse him?'

'I've always been independent right from the cradle, and some sixth sense told me that being married to Craddock – well, Henry as he was then – would be suffocating. He would have expected complete loyalty, complete absorption in his business affairs, because it was obvious even then that he was going to be a business-man, and I baulked at the idea of being so completely taken over. I engineered a row and that was that. He hated the idea that anyone owned him, you see, so I deliberately said something, whatever it was I can't remember exactly, to annoy him and he blew his top.'

'And now?'

'Now he's different. He respects me, which he didn't before. I can answer back without him freezing me out with his stony silences. We can discuss and argue and he listens to my opinion. And what's more, I still find him fascinating. He's not the chilly person he appears to be. Oh no! He wants to be a warm loving man, and he's trying very hard.'

'Look, Mother, if you love him, for heaven's sake marry the man. Whyever not?'

'You may be right, but . . .'

'Yes?'

'This mail-order business. I've built that up myself. Agreed, it stemmed from an idea of yours, but the work and the success has been mine – agreed? I've felt fulfilled making a success of it. I love Harriet's Country Cousin marmalades and jams, and the labels! I get a thrill every time I look at them. And the Christmas hampers are bliss! It's about the only thing apart from you that I can look back on as an achievement which is wholly mine.' Harriet nodded. 'I can hardly bear the thought of giving it all up, which I would have to do.'

'I can't stand the idea either. I'd have to get someone else to do it.'

'Obviously I'd give you my shares.'

'Well, thank you. I shall miss you and so will Jimbo.'

'I haven't said yes yet.'

'No, but I think you will. At the very least you'd keep a rein on his more blatant excesses.'

Sadie looked annoyed. 'What on earth do you mean?'

'You know, buying himself a position here in the village.'

'Oh that. They all know what he's up to, so why not if the village benefits?'

'Why not indeed!'

Sadie sat for a while staring at the carpet. She finished the last of her whisky and then said, 'I might say yes. I could very well say yes. You must understand that my will leaves everything to you and the children, so I wouldn't want you to worry about that. Craddock has quite enough. He doesn't need my money, neither do you really, but it's all yours.'

Harriet got up and went to give her mother a kiss. 'Your money is the last thought in my head. If you do decide to go for it I hope you'll be very happy. I hold no brief for my father so I certainly shan't get in the way if it's what you want. Mr Fitch would definitely be able to keep you in the style to which you would like to become accustomed!'

Sadie grinned. 'I shan't let him take my grandchildren over, though. Definitely not – they're mine. I do hope it won't make a difference to Jimbo's business relationship with him.'

'I shouldn't think so.'

Sadie stood to go. 'Harriet, before I leave you in peace, I should tell you that there was a scene in the Store today.'

'Really?'

'Jimbo's new assistant was serving and I could hear a lot of noise and shouting, so I went to take a look. Simone Paradise was in there with that crowd of little louts she calls her sweeties. They were causing mayhem. Pulling the greetings cards off the shelves and throwing them down. Picking up chocolate and sweets and trying to open the packets up. One took a bite out of an apple . . . I can't remember all they did. I protested and told her to get them all out. She hitched the baby up in that ridiculous sling thing she makes from her shawl and said in that slow drawling way she has, "Sweeties, come on we're leaving now." I was furious. I asked her what about the cards they'd stamped on and we can't sell, and the apple they'd bitten a piece out of? To say nothing of the sweets. She said she couldn't afford to pay for them and it was our fault for having the goods displayed where the children could get hold of them. I'm afraid I saw red. Did my Dame Edith Evans bit, you know the kind of thing. Told her in my most superior manner that she needn't come back in the Store again with her horde of brats because her kind of business we could well do without. Time she got them under control. Et cetera. Et cetera. Simone fixed me with what can only be described as the evil eye. I'm shuddering now when I think about it. I'm not an imaginative person but I felt as though time had stood still. Then it jerked back into rhythm again and there were the children standing beside her angelic and quite still.' Sadie visibly pulled herself together. 'However, what I was going to say was, do watch out for her. She really is odd. Night, night, my dear, take care.'

'I will. I'll tell Jimbo. Good night, Mother. Thanks for talking to me about it. The decision is yours in the end, you know.'

'Yes, but it's nice to know you would approve if I said yes, which I probably shall. I love you for it, my dear. I hope to be as lucky as you. I adored your Jimbo from the first moment I saw him; you did well there, my love, very well. And thank you for all my grandchildren, too. I'm so proud of them all.' She leant forward and kissed Harriet and patted her arm. 'Good night, Harriet. See you tomorrow.'

Harriet closed the door after her mother and decided she couldn't go back to concentrating on accounts and in any case the boys would soon be home. She switched off the computer and sat for a while in Jimbo's armchair – his 'thinking chair' he called it. If her mother could be as happy as she was with Jimbo then she should go right ahead. Sadie had endured years of loneliness, somewhat alleviated by coming to live in the village just after she and Jimbo bought the Store, but even that wasn't quite the same as sharing one's house and one's bed. A stepfather. Wow!

Harriet felt glad to have been consulted. It wasn't often her mother let down her guard and spoke of herself and her feelings; it had indeed been a rare moment between the two of them.

Chapter 12

The news that Sadie had died in her sleep that night shocked the entire village. More than one of them had been on the receiving end of Sadie's forthright opinions, and she had in the short time she'd lived in Turnham Malpas become something in the way of a legend. But Sadie *dead*? Her strong life-force, cut down at one stroke? No one could remember ever having seen her looking anything but at her best, always full of pep and get-up-and-go. And so stylish. They'd envied her style. It wasn't that she spent loads of money on clothes, just that she knew what would flatter her and she'd worn it well. Chic was what she was. Every customer spoke of their horror at the suddenness of her going, or savoured over and over again the times when they'd clashed with her. And no chance to say goodbye even – that was sad, real sad. But then Sadie would have hated any kind of sloppy sentimentality so maybe it was best she went the way she did. All the same. So suddenly . . .

On the day of her funeral the church was packed with mourners. Not a few noticed that Mr Fitch, grim-faced and silent, was there sitting with the family. But then he would be grim-faced, wouldn't he? He'd no heart. But what was he doing, sitting with the Charter-Placketts? That he was a close business associate of Jimbo's they all knew but in the front with family mourners . . .?

It was the three grandchildren for whom the villagers felt the most compassion. They were devastated and quite uncomprehending of this terrible blow, for Sadie must have been a real fun grandma to have. The two boys wore their Sunday suits and little Flick, bless her, that new coat she was so proud of with its fur collar. They remembered how distressed Sadie had been when Flick had her accident. But it was Sadie now they were mourning.

When the service was finished and Sadie had been laid in her grave, they all noticed that Harriet went to speak to Mr Fitch. Funny that; she'd drawn him to one side so they couldn't be overheard. Pity – would have been nice to know what they had to say to each other.

'Craddock, thank you so much for coming,' Harriet said gently. 'I do appreciate it. The night before my mother . . . died, she told me about your proposal.'

'Did she? Did she?' Mr Fitch blew his nose and turned away his face and looked across the churchyard towards the yew tree, so she could only see his profile. 'What did she say about me?'

'That she found you fascinating.'

He turned back to face her. 'Was that all?' The longing in his face overrode anything Harriet might have decided to say and she impulsively said 'She told me she was going to say yes.' No one but she knew Sadie hadn't absolutely made up her mind, but the grief in Craddock's face was unbearable, and if she could give him some comfort, why not?

'Really! I'm so glad. When we were young I loved her very much. My word, she was a spirited young thing. Still is. Was, I mean. If we'd married then, we'd have had some rare old fights. But now it would have been very rich, but without the fights. I think. Maybe not! I'm very sorry for you, Harriet, but it was a lovely way for her to go. She would have hated being less than herself – you know, crippled or senile. This was the best for her, but not for you and me. Thank you for telling me that.'

He clasped both her hands in his and then raised them to his lips and kissed them. 'Thank you, my dear. You would have made a lovely stepdaughter. I should have been proud. So proud.'

Harriet kissed his cheek, Mr Fitch turned away and left the graveyard. Then Jimbo gathered the children and Harriet, and took them home, so the other mourners never did find out what they'd said, but then they remembered that Sadie and old Fitch had known each other years ago. That's right. That'd be why.

'I'll pick up Fran and we'll take off these black things and put on something jolly. It's what she would have wanted, Harriet.'

'We ought really to be having a big party with lots of drink and fun. She always loved parties.'

'I know, but we both agreed it would be too hard on the children. They wouldn't understand.'

'No, perhaps you're right. Oh Jimbo!' Harriet laid her head against his shoulder and wept the first tears since her mother's death. Jimbo hugged her tightly until the tears slowed. 'There, there, darling, you'll feel better for that. It's no good thinking we shall all be over it in no time at all; it's going to take an age, but she wouldn't have wanted us to be miserable, she'd rather we were brave and carried on. She's left such lovely memories for us all.'

'I know, but I shall miss her. She was so young to die. I thought she'd be a grand old lady for years and years.'

'So did I. I had the distinct feeling she'd outlive us all, but there we are.'

'I'm so glad she came to see me the night before. We had the closest conversation we've had in years. Do you think she had a premonition?'

'Bit too practical a chap I am to know about those kind of things. Just be grateful she did come and you did talk.'

'I can hardly bring myself to speak about it, but you know the post mortem? Well, it wasn't really conclusive, was it? They couldn't really find out why her heart had stopped, could they?'

'No. All very odd. Felt sorry for old Fitch.' Jimbo wiped Harriet's face for her. 'All that happiness snatched away.'

'I told him she'd definitely been going to say yes.'

'That was a bit of a fib, darling.'

'Only a teeny weeny bit of a fib, but it did bring him comfort.'

Flick appeared in the hall. 'There, look, I'm wearing the dress Grandma bought me in the summer. She loved it and so do I. It still fits me, look. Mummy, Fran won't remember Grandma, will she?'

'No, darling, she won't.'

'Don't cry any more, Mummy, please. I'm going to get lots of photos and put them in an album and call it Grandma's and then we can show it to Fran when she gets older, and we'll tell her about playing cards for big money, and all the naughty things Grandma did, like having her hair dyed, although you'd never have guessed if you didn't know, would you, and such.'

'Thank you, Flick, that will be lovely. I think you'd better put a cardigan on, darling, or you'll be cold.'

'All right, I will. Daddy, who will do the mail-order now?'

'I haven't worked that one out yet. Do you have any ideas?'

'If I was older it could be me.'

'You'd do a very good job, I'm sure. I shall have to put my studying cap on.'

'It'll have to be someone good. Grandma wouldn't like it all to fail, would she?'

'No, she wouldn't.'

Suddenly Harriet was crying again and she fled upstairs and shut the bedroom door with a slam.

'Daddy, shall I . . .?'

'No, I'll go and collect Fran from the rectory then we'll make a cup of tea and take it up to her in a little while, that'll be best.' Jimbo patted Flick's shoulder and strode away to the rectory. Little Fran screamed when she saw her Daddy had come to collect her. She wanted to stay with the twins and she wasn't going home. No! No! No! But Jimbo insisted. He knew that cuddling Fran would be a great comfort to Harriet right now.

'Thank you, Sylvia, thank you very much. Hope she's not been too much trouble.'

'Certainly not. Good as gold.'

Trying to get the mail orders off in between all his other activities was too much for Jimbo. He knew Sadie had liked to send orders off by return if it was at all possible, and he was failing dismally on that score.

The morning after the funeral, Barry Jones' mother came in and asked him how he was coping.

'Not too good. One never really appreciates how much work people do until they're not there any more. The mail orders are piling up and Sadie would be angry if she knew.' He took off his boater and rubbed his bald head in agitation. 'Now, what can I do for you?'

'What can I do for you, more like. If it's just a question of reading an order, picking the items out and packing them up in them lovely boxes you 'ave and addressing a few labels, I could do that temporary like till you find someone. Wouldn't be any good with accounts or anything, but the rest is a question of common sense, isn't it, really?'

'Do you mean that?'

'Wouldn't say it if I didn't. You and I, Mr Charter-Plackett, have not always seen eye to eye, but I don't mind 'elping someone in trouble. A bit of extra money towards our Barry's wedding would be very useful too, but we'll discuss that later when we see if you're satisfied with what I've done. What do you say?'

'I could run the money side and pass the orders to you, couldn't I?'

'You could. And I haven't got far to go to post the parcels, 'ave I?' Mrs Jones twinkled her fingers at Linda behind the post-office counter.

'You're on. Temporary.'

'Right, I'll get my sleeves rolled up. I'll just ring Vince, if that's all right and tell him where I am, otherwise he'll worry, I don't think.'

'Be my guest.'

'I always liked Mrs Beauchamp – bit like me, spoke 'er mind when necessary. I was in 'ere when she 'ad that row with Simone Paradise. Nasty, that was. Yer could feel it in the atmosphere. Charged it was, like they say in books. That Simone is cracked, yer know. Got friendly with that Kate from the school. Right! Show me where to start. I shall enjoy this.'

And Jimbo's newest assistant attacked her job with zeal.

Chapter 13

'Hetty! We've met the most marvellous man at the museum this morning. He's promised to come and give the children a talk. He's one of the senior archaeologists! Aren't we lucky? I'm sure your class would enjoy it too, wouldn't they?'

'I'm sure they would. When's he coming?'

'Tomorrow. It was either tomorrow or not for four weeks, and that's too long for my class to wait. We shall have moved on from the Romans before then.'

'What's his name?'

'Gilbert Johns.'

Hetty stopped marking exercise books and looked up at Kate. 'I'm surprised you don't know him already. He's our church choir-master.'

'Really? I didn't realise.'

'Not having been to church you wouldn't, would you?'

'Now, Hetty, don't get me into trouble, please. He's giving the talk at half-past nine, and bringing lots of artefacts for the children to handle. Nothing like "hands on" is there?'

'He's a very sweet man.'

'He is – a soul–mate, I think.'

Hetty was amused. 'I don't know about that.' She returned to marking the books. 'There were Roman remains found in the grounds of the Big House last year.'

'Can we see them?'

'No. Gilbert rescued what he could and they were taken to the museum for display, but it's not finished yet.' Hetty slapped the last of her exercise books on to a pile and, clasping them to her chest, stood up to go. 'There, that's that lot finished. In your classroom or mine?'

'Oh, mine I think. We have all the pictures and things up so it'll be more appropriate. Does Gilbert live in the village?'

'No. Down the lane from me in Little Derehams – Keepers Cottage. I called there once collecting for Christian Aid, and it was so untidy! Mr Fitch's secretary Louise seems to be a very frequent visitor.'

'Oh, I see.'

'Don't think the rector won't have noticed.'

'What?'

'That you're not going to church; he misses nothing. It is expected in your position.'

'Yes, well. I'm not breaking a *rule*.'

'No, not a rule as such, but it won't be in your favour.'

'I shall come to it all in good time.'

'Yes?' Hetty raised a sceptical eyebrow and returned to her classroom. Kate watched her leave. Hetty had a point. The job had been offered to her partly because of her having worked in the mission school in Kenya, the assumption being that she was a communicant member of the church, which in fact she had been. But now . . .

Kate had expected Gilbert to arrive a few minutes before half-past nine. In fact, he was there before nine.

'Too early, am I? Car won't start so I've begged a lift.'

'Not at all. We're all bright-eyed and bushy-tailed quite early here, so please feel free.'

'Where?'

'Oh right! In this classroom, please.' With a wide gesture of her hand, Kate indicated the classroom walls for his closer inspection. 'Well, what say you?'

'Oh, very good. I like this. Very good indeed. What clever children you must have and what a clever teacher to get all this from them.' Gilbert turned to smile at her. What a sweet smile he had. Nothing sexual or patronising, just a genuine smile of praise. She liked him for it.

'Here, are we?'

Gilbert turned to face the door. 'Ah! This is Louise. She gave me the lift. Yes, here please, by the table. Mind – that's quite heavy.'

'I can manage, don't worry.' Louise put down the box and went to shake hands with Kate. 'Hello, we've not met before. I'm Louise Bissett, secretary up at the Big House. You must be Kate.'

'Yes, I am. Pleased to meet you.' Kate was surprised that Louise, well-dressed and businesslike, could attract such a sweet gentle man as Gilbert Johns. She would have imagined he'd go for someone in long swirling skirts and lots of beads and long braided hair. However, each to his own – they obviously thought a lot about each other. Louise and Gilbert brought in two more boxes and then Louise wanted to hurry away to work. 'Got to dash. New lot of students today. Busy. Busy. Can I pick this lot up after work, Kate, please, if Gilbert's car isn't repaired?'

'Of course. Give me a knock on my door.'

'Fine. Bye, Gilbert.'

They were the same height. Gilbert kissed her, on the mouth, and Kate couldn't miss the quick flushing of

Louise's face as he did so. Two of the children watched from the doorway. Kate coughed. Eventually they broke apart and Louise fled. Gilbert winked at Kate, wiped some beads of sweat from his forehead with the back of his wrist, and began unpacking the boxes.

Gilbert attended prayers sitting quietly on a small chair at the back, his bony knees almost to his chin, joining in the hymns with his powerful tenor voice. The children began to giggle and Hetty had to still them with a piercing look from her eagle eye. When Kate took over for meditation Gilbert sat with bowed head, quite motionless. As she gave her short speech to help the children direct their thoughts she was intensely aware of him. Of his red shirt unbuttoned almost to his trouser belt, of the brown sinewy arms revealed because he'd rolled up his sleeves. The dark hair dropping forward over his forehead. The well-tanned face, the hollowed cheeks, the dark dreamy eyes. She shook herself mentally. This wasn't what meditation time should be used for.

'Thank you, children. Our five minutes of tranquillity is over. Stand quietly and go to your classrooms. I'll see Class Two in my room at half-past, Mrs Hardaker.' Kate stood up.

The children left the hall. Gilbert returned to the classroom to finish sorting his boxes.

They all had the most wonderful hour and a half listening to Gilbert, looking at what he'd brought, handling the combs, the spoons, the jewellery, the toys. Acting out little happenings for him and generally getting the feel of being a Roman. For that was how he'd presented his talk. Encouraging them to imagine they were Roman children, getting up, washing, eating, working, learning, playing, helping in the house. Everything a Roman child might do. He brought it all so vividly to life.

At the end, the children ran out to play leaving Hetty to make the coffee and Kate to help clear up.

'I can't thank you enough for what you've done today. You were absolutely brilliant.'

'Louise's idea actually. A day in the life of et cetera. Worked well, didn't it?'

'Indeed.'

'This meditation business – what's it all about?'

'A New Age approach.'

'Does Peter know?'

'Yes. He doesn't object.'

'How do you know he doesn't?'

'He hasn't said anything.'

'That's Peter all over.'

'It *is* my school.'

'Don't develop it any further.' Gilbert stored the last of his things and glanced around to make sure he'd not forgotten anything.

'It's none of your business.'

'No. But don't develop it any further. Not with the children.'

'I shall do as I please.'

'Not with other people's lives, especially children's. You're not at liberty to do that.'

'You don't know what you're talking about.'

'Maybe not. But despite being male, I am very sensitive to the fact that things are not quite as they should be.'

'Pity you haven't used your sensitivity where Louise is concerned. Not your kind at all.'

Gilbert's sweet expression changed alarmingly quickly. He almost snarled his reply to her. 'Louise is my concern and no one else's.'

'My affairs are my concern.'

'Not when it affects the children.'

'Sitting silently is a crime, is it?'

'No, but I suspect you're leading them on to your own agenda, which has no place here in this school.'

'What a pity you've spoiled such a wonderful morning.'

'What a pity you can't or won't take on board your proper responsibility for these children. They are in trust to you, they are not yours to do with as you will. They're not guinea pigs. Where shall I leave these? They must not be touched.'

'Here, in this corner, where I can keep my eye on them.'

'Right. Sorry for speaking out, but it had to be said. Any time, I'll come any time.'

Kate preceded him into the hall. 'Coffee?'

'No, thanks, someone to see and then I must catch the noon bus into Culworth. Bye, Hetty. See you Sunday about ten, Margaret. That OK?'

'Yes, I've got everything ready. Louise coming too?'

'Yes, she'll be there.'

'Good. We'll need her organising ability.'

'We will indeed. Goodbye, Kate Pascoe.'

'Thank you again.'

'Not at all. Any time, like I said.'

It was Peter he called to see before he caught the bus. He was in, and led Gilbert to his study.

'Just a quick word, Peter.'

'Sit down, please. Not had a chance to talk to you for a while apart from hymn numbers and tunes and things!'

'No, that's right. Been very busy.'

'How's life treating you?'

'Very well, thanks. And you?'

'Ditto, thanks. If you've come to see me about Sunday, I've been through——'

'I know you will have. No, it's not about Sunday. It's about Kate Pascoe.'

'Why Kate?'

'I'm not sure. I'm uneasy, that's all. Can't put my finger on it but I've told her this morning – been doing a Roman Times thing for the older pupils – that the children are not guinea pigs and she's not to have her own agenda for them. Sounds stupid, when I say it in broad daylight, but I was there and I saw and I felt. You should drop in some time, unexpected. You are allowed to do that, surely?'

'Yes, I expect I am but I don't.'

'Wish you would. Please?'

'Very well, I will. Although I'm sure you're wrong.'

'Maybe. But keep an eye out, OK?'

'OK. Will do.'

'It's the children I'm concerned about.'

'Of course.'

'Good grief! Is that the time? I shall miss the bus. He never waits a moment after departure time – in fact, I swear he goes early sometimes on purpose! Still, he has to have some excitement, doesn't he? Who'd want to drive a bus all day?'

'Goodbye. I'll bear in mind what you say.'

Chapter 14

The following Saturday night the bar of The Royal Oak was exceedingly busy. Every table was occupied and the dining room constantly full. The low-ceilinged room was hot, for massive logs were burning in the inglenook fireplace and great waves of heat poured out across the room. The customers were grateful, for the night was cold. It had taken three years for the villagers to come anywhere near accepting Bryn and Georgie Fields, the licensees, into their lives. Three years wasn't long enough though for the couple to have been initiated into the centuries-old undertow of prejudice and bias which coloured present-day arguments. Cricket was the subject under discussion at the small table beside the fire.

'My grandfather played in the cricket team before the Second World War, and his father before him played as well. They had some grand times in here after they'd won a match. Drunk as lords they were, singing and dancing. By jove, my grandad said the beer flowed and not half. Him' – the speaker jerked a derisive thumb in the direction of the Big House – 'up there's no business to be president. Should be Sir Ralph. Tradition counts. They always had a party up at the Big House to celebrate the end of the cricket season. My grandad said they used to eat till they could hardly stand. Wonderful cook they had up there. None of this daft French business with a couple of peas on your plate and hardly a mouthful of meat but plenty of fancy sauce. Great piles of food they had. Delicious. They didn't eat for a week after. And the ale and cider never stopped coming. They was gentlemen, was the Templetons. Everything given with a good heart. Him' – he jerked his thumb again – 'him, he likes *gratitude*.'

Vera Wright laughed. 'You're right there, he does.'

'Sir Ralph's a real gentleman, yer see. Can mix with anyone, high and low. Grand chap.'

'You're only saying that because he came in here the other night and bought you a couple of drinks. Sat here an hour or more you were with him, raking over old times.' Vera glanced up as the door opened and in came Willie and Sylvia. 'I shall have to go, me friends have just come in.'

'I'm off, they can sit here if you like.'

'Oh, thanks.' Vera waved to Sylvia and she came across.

'Isn't it busy? Bryn and Georgie must be making a bomb tonight. Doing really well out of it.'

'Yes, they must be. Everybody seems to be doing well except me, good old Vera Wright. There's Pat marrying the best pair of thighs in Turnham Malpas, and she's got that wonderful Garden House 'cos of her Dad's job, there's that awful Alan Crimble grinning his head off behind the bar, got married and got a lovely house as well. Mr Charter-Plackett's like a dog with two tails, his business is doing so well. Though I shouldn't say that, not since Sadie died. Unnerving, that was. Even so, everybody seems to be doing well but me.'

Sylvia watched Willie threading his way between the tables carrying their drinks. 'Come on, Vera, things can't be that bad.'

Willie put down the drinks. 'Evening Vera. There's your drink, my Sylvia.' He leant over and kissed her as he handed her the drink.

'See what I mean? You two's happy as sandboys as well.'

'Look, life's what you make it. You've got a lovely steady husband, couldn't be steadier, and a nice grandson.'

'Nice grandson? I don't think. Out all hours, he is. Must have been three o'clock this morning before he got in. At least tonight we'll be able to get to sleep. He's gone to stay with a friend top of Ladygate in Culworth. So we'll have two nights of peace at least.'

Willie proffered the idea that maybe he'd got a girlfriend.

'Come on, Willie, he's only sixteen, he's got no girl. Having said that, in the paper last Sunday there was this story about a boy of twelve, put in care he was because . . .'

Their three heads came close together in conference as Vera revealed the details of the story. But they were interrupted by the bar door crashing open so hard that it swung back and smacked into a chair which fell over with a resounding clatter. Everyone looked up to see who was coming in. It was Jimmy. He staggered in, looking as if his legs would give way at any moment, and headed straight for the bar counter. Leaning on it he heaved in several deep breaths and feebly requested a double whisky, which he proceeded to swallow in one gulp.

Jimmy – a double whisky? He hadn't had one of those since the night he won the pools. Surely he couldn't have won again, could he?

But Jimmy's face, not as tanned as it used to be when he was an idle good-for-nothing who spent most of his waking hours in the woods and fields poaching, was ashen. He tremblingly placed his empty glass on the bar counter and dragged the words 'another double' out of his throat.

Bryn said, 'Now look, you're not used to drinking whisky. Let this one settle first and then I'll serve you another.'

But Jimmy would have none of it. He gestured pleadingly at Bryn, so he was served another double.

Sylvia said to Willie, 'I really think you should go to him, you know. I can see him shaking from here. Go and find out what the matter is.'

Someone had put a bar stool under Jimmy's bottom and he'd sunk gratefully on to it as he downed his second whisky.

The colour was beginning to creep back into his cheeks when Willie said, 'Now then, what's the matter, seen a ghost?' Jimmy's colour receded again and he clutched Willie by his lapels and whispered in a voice which sounded as though he was being strangled, '*Sykes.*'

Willie, thoroughly startled, whispered back 'Have you seen something horrible in Sykes Wood, is that it?'

'No, no.'

'Well, what is it then? Tell me.'

Jimmy shook his head and the trembling grew worse. He took out a handkerchief and wiped the sweat from his face.

'It was 'im. It was 'im.'

'Who?'

Jimmy struggled to speak and eventually came out with, 'I treated him like a son, I did. Loved him like a son. And now this.' Tears began to roll down his cheeks.

Willie had never seen him cry, not even when his wife and baby died. He stood in front of him to shield him from the other customers; he didn't want all the world to see Jimmy's tears.

'I can't help yer if I don't know what yer talking about,' he said gently.

'It's Sykes. I saw Sykes.' The tears continued to rain down his cheeks.

Willie was so surprised he said loudly, 'Saw Sykes?'

Someone said, 'Sykes? Who's that?'

'His dog. Died three maybe four years ago.'

'What's he on about then if he's dead?'

Jimmy asked for another whisky.

Bryn shook his head. 'No, I'm sorry, no.'

Jimmy was by now too distressed to protest. 'It's punishment, you know.' He gestured to the ceiling with a thin shaking hand. 'Him, Almighty God, He's punishing me for what I did. For the way that poor dog of mine died. It was all my fault.'

'No, it wasn't. Of course, it wasn't. You weren't to have known.'

Jimmy's lips trembled as he said, 'It was my rabbit snares that killed him – let's face it. Best Jack Russell terrier any human being could have.'

'But how can yer have seen him when, he's, yer know, when he's as you might say, dead . . . like?'

Jimmy raised his voice to convince Willie. 'I 'ave, I tell yer I 'ave. Out in Church Lane.'

'It's dark, it'd be a cat.'

'It barked.'

Willie, taken aback but reluctant to believe Jimmy, protested, 'Yer can't 'ave. There's no such thing as ghosts.'

'Sez who? You've seen ghosts. What about that tomb in the church you say is haunted.'

Willie agreed, but then ghosts near tombs in churches were only right and reasonable, not like a dog out in Church Lane.

Sudenly there was a commotion at the table where Jimmy and Willie and Vera and Sylvia usually sat. One of the customers had stood up and said, 'There's a dog under here.'

'Don't be daft.'

'There is — I can smell it. That wet warm woolly smell yer get when they've been out in the rain and they're drying off. It's brushed past my leg. Get the damn thing out. It'll be ruining my new trousers.'

They all looked under the table but there was no dog there.

'But there *was* a dog, I felt it!'

Willie and Jimmy were electrified. Jimmy pointed towards the table with a shaking hand, and proclaimed in a loud voice filled with fear: 'See? He's followed me in here. He's there where he usually sat. Remember, I allus put me glass down there and he'd have a drink. Come back to haunt me, he has. Come back to haunt me. Divine retribution. That's what.'

The group finished their drinks and left in haste, unnerved by Jimmy's assertion that they'd felt a ghost. The chatter in the bar rose to a crescendo and more than one was visibly shaken by the idea of Sykes revisiting his old haunts. Not a few ordered more drinks to calm their nerves.

Bryn laughed. 'It'll be good for trade, then. A haunted pub.'

Georgie, furious, nudged him sharply and said, 'Shut up!' Patting Jimmy's arm she said comfortingly, 'Look, love, go home, Willie will take you, and you get to bed with a couple of headache tablets. You'll feel better in the morning.'

Resolutely Jimmy shook his head. 'Can't do that, he might follow me 'ome.'

Sylvia stood up. 'Now look here, this is all getting absolutely ridiculous. We'll all go – Willie, Vera, Jimmy and me – and we'll sit at our usual table and you can put a glass of ale down where you used to, Jimmy, and we'll all sit there and prove there's no smell of a wet dog and the ale won't be touched and we'll know it's all imagination. It's worth trying it out as an experiment, isn't it? Jimmy can't stay here all night, can he? We'll settle our minds once and for all. Come on, bring yer drinks.'

Rather hesitantly the three of them drifted across to the table where Sylvia had already plumped herself down on a chair. Bryn carried across the glass of ale and Jimmy placed it just where he always had done when Sykes was alive.

At a loss for conversation while the experiment took place, Sylvia began talking about the shoes Willie had bought that afternoon in Culworth. She was just describing how rude one of the shop assistants had been to her when all she'd said was 'these same shoes are two pounds cheaper down the road', when they distinctly heard the sound of a dog lapping. Everything stopped. Conversation. Drinking. Laughing. The entire bar froze. The only noise was the lapping which sounded almost indecently eager for a ghost. Sylvia looked at the three of them to see which one of them was going to dare to look under the table. But Willie and Jimmy and Vera were paralysed. Their only movement was their eyes, swivelling from side to side in terror. So it was she who bent down to have a look. Everyone heard the sound of breath being rapidly drawn in through tightly clenched teeth, then, energised by some unknown force, Sylvia's head shot up from under the table, she leapt up onto the seat of her chair, clutched her skirt around her knees and screamed, 'It's 'im! It's 'im!'

Someone muttered a heartfelt, 'Bloody hell.'

Vera slid off her chair in a dead faint.

'So there I was, Rector, up on the chair screaming my head off! Bryn came and enticed it out from under the table with a biscuit. I was still standing on the chair, my heart was absolutely pounding. The relief was unbelievable. It's a nice little dog and the absolute spitting image of Sykes. Same size, same colouring, even to the placing of the black patch round his left eye. Just like Sykes it is. 'Cept perhaps the black isn't quite as black as Sykes' patch but, as someone said, what else could you expect when he'd been buried in the wood for three years? Jimmy didn't take kindly to that remark, I can tell you!! It hadn't a collar on, so we still don't know whose it is.'

'Where is he now?'

'Well, Saturday night what could Jimmy do but take it home with him. He tried turning it out on Sunday morning and it went straight to church. Like you saw him when you went to Matins at eight. Then when the ten o'clock service was over it went back to Jimmy's and it's been there ever since. Anyway, Willie saw Jimmy first thing this morning. He was off to see the Sergeant, ask him if anyone had reported a dog missing, and the dog was trotting behind him for all the world like Sykes used to do. I've half a mind to think he'll keep it if the real owners don't turn up.'

'I wish I could have seen your faces!'

'I'm glad you didn't. I felt such a fool afterwards. I don't mind telling you we were scared and not half! But you know, there is something very odd about that dog. First it had a liking for ale which Sykes did – he loved it, would've been drunk as a lord every night if he'd been allowed. Then when Jimmy got it home it knew exactly where to go to look for a drink, the exact place where he always kept Sykes' water bowl, and when it was time for bed it went to stand where Sykes' bed had been, but Jimmy's got a little table there now so it couldn't lie down. Anyway, Jimmy moved the table and the dog laid down on the carpet with its back against the skirting board in exactly the same position as Sykes. So Jimmy got an old blanket out Sykes had used and put it down and he settled on it as if he'd been sleeping there for years. I don't mind tell you it's put Jimmy's thinking cap on and no mistake. He's not the man he was. What do you think, sir?'

'It does all seem very odd, Sylvia. I mean, the dog appearing is not so peculiar; obviously it's lost and happened quite by chance to appear in Turnham Malpas, but what you say about it knowing where Sykes slept and where to look for his water bowl is certainly more than a bit disconcerting. I don't know much about dogs really; maybe they have a sixth sense of where the best place is for sleeping and such. I just don't know.'

'There's something else I've got to tell you, nothing to do with the dog. Have you got a minute?'

'Yes.'

Sylvia told Peter about finding Mimi's collar. 'So I've still got it here in my bag. I'll give it to you and perhaps you can decide what's best. It's been weighing on my conscience and it's time I did something about it. I couldn't tell Dr Harris, just couldn't find the words. Don't you think, sir, that there's a strange series of coincidences nowadays. First Mimi missing, then poor Sadie Beauchamp dying so sudden and now this blessed dog.'

'All perfectly explainable.'

'I know, but *together* all very odd. Here's the collar. Make sure you hide it; can't have her coming across it by mistake. Shall you tell her?'

Peter fastened the collar and tried to pull it open with a crooked finger. But he couldn't. 'Unfastened, you say?'

'Oh yes, and half kind of buried in the soil.'

'I'll think about what to say. Thanks.' Peter smiled. 'Vera came round all right, did she?'

Sylvia chuckled. 'Well, it took a double brandy to bring her round properly, but then we had had a terrible fright!'

Chapter 15

Many of the children at school that morning had been in church on the Sunday when the little Jack Russell had been found sitting for all the world like a regular worshipper on top of the tomb Willie claimed was haunted. They were full of the story and could talk of nothing else.

'What do you think, Ms Pascoe?'

Tight-lipped and dismissive she snapped, 'Just a stray dog from somewhere, just happened to be like Mr Glover's.' Then, to avoid the children's questions, Kate went to her office.

'My mum says it's just like Sykes was.'

'It is. That black patch that makes him look like a pirate.'

'That's right and they say he knows Mr Glover's house like the back of his hand, er paw.'

'Pissed as a newt he . . .'

Hetty Hardaker interrupted. 'Brian, that will do! You know better words than those with which to describe the condition he was in.'

'He was just like Mr Glover then!' The children burst into hysterical laughter at Brian's joke.

'Children, time for prayers, now come along.'

'My dad says old Jimmy was as white as a sheet. Shaking, he was.'

'I 'opes nobody claims 'im. Be nice for Mr Glover to have a dog again. Perhaps he'll dig up his snares in Sykes Wood and start poaching again.'

'I hopes not. There'll be Sykes' skellington there. Ugh!' Stacey shuddered.

'No, there won't 'cos he's been spirited to life. That's what my mum says. Brought back to life! She's certain it's the real Sykes, she is. She was there when they found him.'

'Something funny going on, my dad says. Lights in Sykes Wood at dead of night. He's seen 'um.' Stacey rolled her eyes, enjoying the sensation she was creating.

Brian asked what Stacey's dad was doing in Sykes Wood at dead of night?

Stacey tapped the side of her nose. 'Ask no questions, get told no lies.'

Hetty Hardaker said, 'I think it best you don't ask what Stacey's father was doing in Sykes Wood at night, Brian. Now, you can be leader and take us into prayers. Stand tall and lead the way. Miss Booth is already playing the "settling down" music. Come along, Class Two. Chop chop! Nice straight lines, nice straight backs. Lead on Brian, quietly, and *don't* stamp your feet, please. We're not on Horse Guards Parade, and there's definitely no need to salute.'

As they settled down for prayers Peter came in from the playgroup room. The children all turned and without prompting chorused, 'Good morning, Rector!'

'Good morning, children. May I join you for prayers this morning, Ms Pascoe? Mrs Hardaker?'

Kate said, 'Certainly. Can someone fetch a chair for the rector?' A flurry of hands shot up. 'You Flick, get my chair from our classroom. The rector needs a grown-up's chair.'

'I'll sit at the back.'

One of Ms Pascoe's children gave him a hymn book and he seated himself on the chair Flick brought for him.

It was a dull dark morning but the children's enthusiasm for life seemed to Peter to fill the room with light. Mrs Hardaker announced the first hymn. Those who could, found the number for themselves and then helped those who couldn't.

Miss Booth played the first line and the children began to sing '*If I were a butterfly*'. Peter joined in and the children had to restrain their giggles for he sounded like Mr Johns except his voice was deeper and louder even though he was trying to sing quietly.

When Hetty Hardaker asked the children if they had anything they needed to thank God for this morning, Brian suggested, 'Sykes. Let's thank God for bringing Sykes back.'

Several of the children agreed. 'Yes, that's a good idea!'

'I don't think that Sykes has actually come back, Brian. Not really Sykes, just a dog who *looks* like Sykes.'

There came a strong murmur of dissension from the floor of the hall. 'How come he knowed where Sykes' bowl was then?'

'Yes, and he knowed Mr Glover. Stuck to him like glue he did.'

Mrs Hardaker began to flounder. 'Perhaps we should pray that the real owners will come to claim him. After all, they must be very sad to have lost their dog. I expect they love him very much.'

'How can they, when he's Mr Glover's Sykes?'

'Let's pray for all pets, that they are all as well cared for as your animals are. Hands together, eyes closed.'

By the time Mrs Hardaker's part of prayers was over Peter could see she was more than glad to hand over to Kate Pascoe.

Kate stayed sitting on her chair to the side of the children. She looked around at them all to catch their undivided attention before she began to speak. 'Some days ago, Class Three went with me into the woods on a nature walk. Because it is winter most of the trees were bare of leaves, but we could see the beautiful symmetry of the twigs and branches reaching skywards high up above our heads. The trees were sleeping – no growing, no leaves rustling in the wind. They were biding their time, waiting for the sun to shine, the earth to warm up, for longer days and shorter nights so they can begin to stir to life. It won't be long now before that happens; we call it Spring. Let us think about those trees and plants in the wood, waiting quietly through the cold months for the whole wonderful miracle, which comes every year, without fail. Imagine yourself like a tree, able to feel pain and hurt if you get damaged or chopped down, silently waiting like all nature is, for the right moment to wake up. Imagine yourself feeling the first stirrings of life.'

The children sat for fully five minutes quietly but not necessarily meditating on Kate's theme. Peter sat quietly too. Mentally he checked his diary for the day – yes, he did have a spare hour around four if he cut short his usual Monday-morning visit to Penny Fawcett and thus got back from hospital-visiting early. And it didn't matter what Ms Pascoe had in mind for after school, she was seeing him. Trees feeling pain, indeed! Whatever next!

Peter got to the school just as the children began to leave for home. Hetty Hardaker was running across the playground calling out to one of them:

'Craig! Craig! Your stamps; you've forgotten your

stamps! Catch him for me, Flick. Why hello, Rector, twice in one day, we are honoured! There you are, Craig, I've put the album in this plastic bag then you won't lose anything out on the way home. Mind how you go. See you tomorrow. Come to see Miss Pascoe?' She went back into school followed by Peter.

'Yes, I have.'

'She has a parent with her at the moment, but she won't be long. Do I know what it's about?'

'Very likely.'

'If you need my opinion which you don't but I'm saying it just the same, it's not right. Believe me it's not right. Well-meaning, I think, but misguided.'

Peter nodded his head and gave a noncommittal 'Hmm.'

Kate offered him a cup of tea, but he refused it. She felt that he filled the small room not just because of his size but with the strength of his persona. She was really into this business of aura and she could feel his almost touching hers.

Kate looked into his face and saw he was troubled. 'Is there something I can help you with, Rector?'

'There certainly is.'

She placed her empty cup on the desk and, having offered Peter the one and only chair, she perched herself on the edge of the washbasin and waited.

'While I am well aware that the church does not have quite the same influence on the education of the children in its schools as once was the case, I really feel that I must speak up. During your short speech directing the children's thoughts to a subject for meditation, you never once mentioned the One to Whom we should give thanks for the beautiful world in which we live. Nothing was attributed to Him and I should like to know why in such a context God's name was never mentioned.'

Kate didn't answer immediately and Peter, as so many of his parishioners knew to their cost, didn't fill the silence for her.

'That's a sticky one.'

'It was meant to be.' Peter waited patiently.

Kate turned her face from his scrutiny and looked out of the window. Her view was of the school dustbins and the cycle shed. She heard the slip slap of Pat Duckett's old shoes and watched her come into view to empty waste paper into the recycling bin. She wished she lived Pat Duckett's uncomplicated life. With Peter present, she had been a fool not to have mentioned the Deity. Now what? Abject apology was called for. 'You're quite right, I should have. It won't happen again.'

'Good. Talking about trees feeling pain, that is ridiculous, and has no place being presented to these impressionable children by someone whose word they see as absolute truth. They have to believe what you say, otherwise they can't learn. If you say two and two make four then that's the truth to them. If you say trees feel pain then, in just the same way, they believe you. It's a most tremendous responsibility. And hugging trees? Come, come!'

Kate opened her mouth to protest but Peter held up his hand and silenced her.

'There is another matter I need to speak about. At one time the absence of the head teacher from Communion and indeed from any service in the church would have been a matter for stern admonition. Not nowadays, however, but you're never there *at all*. Is there a reason for this?'

'None. I've just not got round to it.'

'You've an example to set. Your behaviour doesn't go unnoticed in such a small community.'

Kate swung round from staring out of the window, and looked him full in the face. 'What do you mean by that?'

'Nothing sinister, I assure you. But straight from a mission school to nothing? It doesn't add up. Well, I'll be on my way. Won't take up any more of your time. No offence meant, only the very best of intentions. I know you'll think over what I've said.' Peter stood up. 'I expect you'll be pleased Beth has settled better. We do have the occasional dodgy morning, but mostly she comes quite happily. If there's one thing you learn about children it's that they are full of surprises.' He smiled. 'God bless you, Kate.' He left and so didn't see her shudder.

Peter got home late from a meeting that night, to find Caroline already in bed. He called upstairs, 'All right, darling? I'm just making a drink – want one?'

'Yes, please, don't mind what. You're late.'

'I know, lot to discuss. Won't be long.'

He glanced appreciatively at her as he took the tea into the bedroom. She was sitting up in her dressing gown on top of the duvet reading a book. He placed her cup on her table and bent to kiss her. 'You feel damp and deliciously perfumed.' Peter bent still further and kissed the hollow at the base of her throat. His tongue trailed up her neck, up her chin as far as her mouth and he kissed her again, tasting the toothpaste. 'Love you.'

'Love you. You look tired.'

'I am. Long day. Looking back on it I'm having doubts if I should have reproved Kate the way I did. Perhaps I came down a bit too heavily.' He sat beside Caroline and sipped his tea. 'What do you think?'

'Not heavily enough in my opinion. I don't want our offspring learning to hug trees and things.'

'Neither do I. There are rumblings from the parents, too.'

'Hardly surprising.' Caroline put her cup down and leant forward to kiss him. 'Don't worry, it'll all come out in the wash. Believe me!' She kissed him again and tasted the hot tea in his mouth. 'Isn't it odd, there's no other person in the whole world I would want to kiss like that but you.'

'Thank heavens for that! I'd have a lot to say if there was.'

'Never. You'd take it patiently and wait, and leave the decision with me.'

While Peter thought over what she'd said he held her hand to his cheek. Kissing it, he said, 'I wouldn't stand by in circumstances like that. I'd be in there hauling my woman back to my cave!'

Caroline laughed. 'And you a pacifist!'

'Darling girl!' He relished the taste of her toothpaste again and was thinking of stripping off his clothes and stretching out on the bed beside her when the phone rang. 'Blast.' He climbed over her to pick up the receiver on his side of the bed.

'The rectory. Peter Harris speaking.'

'That you, Rector? It's Vera. Vera Wright. Can yer come? I know it's late but it's our Rhett. He's out of his mind and we don't know what to do. Please, come, please tell us what to do. He's going mad.'

'I'll come, though it sounds as if you need a doctor rather than me.'

'If we get a doctor they'll cart 'im off. *Please*, Rector!'

'I'm on my way.' He put down the receiver and stood up to straighten his cassock.

'What's the matter?'

'Rhett Wright appears to be going out of his mind. Sorry, I've got to go. I'll try not to wake you when I get back.'

'I could be unprofessional and give him a jab if things are difficult – I've got my case with me. If you ring for a night-call it could be hours before anyone comes.'

'Thanks. Let's hope it doesn't come to that. Is Rhett on drugs, do you think?'

'Not that I know of, but then we don't see much of him.'

Don Wright let Peter in. 'Thank God you've come, Rector. I didn't want Vera to ring but it's just that we don't know what to do. He's gone stark raving crackers.'

'Tell me, Don. Have you ever thought he might be on drugs?'

Don looked embarrassed. 'Well, a while back I might have said yes, but not these last months now. Got in with a different crowd.' From upstairs the sound of howling drifted down to the hall.

'Come on, then. Show me the way.'

Vera was in Rhett's bedroom on her hands and knees, peering round the door of the built-in cupboard.

'Thank God you've come. He's in here.' She pointed to the bottom of the cupboard and moved aside so Peter could see him. The howling was spine-chilling.

Rhett was crouched in the bottom of the wardrobe amongst the shoes and boots; he'd made his body as small as he could. On his head he'd rammed a sports bag and with his arms through the handles his head was completely hidden. His hands were gripped around his shins. Although his howls were muffled by the bag they were still loud enough to wake the dead, as Vera observed.

Peter shouted above the howling. 'Hello, Rhett, Peter here from the rectory. Come to see if I can help at all. Is there anything I can do?'

There was a violent shaking of his head, but no dislodging of the bag.

Peter retreated from the cupboard and asked Vera how long he'd been like this?

'Been to a friend's to stay, got home about five, went out in the garden for a drag, beggin' yer pardon Rector, but I won't have him smoke in the house, and next news he's deathly white, shaking from head to foot, and can't speak. He raced in and hid in 'ere and he's never moved since. Just howled.'

'Did he seem odd when he came home or do you think he saw something while he was outside, or perhaps he spoke to someone? Did someone threaten him, perhaps?'

'Only Jimmy spoke to 'im. I was outside there getting some coal in and Jimmy called over the fence.'

'What did Jimmy say?'

Vera tried to remember the exact words. 'He said "Now, Rhett, how about that then? What d'yer think, eh?" Then he laughed and pointed at that dratted dog he's found. Rhett peered over the fence and was took bad immediate like. That's all.' Vera wrung her hands. 'Oh God, Rector, I'm at my wits' end. He hasn't eaten or drunk anything and not been to the you–know–what for nearly six hours. What shall we do?'

'He must be thirsty. Get him a drink — whatever he favours.' Peter bent down inside the cupboard. 'Rhett, we're just getting you a drink; you must be ready for one after all this time. Your grandmother is very worried about you, Rhett, so how about coming out and sitting on the bed? I'm a very good listener; I've heard some rare tales in my time. You can tell me absolutely anything and it will be entirely confidential.'

Rhett's howls grew louder and he began thrashing about inside the wardrobe, hammering with his fists against the back and slamming his feet at the end panel. Still with the sports bag over his head he said, 'Go away, the devil'll get you. Get away.'

With absolute conviction Peter said, 'He can't get me, because I'm wearing my cross. I believe the devil always runs from absolute goodness and that is what Christ is – total goodness. Here, you hold it.' Peter unhooked the cross from his belt, took the chain from around his neck and reaching inside the cupboard touched one of Rhett's hands with it. He clawed it into his grasp. Almost imperceptibly the howling began to lessen.

Vera came up with a glass of shandy. She whispered, 'He's a bit quieter. Thank Gawd for that.'

'Indeed. Here we are, Rhett, your grandmother's brought you a drink.' There was a violent jerking of Rhett's whole body and the glass of shandy spun out of the cupboard, spilling its contents over Peter and the carpet.

'Oh sir, I am sorry.' She shrieked at the cupboard: 'Rhett, you stupid ungrateful boy! Look what you've done!'

Peter put his finger to his lips and waved her away. Vera went to stand by the bedroom door. She heard Peter telling Rhett that he wanted him to bring the cross out into the open into the light, and he'd be quite safe while he did it.

'Come on now, come out, Rhett. Slowly. Slowly.' Peter opened the door, shielding Rhett. 'Let your hands go. That's it. Hold the cross. That's right. I'll lift the bag off. Slowly. Yes, yes, I'll do it very slowly. That's great. Now your legs, one at a time. Don't hurry. That's it. Slowly. Grip my arm.'

'Lights, is the light on? Mustn't be dark. I want the light.'

'If you open your eyes you'll see it is.'

Inch by inch, Peter extricated Rhett from the cupboard. When he was finally standing on the carpet he raced for the bed and shot head–first under the duvet, his dirty trainers resting on the pillow.

'Oh thank Gawd.' Vera shouted downstairs, 'Don, he's come out! What is it, love? Tell your old gran.'

Peter said, 'Let's leave him for the moment. I'd love a cup of tea, Vera. I'd just poured one out when you rang.'

'Of course, Rector. Cup of tea coming up.' Vera scurried away downstairs, leaving Peter alone with Rhett.

'Now we've got your grandmother occupied, can you come out?'

'No.'

'You've got the cross. No harm will come to you. Remember, you can tell me anything and I shan't tell a soul unless you want me to. I've heard it all; there's nothing can shock me.'

Very slowly, Rhett began to emerge from the bottom end of the duvet like a mole testing the night air. Peter's cross was gripped in one hand and his eyes were covered by the other. Peter felt compassion for him. He was a typical teenager, lean and gangling, three rings in each ear, close-cropped hair, smooth-skinned but with a spotty chin.

Rhett opened his fingers slightly and peered at Peter through the gaps. 'Can't go to sleep. Daren't go to sleep.'

'If you could let me know what's troubling you, then perhaps I could help to make you feel better.'

'Can't tell you, sir. Oh no, not you.' Quietly he began howling again, rocking from side to side.

'Look, Dr Harris – my wife – could give you something to help you to sleep. Then we could talk in the morning when you've rested. We'll ask your grandfather to help you undress and get you into bed, and then she could come across.'

Rhett nodded his assent and whispered, 'Can I keep your cross? Till tomorrer?'

'Of course. I'll come back and we'll talk. Right?'

'Right.'

Chapter 16

'It's that blasted dog, Mr Charter-Plackett. The thing's damned, that's what.' Mrs Jones snipped the parcel tape on her twelfth package of the afternoon and neatly pressed the gummed address label onto it. 'Poor Rhett's clean out of his mind and now it's affected the sergeant's wife.'

'Really, I hadn't heard that?'

'Oh yes. Jimmy went round to ask if anyone had reported a dog missing, took the blasted thing with him, and the sergeant's wife was doing her bit of dusting and that in the office – when lo and behold she collapsed against the counter and they had to get her to bed. Incoherent, she was. Drip white. Her eyes rolling all over the place. They say her hair stood on end, like she'd been electrocuted, but I think that's a bit of an exaggeration. Still in bed and won't talk. The sergeant did think of sending for the rector but when he mentioned it he thought she was going to strangle him.'

'Really?'

'Oh yes.' Mrs Jones selected another jar of Harriet's Country Cousin Apricot Chutney from the shelves. 'This is going well; we'll soon be needing some more. Will I ring her that makes it, or will you?'

'You can.'

Mrs Jones nodded her agreement. 'So, she won't hear of the rector going to see her, hysterics she 'as if his name's even mentioned. Rhett's started sitting in the church which is a first for him, I don't mind telling you, and Vera's gone out and bought him a cross of his own so the rector can have his back again. Said she felt a complete fool buying a cross, but it seemed the only way to give Rhett peace of mind. I tell you, Mr Charter-Plackett, there's more in this than meets the eye.'

'Such as?' Jimbo took a huge bite out of his lunchtime pork pie, and looked up expectantly at her.

Mrs Jones settled herself on Sadie's old chair, pushed a strand of hair back into place and told Jimbo what she thought. He hadn't imagined when he'd taken her on all of three weeks ago that he would find such satisfaction in talking to her. She was a window on the village in a way that Sadie could never have been. She had her finger on the pulse.

'Well, Rhett won't tell the rector why he's so upset. Refuses point blank. The rector's tried and no mistake but to no avail. But whatever it is, the sergeant's wife is affected the same way, isn't she? One sighting of that blasted dog and they're off their heads. Nothing could be more out of character than Rhett Wright going about with a cross round his neck and sitting in church. I mean, all this because of that dog. Now, where has it come from, eh? Answer me that.'

'A stray, that's all, just a coincidence.'

Mrs Jones glanced around the mail-order office as though expecting someone who shouldn't to appear from behind the boxes. 'Well, there's more than me think it's from the devil. Why should a dog cause such an upset otherwise?'

'I've seen it, you've seen it and we're not behaving oddly.'

'No, you've a point there, but couple it with lights in Sykes Wood in the night and what have you got?'

'Badger-watchers?'

'No! Badger-watchers?' Mrs Jones snorted derisively. 'No way. No, this is something more sinister.'

'Such as?'

'Sykes the dog, Sykes Wood – there's the connection, you see. He was buried there, wasn't he?'

'Mr Charter-Plackett! Can you come, please? The rep's here you were expecting.' It was Linda calling from the Store.

Jimbo left Mrs Jones to her parcels. There were times when the villagers' logic completely baffled him and this was one of them.

Peter had already called to see the sergeant's wife but she had adamantly refused to meet him. The sergeant had leaned his elbow on the station counter and confided in him.

'You see the thing is, Rector, I know you won't take this any further,' Peter had agreed he wouldn't; of course not. 'I thought, well, I thought she'd got another man. She suddenly started going out late at night, 'bout once a week, like. At first she told me it was the drama society. Well, I knew different. I mean, who'd want my Ellie on a stage? There weren't no rehearsals, neither. And you don't rehearse for a play at midnight, do yer?'

'Indeed not.'

'I asked her straight out one night. I said, "Ellie, what you doin' coming 'ome this time o' the mornin'? Have you got yourself another man?" "What if I have. You mind yer own business," she said. "I've slaved for you all these years and now I'm having a bit of life of my own." I tried all ways – police techniques and that I learned at Hendon once when I went on a course, but to no avail. Now she's bedridden. Can't speak, and near throttles me if I mention getting help. Women! There's no weighing 'em up is there, sir?'

'It can be difficult. The dog upset her then?'

'Oh yes. Didn't bite her nor nothing. She just took one look and she hasn't spoken since.'

'Has anyone laid claim to it?'

'No, and there ain't going to *be* nobody coming to claim it. Had a fax from Culworth yesterday. Turns out it was in a car what was involved in that massive smash-up on the by-pass that Saturday tea-time. It escaped completely unhurt, which considering its owners were squashed to a pulp is nothing short of a miracle. Vicar and his wife from up North travelling back off their 'olidays, perhaps that accounts for 'is liking of going into the church. Anyways no one noticed it running off, and the relatives never gave it a thought, they was that upset yer see, then they remembered it but they don't want it, and they're glad it 'as a good 'ome. But it ain't no good me telling our Ellie that. She says she knows whose it is, it's Jimmy's Sykes and there ain't no one who can persuade her different. So now we know where it came from, but it's still frightening. Seems too much of a coincidence, both dogs being so alike.'

Peter didn't take him up on this idea; everyone was quite superstitious enough without him encouraging them. 'Is Ellie eating?'

'Well, she is now. Spends most of her time moaning under the bedclothes, but she will eat so long as it's under the covers like. Won't have the light turned off at night, though. I can't go on like this. Hospital it is, if there's no improvement.'

'If she decides she wants to see me, ring me any time – night or day.'

'Well, that's very generous of you, Rector. I'll do what you say. This isn't like my Ellie at all. Not at all.' He lifted up the flap on the counter and came out to see Peter to the door. 'Be retiring soon. Police house goes with the job. Be moving away.'

'That's a pity.'

'Might be for the best, all things considered.'

Peter had waved and driven away, puzzling about the whole situation. The village was getting very twitchy about Jimmy's dog. Everyone appeared affected by its arrival. Yet the dog seemed harmless enough. Nice little thing, very friendly. Quiet as a mouse in church on Sunday. Bit unorthodox allowing him to stay. But poor Ellie! Poor Rhett! Being jobless at sixteen couldn't be much fun. Peter had wondered who might possibly employ him. As he'd turned up Pipe and Nook Lane to put the car in the garage he thought of the Big House and the grounds. Surely *they* might be able to find him work, even if it was only part-time. He did a U-turn immediately and drove straight up to the Big House.

As he'd expected, Louise was at the reception desk.

'Good morning, Louise.'

'Good morning, Rector.' There was no longer a hint of the constraint in her voice which had been present ever since her misguided predilection for him. 'What a lovely surprise! What can I do for you?'

'I'm looking for Jeremy.'

'He's here, I'll give him a buzz. Do sit down if you wish. He won't be long.'

While Louise tracked Jeremy Mayer down, Peter went to look out of the hall windows. The lawn, now restored to its former glory after the disastrous episode with the new sewers, was a joy to behold. Peter caught a sense for a brief moment of how hard Ralph must find it to come up here and see his old home. Especially now it was in the hands of an insensitive entrepreneur like Craddock Fitch; though since Sadie's death the man had been a little less assertive than before. He felt as much as heard the heavy ponderous step of Jeremy Mayer.

'Good morning, Rector. Pleasure to see you.' Peter turned and shook the outstretched hand. Jeremy was not getting any thinner. His upper arms resembled large hams, and his feet looked ridiculously small at the end of his necessarily wide trouser legs. Peter surreptitiously wiped his palm dry on the handkerchief in his cassock pocket.

'And to see you. I've come on a begging mission.'

'Donation is it, to some worthy cause?'

Peter quelled his indignation at Jeremy's assumption and said, 'No. I'm speaking to you in your capacity as estate manager. I wonder, are there any vacancies at the moment, or likely to be in the near future, for unskilled teenagers? Anything would do – kitchens, gardens, handyman, anything. I have a particularly needy case in mind.'

'I don't think we have. I wish I could help.'

Peter was disappointed.

Then Louise pushed a piece of paper across her desk. 'You've come on the right day, Rector. There's this advertisement I've just written out for a garden labourer.'

Jeremy, angry with himself for appearing out of touch, said: 'Ah yes, I'd forgotten about that. Gardening any good?'

'Anything at all.' Peter flashed a grateful glance in Louise's direction. 'Before you put it in the paper, could I be given the chance to speak to this young chap?'

'Someone in the village?' Louise asked.

'Yes, Rhett Wright.'

Jeremy laughed. 'Poor chap needs all the help he can get with a name like that. That's the one who's gone off his rocker, isn't it?'

'I wouldn't quite put it like that.'

'Whole village seems to be jumpy. All over a dog. Amazing!' Jeremy's mountainous body shook with laughter.

'Worrying, actually. I just wish I knew what it was all about. Neither Rhett nor the sergeant's wife will tell me why they're so terrified. I'll be in touch, Louise, about the job as soon as possible. OK?'

'Fine.'

'Bye, Jeremy. Thanks for the chance. I'll return the favour one day.'

In The Royal Oak that night Vera expressed her eternal gratitude. 'The drinks are on me and if the rector was in 'ere tonight I'd be buying him one as well. Gawd! Am I grateful. Rhett's been up there meek as a lamb and Greenwood Stubbs, head gardener though he might be, 'as been that lovely with him. Told him there's a career waiting for him if he puts his mind to it. Promised to teach him all about the greenhouses, growing them grapes and peaches and whatnot as soon as he proves himself diligent-like. And he's promised him a day a week at college if he shows interest! Can yer imagine our Rhett at college? Never thought I'd live to see the day.'

'Wouldn't have thought your Rhett would know one end of a spade from the other,' Jimmy wryly observed.

'He doesn't, but he soon will. I've promised him a nice packed lunch each day and I'm keeping my fingers crossed.'

'Better now, is he?' Willie asked.

'Much improved. But it's unnerving, this business of 'im sitting in the church such a lot.'

Willie became indignant. ''Armless enough occupation. Might do 'im a bit o' good. Better than sniffing drugs. Saw him in there this morning when I was clearing up. He isn't praying. Just sits there or walks about reading the memorial tablets and the like. This job could be the making of 'im.'

'I 'ope so. Teenagers need money in their pockets nowadays; it'll be grand for 'im. Here's to the rector and Greenwood Stubbs and our Rhett. Let's 'ope he sticks with it.'

Willie and Jimmy raised their glasses and joined in the toast.

Jimmy wiped his lips, put down his glass and said, 'What d'yer reckon made him go crackers then?'

Vera looked shiftily at Jimmy and chose her words carefully. 'To be honest, Jimmy, and I 'ope you won't take offence, but he went funny after he'd seen that dog of yours.'

'Sykes?'

'Have you called him Sykes?'

'I have. I'd no alternative and no one's reported him missing as yet, so I'm keeping 'im.'

'Really?' Suddenly afraid, Vera asked, 'Is he under the table now?'

'Yes.'

'Oh Gawd!' She leapt up and made to leave.

'He's pulling your leg, Vera. He's not here.' Willie laughed. 'It's all daft, this being frightened. I mean, he's only a stray.'

Jimmy shook his head. 'Don't you be too sure about that, Willie Biggs. He's far too wise just to be a stray. Mark my words.'

'If it's Sykes, who was it brought him back to life, then? Answer me that.'

Vera whispered, 'The devil? Our Rhett's frightened of the devil getting him, that's what he says. That's why he's so scared.'

'For heaven's sake, don't let the rector hear you talking like that.'

'There's lights in Sykes Wood at night. I reckon there *is* someone dabbling with the devil.'

'Let's hope they have a long spoon then if they're supping with *him*.'

'Ms Pascoe's cat's been seen late at night in the woods.'

'That's nothing to go by. Dr Harris' Mimi used to go huntin' there. Rector's Meadow, Sykes Wood – you name it.'

'Yes, and look what happened to her. She's never been seen since.'

Willie saw he was on dangerous ground and, fearful of betraying what Sylvia had found in the wood, he tried to change the subject. 'Pat's still at the school then.'

'That's another thing. Ms Pascoe, what's she up to?'

'Teaching if she's any sense,' Willie replied.

'And some. I reckon she's up to something funny with them kids. The rector's been and given her a telling off.'

'How do you know?'

'Pat told me. They left the office door ajar and she was dusting in the hall, quite by chance.'

Jimmy and Willie both said, 'Of course.'

'She couldn't hear everything but she did hear him tell her she'd no business teaching the children about bloody trees feeling pain.'

'That's not evidence she's doing deals with the devil, is it?'

'I haven't finished.' She leant towards the two of them and said softly, 'Last night my Don was coming back 'ome later than usual after one of his late shifts, two o'clock in the morning it was, and he passed Ms Pascoe walking along towards the village, with that cat of hers. *From the direction of Sykes Wood.*'

'Is this true or have you made it up?'

'True as I'm 'ere – ask him if you like. You know Don don't exaggerate, and he 'adn't been drinking 'cos as you well know he doesn't. So what's she doing that time o' night walking home from Sykes Wood, eh?'

Chapter 17

It was not only Don Wright who'd seen Kate walking home in the night. Ralph and Muriel had been to dinner with an old Diplomatic Service colleague of Ralph's and the two men had been reminiscing with such enjoyment that Muriel had not wished to spoil their pleasure by reminding them how late it was getting, with the result that they hadn't left his house until a quarter past one. Muriel was very tired and dozed for most of the way home.

Ralph had woken her when they were about five minutes away from Turnham Malpas. 'My dear, time to wake up. Five minutes and we shall be there.'

Muriel stretched. 'I wasn't really sleeping, just dozing. I'm glad you had such a wonderful evening, Ralph.'

'We rather neglected you, I'm afraid.'

'No, you didn't, I enjoyed hearing about your exploits. He seems to have been great fun.' In the beam of the car headlights Muriel spotted someone walking by the side of the road. 'Oh look, Ralph! Be careful, there's someone there. Look!'

'So there is. Who on earth can it be?'

As they passed, Muriel saw it was Kate Pascoe with Cat.

'What is Kate doing out at this time of night? Quick! Do stop and give her a lift.'

'No.'

'Ralph! Perhaps her car has broken down. Do stop.'

'I don't want that cat in my car.'

'I think that's most unkind, and not at all like you.'

'She's nearly home anyway. I don't like cats, Muriel. Particularly ones the size of a young panther.'

'You're not succumbing to this village superstition thing, are you?'

'Of course not.'

'You don't sound very sure.' She turned her head to look into his face. There was a half-smile on his lips and she said, 'You are, just a little bit, aren't you?'

'I was born and bred here, so perhaps I am in tune with the spirit of the village.'

'Well, really, I'm ashamed of you. I truly am. I was born here too, but I don't feel like that. It's nonsense.'

'There's an atmosphere in the village at the moment that I don't like – a kind of wary atmosphere – and people are finding it difficult to meet one's eye. Have you noticed that? But then there have been some strange happenings recently, haven't there?'

'Ralph – you're as bad as everyone else! Sadie dies in her sleep, which I'm very sorry about because I envied her her *joie de vivre* and I shall miss her, one cat goes missing and a stray dog turns up. No connection at all.'

'Two people, one quite young, are both quietly going out of their minds. You've forgotten that.'

Muriel shivered. 'You're right.'

'I am. Somewhere there's evil about. Someone is toying with the devil.'

As Ralph was putting the car away in the garage, Muriel remarked, 'I overheard in the Store that there's been lights seen in Sykes Wood at night.'

'Ah!'

'Why "Ah!"?'

'We've just seen Kate Pascoe, with a torch, walking along in the early hours of the morning, haven't we?'

'We have. Ralph, how about if *we* go and take a look one night? Very late.'

'Muriel!!'

'Why not?'

They walked down the back garden path full of their idea, and Muriel fell fast asleep with an image of Enid Blyton's Secret Seven in her mind. She'd so enjoyed those books when she was a girl, and she and Ralph setting off to investigate a mystery made her feel like a schoolgirl again.

A week after seeing Kate coming home in the early hours Ralph made up his mind to do something about it. He had to find out for himself what it was that the village was so upset about. That evening, he made one of his rare appearances in the bar of The Royal Oak. It was nine o'clock. Being midweek the bar was only half-full but the two people he was hoping to see were there. He ordered his whisky, exchanged views with Georgie and Bryn about the long winter they were experiencing, and then took his drink across to the table where Willie and Jimmy were conferring.

They both looked up as his shadow crossed the table. 'Hello, Ralph.'

'Hello, Jimmy, Willie. Can I join you or are you expecting someone?'

Jimmy moved further up the settle. 'Sit here. There's just the two of us. Sylvia's sitting in at the rectory and Vera's having to fill in on the late shift at the nursing home.'

'Thank you, I will then. How's Sykes?'

Jimmy put his finger to his lips. 'Sssh – he's under the table, but don't let on; it only upsets everyone. I can't leave him by himself at home all evenin'.'

'Saw you taking him out the other morning. He's indistinguishable from the old Sykes, isn't he?'

'Yes, and a grand dog he is, too. We're becoming real friends. He's good company.'

'Capital. There's something a bit special about dogs, something extra in their companionship which you don't get with a cat.'

'Exactly.'

'I keep wondering if Muriel should get another dog, but she can't forget Pericles.'

'When you've 'ad a good dog, yer can't replace 'em easily. I've taken to 'im,' Jimmy pointed under the table, 'only 'cos he's so like old Sykes in looks and that.'

'And that?' Ralph queried.

'Habits an' that. Uncanny it is sometimes.'

'Uncanny?'

Willie interrupted. 'This is leading somewhere, Ralph?'

'You've both finished your drinks – will you allow me to get you another?'

Willie pushed his glass across the table. 'Thanks very much. Same again, please.'

'And me,' echoed Jimmy. Ralph took their glasses to the bar. 'He's got something on his mind, he 'as.'

Willie agreed.

Ralph settled down again at their table and when they'd thanked him for their refills, he said heavily, 'Sykes Wood.'

'Yes?' Jimmy said. 'What about it?'

Willie looked away, tried to pretend he hadn't heard. Jimmy lifted his glass and having taken a long drink, wiped his mouth on the back of his hand.

'You've been there, haven't you, to take a look?' Ralph asked.

'I 'ave, yes, but I saw nothing unusual at all, 'cept for a dead bonfire.'

'I think there's something untoward happening there. Do you?'

Jimmy put down his glass, and fiddled with the beer mat, making it straight and placing his glass right in the centre of it.

'Per'aps.'

Willie looked anxiously at Ralph. 'What do yer mean?'

Ralph leaned towards them both. 'I think it's witch-craft or black magic. Something of that ilk.'

Jimmy nodded. 'Some years since we 'ad any of that round these parts.'

Ralph glanced about and then asked quietly, 'Remember what happened then at the time?'

'Must have been twenty years ago – no, maybe twenty-five. Tell yer who was involved,' he counted them off on his fingers, 'the Senior sisters, Simone Paradise's French grandmother, Gwen Baxter's mother and a woman who'd been evacuated 'ere during the war and stayed on – forget her name. Used the old cricket pavilion for services or whatever they called 'em. Right uproar there was. Old Reverend Furbank, not so old then o' course, was at his wits' end. Thelma and Valda's mother finished up running screaming through the village in the night in her nightdress, got herself so frightened she 'ad. Blamed it on a black cat of Valda's, said it was Valda's familiar or some such. Looked damned ordinary to me.'

Willie joined in. 'I remember that. They held a meeting in the churchyard one night – Hallowe'en it was. I 'ad a grave dug ready for the next day, and one of 'em fell in it and nearly died of fright. She dislodged a lot of soil and, before we could use it, I 'ad to get down in it and clear it out a bit and I found a dead cat. Horrible it was. But yer don't have that kind of thing in this day and age. Heavens above. Course not.' Willie shuddered.

Jimmy disagreed. 'Don't you be too sure, there's a sight lot more going on in this village at the moment than meets the eye. There's something nasty and I reckon Ralph's suggested the very place where it's all 'appening. And you know more than you're saying, Willie Biggs.'

'I don't.' Willie shook his head emphatically and tried to signal to Jimmy not to say any more.

'You do.'

'Care to investigate?' Ralph said this very casually.

The hairs on the back of Willie's neck stood up. 'Investigate?'

Ralph raised a questioning eyebrow and said softly, 'Tonight?'

Willie shook his head. 'Rector and Dr Harris are out very late tonight. Gone to a party at the George. When I've finished here, I've promised to go and keep Sylvia company, seeing as she's staying so late.' The relief on his face was noticeable.

'Very well – can't be helped. I need you, Jimmy, because you know the woods so well. I have a powerful torch I keep in the car in case of a breakdown, so we'll take that. Anything else we need?'

'I'll bring Sykes.'

'Good – he might give us early warning if there's anything wrong. Midnight, at my house, right?' Ralph downed his whisky and said good night.

Jimmy surreptitiously put his glass down under the table for Sykes to drink the remains of his ale. 'Well, well,' he said slowly. 'Who d'yer reckon we'll find?'

Willie answered Jimmy's question with a shake of his head. 'You'll see nobody. Not a bloomin' soul.'

The church clock was striking midnight as Jimmy knocked at Ralph's door. It was a cold night so he was well wrapped-up. He'd unearthed his old poaching jacket and Ralph answered the door wearing his Barbour jacket with a corduroy cap Muriel never liked him to wear in daylight.

'You carry the torch, Ralph.' Muriel appeared and handed it to him. Ralph looked at her in astonishment. She was dressed for going out, wearing that jaunty wool hat she loved, a thick winter coat and wellingtons.

'My dear, you're not coming.'

'I am. I'm all dressed ready to go.'

'I can't possibly allow you—'

'I'm sorry, Ralph, three heads are better than two and I'm coming.'

'Absolutely not. It could be dangerous.'

'Phooey! Dangerous? This is Turnham Malpas, not downtown New York.'

'Jimmy! Say she mustn't come.'

'I'm having nothing to do with it. I'm not coming between married folk. But make up yer minds, please. It's cold standing 'ere.'

Disappointed at not getting immediate support from Jimmy, Ralph sighed. 'Very well, my dear, but at the first hint of—'

'Ralph! Don't mollycoddle!'

They climbed the stile into the woods and Ralph led the way followed by Muriel and then Jimmy. Somewhere close an owl hooted. Muriel jumped. The deep silence in the wood, to say nothing of the very deep blackness of it, unnerved her, though she would have died rather than admit to it. She'd lived in the country the first fourteen years of her life, but had never been what could be called a countrywoman. Now, take Jimmy, he was a countryman right to the tips of his toes. So too was Ralph. They actually enjoyed field sports – but not Muriel. The fields and woods gave her pleasure and they gave her space to breathe and she wouldn't have wanted to live anywhere else, but . . . she tripped over a tree root.

'Mind out,' Jimmy whispered hoarsely. 'Be careful, watch where you're going.'

'Sorry!' Muriel stumbled on. They'd be there all too soon at this pace. Ralph wasn't half determined once he'd made up his mind – just like he'd been as a boy at the village school. A twig flicked against Muriel's cheek and startled her. Anyway it was more than likely they'd find nothing, absolutely nothing. She wished she'd brought a torch for herself; Ralph's torch going on ahead wasn't much use to her walking behind him, but the path was too narrow to walk alongside each other. Sykes ran back to check on Jimmy, and Muriel had to pause for a moment to avoid tripping over him.

It was Sykes' low rumbling growl which upset Muriel; there was a menacing note in it which boded ill.

'Quiet, Sykes! Shut up!' Jimmy snarled, but the dog wouldn't be hushed. 'Wait, Ralph. Listen.' The three of them stood quite still straining to hear what Sykes had already detected. Ralph had switched off his torch so that darkness was even deeper. The owl hooted again, fraying Muriel's nerves once more. An unexpected gust of wind rustled the trees.

Jimmy whispered, 'There's a while to go yet before we reach the clearing. Can't hear a thing, can you?'

Ralph said he couldn't either. 'Let's press on.'

Muriel followed feeling more alarmed than ever. Why ever had she said she'd come? She was always doing this, getting involved and then fervently wishing she hadn't. As for Sykes . . . Dogs knew things human beings didn't and she'd an idea that Sykes knew more than most. She guessed they'd chosen the right night, because . . . Out of the corner of her eye, she spotted a pair of gleaming green eyes, low down amongst the undergrowth. It was only for a fleeting second but very frightening. Oh dear Lord, if she'd been a woman who crossed herself she'd have done it then and there. She poked Ralph in the back, and pointed but Ralph only shrugged: he could see nothing. Then there they were again, the eyes, watching them. Sykes, who was keeping close to Jimmy, renewed his rumbling growl. Muriel poked Ralph again and pointed but, as Ralph's torch flicked the other way, the eyes could no longer be seen. Muriel didn't really know whether she wanted to watch out for them again or whether she wanted to stare straight ahead and ignore them.

Jimmy cannoned into her as Ralph halted unexpectedly. The torch went out and they were in utter blackness again. That owl! It chilled her spine. They sounded so lovely at night when she was safely tucked up beside Ralph, but not out here in the dark. Then she smelt woodsmoke, and through the trees she could just detect a blaze. Oh God in heaven! There they were. Faintly she could hear strange chanting, like in church but different. Sykes' ears were on alert, his head twitching from side to side as though detecting the direction of a sound he'd heard close by. Muriel thought about the green eyes, and her flesh began to creep. Had they got a wild panther in the woods? Was that what had got Mimi?

Jimmy's shoulder was touching hers as they stood listening; he tugged at her sleeve and she felt rather than saw him turning off the path and going between the trees following Ralph. *Towards the green eyes.* Oh heavens above! She couldn't see a thing. She stumbled amongst the closely packed trees, catching her arms, her face, her elbows, her feet on twigs and stones and low-lying branches. Once her coat caught on a branch and by the time she'd unhooked herself she couldn't see Ralph ahead.

A hand reached out and grabbed her arm. It was Jimmy. They moved on stealthily until the chanting grew louder, the light from the fire brighter. Then Ralph stopped and crouched down. He waved his hand behind him to signal that they should do the same.

Between the bushes, they could see there were five of them dancing round the fire, black figures silhouetted by the flames. You couldn't identify anyone, except to say one was short, one was tall, two were thin, one was fat. Then after the chanting had reached a climax and the frenzied dancing had slowed, one of the figures reached towards the fire and then walked towards a pile of stones. They were carrying something they had lit from the fire. Muriel saw they were lighting candles at the top of the pile of stones. The figures stood in a circle around the stones and then one lone voice began a chant. The only sound was the voice. Unchurchlike and yet churchlike. Worshipping and yet not. Fascinating but yet repellent.

The spell was broken by Sykes, who suddenly flung himself out of Jimmy's grasp and hurtled towards the clearing. Muriel saw the green eyes again: Sykes was heading straight for them. Though the two animals were fighting in the light of the bonfire, it was impossible to see what was happening for they were fastened into a tight ball of snarling, spitting, scratching and yowling. Rolling over and over, never letting go. Occasionally Sykes yelped but mostly he snarled. The fight seemed to last an age; the effect it had was startling. The five figures simultaneously snuffed the candle-flames, picked up belongings from around the fire, and fled in five different directions.

Only the cat and dog remained, still fighting as though to the death. Jimmy raced towards them, shouting. Ralph shone his torch between the trees attempting to catch a glimpse of the figures fleeing into the darkness, but he was too late. They had gone. The cat and dog rolled too close to the fire and the cat's shrill shriek as it rolled on the glowing ash at the edge of the bonfire cut Muriel's fragile courage from under her. She screamed. The cat fled. The fight was over.

Sykes stood up panting, laughing in his doglike way at Jimmy, waiting for praise for his efforts. With one arm gripping Muriel tightly, Ralph shone the torch on Sykes. There was a long bleeding gash from his right eye down the side of his face to the corner of his mouth, and a tear down his left flank. But he was triumphant; no one could deny him his victory.

Ralph asked, 'Did either of you catch a glimpse of who they were?'

Both Muriel and Jimmy shook their heads.

'Neither did I. What a pity. No doubt in my mind that cat was Kate Pascoe's.'

'Nor mine. Must have been, 'cos they were of a size. Come here, old lad. Good dog, good dog. Jimmy'll see to them scratches when we get home.' Jimmy patted Sykes where he could without touching his wounds and Sykes wagged his tail. A job well done, he seemed to be saying.

Fired up by the fight and the flight of the participants, Jimmy wanted to find out more. 'Let's look around, see what we can find.'

They found that the candles were black. Muriel shrieked. 'I read about that in a novel once. Oh dear! Oh dear!'

'What did you read, my dear?'

'They had the black candles.'

'Who did?'

'The witches!'

'So we are right, it's just as I thought.' Ralph shuddered. 'Let's be gone from this evil place.'

He held Muriel's arm in a tight reassuring grip. She was shaking with fear. Looking round the clearing, a place she had once thought was lovely, and indeed a place where as a girl she had often picnicked with the Guides, Muriel felt nothing but horror. To think it was people from her own village who were doing these dreadful things. Perhaps dreadful things to Mimi. And whatever it was that had frightened Rhett and the sergeant's wife. Maybe they really *had* reincarnated Sykes. She shook herself. Pull yourself together, Muriel, she thought. You would come on this adventure, it's all your own fault. 'Let's go, Ralph. Come on, Jimmy.'

Jimmy kicked a lot of earth onto the bonfire to damp it down. Ralph pulled one of the candles free from the altar, pinched the wick to make sure it was completely out and stuffed it in his pocket. 'Evidence.' Then he proceeded to kick down the column of stones, till it was just a heap, and the remaining black candles crushed into pieces.

As they left the clearing there was a massive clap of thunder directly above their heads, and huge spots of rain began to drop. By the time they'd reached the stile there was a full-scale thunder and lightning storm raging. Huge flashes of sheet lightning were spreading across the sky and Muriel was wishing she was safely at home in bed with Ralph; she wished she'd been there all night and had never encouraged him to come on this adventure. They'd found out more than they'd bargained for and she was frightened.

When they reached Jimmy's cottage, Ralph cautioned him: 'Not a word about what we've seen, Jimmy – to anyone. I shall speak to the rector first thing in the morning. I'm going to him because I don't know what else to do. I'll let you know developments. Good night, and thank you for coming with us, Jimmy. Someone had to find out. We shall have to put a stop to it, but I'm not sure how, when we don't know who it was.'

'But we do. It was Kate Pascoe's cat, sure as eggs,' Jimmy argued.

'Yes, I'm certain you're right on that score. Good night to you.'

Ralph and Muriel went to their own house and Ralph unlocked the door for Muriel but, before he followed her in, he stood in the road looking round at the sleeping village. Well, well. What next? But they'd withstand this crisis. The village had withstood heaven knew what for centuries – a bit of black magic wasn't going to destroy it. Civil war, world wars, plagues, kings and queens . . . all had come and gone, but here it still was, and here it would be for all time. The canker would have to be plucked out of its heart. He, Ralph Templeton, would see to that. He wasn't going to allow some pathetic people with twisted minds to destroy the peace of mind of this beloved place.

Chapter 18

Hetty Hardaker rang the school-bell at five minutes to nine, as she always did. The children made their neat lines, Margaret Booth came to collect her infants and there was the usual hubbub of happy young voices, eager for the school day to begin. She couldn't help smiling. Where else would she find such satisfaction?

'Sophie, use your handkerchief dear, please. You haven't got one? Go and get a tissue from the box in my room.'

'Mrs Hardaker, it's my birthday today.'

'I know, Brian, I've got the candles all ready. I've put five out – that's right, isn't it?' She laughed at her joke. The children chuckled.

Brian protested. 'Eight!'

'Of course. I know. Just testing! Right, Miss Booth?'

'Right, Mrs Hardaker. Come along, Class One. Gently now.'

The only cloud on the horizon this morning was that Kate Pascoe was late. Hetty looked across at the school-house. The curtains were still drawn. Odd.

'Miss Booth, could you take prayers? When I've done the register I'm going across to the school-house to see what's happened to Miss Pascoe.'

'Will do.'

Hetty slipped on her top coat and strode across the school playground. She kept thinking Spring was on its way but this morning she knew she was mistaken. The wind blowing across the open space between the school and the house was cruelly cold. She knocked on the front door. She knocked again. She tried the knob, but the door was locked.

Only the curtains in the kitchen were open. Shading her eyes she peered in. Everything appeared to be quite normal. Neat, tidy, nothing out of place. Typical Miss Pascoe. But acid green kitchen walls? Hetty shrugged her shoulders. She stood below the bedroom window and shouted, 'Kate! Kate! Are you all right?'

Hetty returned to school. The head teacher's absence made a complete hash of the school timetable. She'd better inform the Education Department in Culworth to see if they could send a teacher to help out. At the back of her mind there was a nagging feeling. This was so unlike Kate. Hetty wished wholeheartedly that Mr Palmer was still here. Those were the days. Still, she couldn't deny him the happiness he'd found at last. His wedding to Suzy Meadows had been so beautiful . . . Maybe Kate was ill, Hetty thought suddenly. That was it! Too ill to get help. Oh dear. She hadn't got a key, so she couldn't get in.

Pat Duckett was just finishing in the kitchen when Hetty hurried back into school. 'No message from Miss Pascoe is there, Pat?'

'No, nothing. Funny she's not here. You'd think she'd have let us know.'

'Exactly. I think she must be ill and *can't* let us know. If I had a key I'd go and find out.'

'Look no further. I've still got one. Mr Palmer always let me keep one for him in case he lost his. Been meaning to give it to Ms Pascoe and never got round to it.'

'Where is it?'

'Safe at home. Too 'eavy to carry around.'

'I must go and see to the children. Is it asking too much to suggest you go home and bring it back here?'

'No sooner said than done.'

By the time Pat had cycled up to the Garden House and back again she was tired, but her curiosity urged her on to suggest Mrs Hardaker oughtn't to go into the house by herself just in case.

'You come with me then. It's better if there's two of us, just in case as you say.'

The decorations inside the school-house appalled Pat. It felt decadent. It *was* decadent. Give her a nice light emulsion and some chintzy curtains any time. This was a nightmare. There'd been two deaths on school premises, Toria Clark's and Mr Palmer's wife before that. Was this to be the third? She shuddered.

There was nothing and no one downstairs so Hetty called up: 'Kate! *Kate!*' Still no reply.

Nervously, she climbed the stairs with Pat close behind. The bed in the little bedroom hadn't been slept in. There was no sign of habitation except for a pair of black velvet slippers under the bedside table, and a book laid on the bedspread, which was dyed the deepest purple Pat had ever seen. Good grief! She'd never sleep a wink under that thing.

Then Hetty looked in that awkward corner under the eaves. There was an object shrouded beneath a black cloth. Two black candles stood sentinel either side. She whisked the cloth off and found a crystal ball.

Pat blanched. 'Lord help us! She's a witch.'

Hetty snapped her reply. 'Don't be ridiculous, Pat.' Despite her anger at Pat's remark she covered the ball with the cloth and went down the stairs much faster than she had gone up them.

They stood at the bottom of the staircase looking at each other.

Hetty said, 'It's not a criminal offence.'

Pat trembled. 'The cat — where's the blasted cat?'

'I've always hated that cat.'

'Unnatural it is. I don't fancy finding it.'

'Neither do I. Where is she though?'

'I've just had a thought.' Pat raced outside. 'Look — her car's not here.'

Classes Two and Three had just gone out for their morning play when Kate's car drove into the school playground. Hetty ushered the children to one side whilst Kate parked it beside the school-house.

'Miss Pascoe! Thank goodness you're all right. Where have you been? We've been so worried.'

In answer to Hetty's questions Kate reached into the car and carefully lifted out a wire cat-carrier. Cat was inside. The animal had a wide bandage all the way round her middle, and looked much the worse for wear.

'Oh dear, I am sorry. Whatever happened?'

'A coal flew out of the fire and burnt Cat before she could get out of the way. It's a terrible burn and I had to take her to the vet's in Culworth. I've been so upset.' And indeed, the head teacher looked strained and hollow-eyed. 'They took ages attending to her. I'm sorry I didn't let you know but it's been terrible. I've been up all night with her. They wanted to keep her in but I insisted on bringing her home.'

The children pressed round to see the horrific injuries and were quite disappointed that the bandage prevented it.

'Oh! Ms Pascoe!'

'Ohhhh! How awful!'

'Awww. The poor thing!'

'It must hurt!'

Kate unlocked her door and said, 'Mrs Hardaker, I'll be in school by the end of playtime. I'll just grab something to eat and then I'll come.'

'Are you sure?'

'Of course I am. I can't leave you holding the fort.'

Hetty had to admire her, but at the same time . . . Crystal balls? What was the teaching profession coming to! At dinnertime when Pat came back she'd have to warn her not to let Kate know that they'd been in the house. At all costs Kate must never find out. It would put their working relationship, already somewhat tetchy, on such a precarious footing if Kate knew she'd seen the . . . well, not to put too fine a point on it . . . *the altar.*

Ralph had rung Peter at nine o'clock that morning to ask if he would be free to see him.

'Of course, if you come in about half an hour. After that I have various appointments which I can't ditch.'

'That will be absolutely fine, Peter.'

'Good, see you then.'

They settled down to talk in the study. Peter said, 'Before you tell me what you've come to discuss, can I say the builders have given me the quote for pointing the church tower and replacing any necessary masonry. When it's been agreed, they'll go ahead as soon as the weather improves.'

'Good – not before time. Can't have the tower falling down. Stitch in time et cetera.'

Ralph mentioned the cricket club and his hopes for the summer, and that the first match in the League was on the first Bank Holiday in May; they would be playing against Little Derehams. What did he think?

'Brilliant!' Peter, a born athlete and keen cricketer, was pleased. 'I understand they're a very good team.'

'They are. They are,' Ralph beamed.

'The pavilion will be finished then?

'Oh yes! Have you not been to take a look?'

'No. I keep meaning to find the time. It's not lack of interest.'

'It is going to be excellent,' Ralph enthused. 'All modern conveniences in every sense of the word, plus a marvellous wide verandah right across the front – old Fitch's idea, and give him credit it's a good one. Best pavilion in the county when it's finished – but then that's typical of the man.'

Peter looked at Ralph with a reproving expression on his face. Ralph apologised immediately. 'Sorry! I truly am grateful for what he's done but it does rather stick in the craw. However, we shall have a superb summer cricket-wise, I'm sure of that, and the pitch is coming on a treat.'

'Is it cricket you came to see me about then?'

Ralph sat forward and rested his hands on his knees as he always did when he was searching for the right words. Looking up at Peter he said, 'It was nearly half-past one last night before I got to bed.'

'Oh, I'm sorry. What was the problem? Muriel not well?

'No, no, nothing like that. I was in Sykes Wood with Jimmy and Muriel.'

'Ah. Yes?' Peter's expression changed.

Ralph told him what had happened in the wood and asked his opinion.

'I am completely bewildered. Who on earth can these five people have been?

'The cat Sykes had the fight with was Kate Pascoe's.'

'Oh good Lord, I don't believe it.'

'It got badly burnt. It actually rolled on the glowing

embers with Sykes on top of it. It's bound to have burns. That will be proof of a kind.'

'I can hardly ask to see her cat can I? What excuse could I give?'

'None. But I won't have black magic or whatever it is they're doing, in this village. People are being affected by it, and it must stop.'

Unable to believe what was happening, Peter said, 'They'll not meet there again, will they, now they've been seen.'

'Exactly. I didn't mean to let them know we were there but Sykes thought differently.'

'I wonder who else is involved?'

Ralph retorted. 'No idea.'

'Hardly a police matter is it? But there's no doubt it is a church matter. They've done nothing criminally wrong, have they?'

Ralph shook his head saying 'No, but morally wrong.'

'Indeed. This calls for intervention on my part. I shall have to act, and quickly.'

'Quite. A sight of the cat is most important. Evidence, you see. And here's the other bit of evidence – one of the black candles.'

He took the candle from his pocket, and put it on Peter's desk. Peter picked it up. 'Oh, my goodness. That is ominous.'

'It is, isn't it? I must go, Muriel will be wondering where I am. She's very upset after last night, but she would insist on coming with us. She can be quite headstrong sometimes.'

'Thank you for telling me, Ralph. Action is called for, definitely, but I'm not yet quite sure what to do.'

'Neither am I. If I get any more information I'll let you know.'

'Very well, and I you.'

When Ralph had left, Peter moved one of his appointments to the afternoon so that he would be free to collect the children from playgroup.

'I *want* to go, Sylvia, I have a particular reason for going, OK?'

'Very well, Rector, but don't let Beth forget her wool hat. Dr Harris and I are taking them both to Bickerby Rocks this afternoon. Wear them out a bit, we hope!'

Peter laughed. 'Got to go, but I will collect them, don't worry.'

When he got to school at five minutes to twelve he went straight to the playgroup room and picked up the twins.

'Just need to see Ms Pascoe for a moment, children. Come with me.'

'Daddy.'

'Yes, Alex?'

'Cat's got a big, big bandage round her tummy and she's in her cage and she's poorly, and you can't see her eyes, she won't open them.'

Beth, not to be outdone, said, 'Ms Pascoe's been crying. Truly crying.'

Peter's heart sank. As he crossed the hall Kate, looking quite dreadful, came out of her classroom.

'Hello, Ms Pascoe. The children tell me your cat's been in the wars.' He felt very two-faced saying this but couldn't see any other way round it. He could hardly tell her outright that he knew the cause.

Kate didn't answer immediately. When she did it was in a low voice. 'A coal shot out of the fire and tangled in her fur and burnt her before I could get it out. She's really quite unwell.'

'I'm so sorry. She'll need good care.'

'Of course, and she'll get it. Cat's a dear friend.'

Peter smiled and said goodbye.

★

'Peter! I'm amazed you didn't realise yourself it was all lies,' Caroline said that evening when they were sitting by their own fire. 'I told you she'd bought a load of logs from Greenwood Stubbs. You remember, they cut down those trees and he'd advertised the logs for sale on the Village Voice board? I heard her in the Store ordering them from Pat, and giving her the money. So she's a liar to boot.'

'Maybe last night she burnt coal instead.'

Caroline sighed. 'Come on, Peter. I saw Sykes this morning. Chang and Tonga couldn't inflict wounds of that size and depth on Sykes, they're not big enough nor strong enough. But *her* cat could. Sorry, but you've got a witch for a head teacher.' Caroline burst out laughing. 'That must be a first!'

'It's all very well you laughing, Caroline Harris, but I've got a monumental problem. It doesn't just concern the school: it's affecting the whole of my parish. It's got to stop.'

'Well, don't ask *me* for advice! I haven't the faintest idea what to do with a witch.'

'Darling, in the light of what has happened, I can't avoid telling you something that I've kept putting off and putting off till now I can't delay any longer.'

Caroline turned swiftly to look into his face. She asked sharply: 'What have you got to tell me?'

'It's about Mimi.'

'Mimi!'

He paused, then looked Caroline full in the eyes. 'Have you accepted the fact that she might be dead?' he asked gently.

'Of course.'

Caroline waited for him to go on. She noticed he was twisting his wedding ring round and round, a sure sign he didn't like what he was going to have to say. 'Her collar's been found,' Peter said at last.

'Her collar? Where?'

'In Sykes Wood, near the bonfire you saw.'

'Oh God! You don't think they used her for—'

'I doubt it. It could just be chance.'

'Who found it?'

'Sylvia, but she didn't dare tell you. She was so frightened, and she didn't want you upset.'

Caroline took out her handkerchief and wiped her eyes. 'I can't bear to think of those dreadful people having poor Mimi in their power. When did she ever do anything unkind to anyone at all?'

'Never. Come here.' Caroline laid her head against his chest and wept quietly. Peter encircled her with his arms and wished he could say something of comfort but there wasn't anything that could alleviate her distress.

Caroline finally put her hands on his chest and pushed him away from her. 'I shall personally strangle the woman,' she said in a quivering voice. 'I shall go round to the school tomorrow and *do it*.'

'Darling, we have no evidence that she is involved – none at all. It's all pure conjecture.'

'No evidence? Of course we have!'

'What evidence? Tell me that.'

'The cat fighting Sykes.'

'But the cat could have been there quite by chance.'

'Why will you go round this world believing the best of everybody? I bet if you'd been on the jury at the Yorkshire Ripper trial you'd have found a reason for letting him off! It won't do, Peter. It won't do.'

'It's the way I'm made.'

'Poor Mimi! I shall make sure that Kate gets her comeuppance. She's got her cat, but I haven't got mine because of her evil ways.'

'Caroline!'

'Don't say "Caroline" in that tone of voice. She'll have to go.'

'I can't sack her! There are no grounds for me to do that.'

At that moment, Chang and Tonga flicked through the cat flap. They'd come in to go to bed. Caroline rushed towards them and hugged them close. 'We shall have to have litter trays and they won't be able to go out ever again.'

'Oh no! That was something we knew we couldn't have once we got the children. You agreed on that. No more litter trays. I never liked them in the first place and we are not having cats doing their business in this house. I forbid it.'

'You *forbid* it?' The ringing challenging note in Caroline's voice made Peter's heart sink. He forced himself to speak calmly.

'You have got to be rational about this. Much as I love the cats, the children's health and well-being come first. As a doctor, you know I'm right. Besides, it's cruelty of the first order to forbid the cats their freedom. I can't bear such cruelty.'

'But if it's to save their lives?'

'Even to save their lives. I refuse to have an argument about it. No litter tray and the cats have their freedom. One year of freedom is better than ten years locked in a house. I won't have it.'

'They're my cats.'

'They're your children.'

There was a split second of stunned silence and then she rounded on him and, in a controlled, ominously quiet voice, she said, 'The cats are *not* my children. I'm not some idiotic sentimental fool.'

Peter was furious that she should think that he knew so little of her as to make such a mistake. He retorted angrily, 'I know you better than to think that of you. I didn't mean the *cats*, I meant Alex and Beth are your children.'

Caroline opened her mouth to protest and then changed her mind. He was right: the children did come before the cats. Peter watched her gather herself together.

Caroline swallowed hard. 'I'm so sorry. Of course you're right. I do beg your pardon. I got everything out of proportion with being so upset. Yes, the cats shall have their freedom, no matter what. But Kate Pascoe is another matter. I shall go to see her tomorrow, and you mustn't try to stop me.'

'No, Caroline. Please, leave it to me.'

'Someone has to confront her with it.'

'I know, but I need time to think how to go about it.' He took both her hands in his and raised them to his lips. 'My darling girl, I'm so sorry about Mimi; so very sorry. I wouldn't have you hurt for the world.'

'Peter, where's her collar now? I'd like to see it.'

'Are you sure?'

'Yes.'

'Wait there.'

When he came back with it in his hand, Caroline smiled sadly. She cradled it against her face, looked up at him and said, 'You know, I used to confide in her about you. When I got back to the flat after being out with you, I told her what you'd said and the things we'd done, and where we'd been. Told her how lovely you were and how much I loved you. Silly, wasn't I?'

'Of course not. I love you for it.'

'Do you think she suffered?'

'I don't honestly know. I just hope not.'

'And so do I. So do I. But Kate Pascoe will have to go.'

Chapter 19

Kate surveyed the paintings Class Three had done that afternoon. They were most unsatisfactory. Almost all of the children had become obsessed with black. There were black cats, black hats, black trees, black people, black clouds and two of them had a dreadful black interpretation of the devil. What on earth had happened to them all?

'Weird, ain't it?' Kate jumped. It was Pat Duckett coming in to clean the classroom. 'Downright spooky. Our Michelle didn't do paintings like that when Mr Palmer was 'ere. He wouldn't have allowed it.'

'But then Mr Palmer didn't know how to encourage children's talent.'

'Well, if that's talent give me mediocre any day. I don't know about him not encouraging them – all three of the kids who've applied for Prince Henry's and Lady Wortley's this year have had interviews. They'll be hearing any day now. So he must have taught 'em something.'

'Indeed he must, but that was the three Rs; this is creative talent.'

'Is it? I wouldn't have known if you hadn't told me.

What about Liz Neal's boys? Guy's turning out real talented at painting at Prince Henry's. Liz says—'

'All right, Pat, there's an exception to every rule.'

Pat began to sweep. 'I'll say this for you, you keep a lovely tidy classroom. No bits to pick up at all and every cupboard top as clean as a whistle. No Brownie points though for the paintings. That one of the devil is the rector really.'

'I beg your pardon?'

'Well, when it's Stocks Day in June the rector dresses as the devil, horns and the lot, but underneath he has his white wedding cassock on and he flings off the devil's costume, blesses the stocks and everything's all right for another year. Something to do with the time when the Black Death came to the village, and we always celebrate it every year or else things worse than the Black Death might 'appen. So that's 'im. Strikes me he'll have to be doing some of that exorcising that a man of the church like 'im can do. There's another one of 'im there, look, with great big horns. You can just spot the white of his cassock at the bottom – see? These kids knows a thing or two, they do.'

'Nonsense!'

'Everybody's scared to death. Talking of death, look at Sadie Beauchamp – alive and kicking one day and dead as a dodo the next. Never ailed a thing. And why's Rhett and the sergeant's wife frightened out of their skins? Answer me that.'

Kate dismissed the ideas as quite ridiculous. 'They are all a load of rubbish, these scaremongering tales. And it's time you got on with your work, Pat.'

'Thanks very much. Only offering a bit of advice.'

Kate swept out of the room ahead of Pat's broom. She went to her little office, and stood looking out at the bins. Cat came in and, sensing the disturbance of Kate's mind, jumped up on the desk and rubbed her head against Kate's hip asking for attention. Cat's huge bald patch caused by her burn was beginning to grow new fur, and she was feeling and behaving more like her old self.

'Hello, Cat. Time to go home, is it?' Kate fondled Cat's ears and tickled her chin. Outside, Pat came round the corner to empty a wastepaper basket. Kate watched her. The paper cascaded into the recycling bin, except for one piece which blew upwards in a sudden gust of wind. She watched Pat reach out to catch it. Pat was right. The children *were* being affected, that was obvious from their paintings. In their own ways, they were suggesting that Peter did something about it for them. Kate shook herself. She was becoming even dafter than Pat, reading such ludicrous things into paintings the children would have forgotten about by now. Exorcism! Whatever next? All of it was pure coincidence, wasn't it? Cat purred. Pure coincidence.

'Tea and toasted teacake, I think, Cat. What about you?' Cat purred louder still; Kate's finger was scratching her in just the right places. Life was good here in Turnham Malpas. Everything had fallen into place. Soulmates, yes indeed, there were soulmates here. Cat jumped down ready for going home. When Pat came in to clean the staff washbasin, Cat, back arched, tail fluffed, spat at her.

Kate usually drank her afternoon cup of tea at the kitchen table, but today she took it into the living room and put a match to the fire. Her technique for lighting fires had improved by leaps and bounds and it was crackling healthily in no time at all. Cat had learned nothing since her accident and was sitting as close as she possibly could to the flames, busy washing herself and licking the bald patch as though to speed the growth of the fur there. Kate watched her dreamily.

She'd definitely done the right thing by leaving Africa and coming home to England. The climate suited her better and suited Cat better too. And here in Turnham Malpas there were such possibilities. The school for one offered her a tremendous opportunity to educate as she saw fit. The tight lines within which Michael Palmer had operated were not for her. All-round education, that was what these children needed, and the next thing she would do on that score was to buy computers. It was nothing short of scandalous that there were none in the school. One wouldn't be enough, not by any means. Kate had just put her mind to how she would fund her computer project when the front door burst open and the sound of children invaded the house.

Cat sprang up and ran to see who'd come, but Kate already knew. It was Simone with her brood.

'Hi! It's me. As if you didn't know.'

'Hello! Come in!'

'We are.'

The children spread like a plague of locusts around the little living room. Simone had the baby enveloped in the huge shawl she used as her baby carrier. Only wisps of dark curly hair showed above the shawl. Simone hitched the baby higher and sat down on the futon.

'Well?'

Kate raised an eyebrow. 'Well?'

'What about it then?' Cat leapt onto her knee, purring gleefully and begging to be stroked. 'What are we going to do?'

'Do?' Kate echoed again.

'Don't be stupid, Kate. You know what I mean.' The fact that the children were playing with just about every moveable object in the room, some of which were in imminent danger of being broken, didn't intrude on Simone's consciousness at all. It made Kate edgy.

'Do I?'

Simone pushed her long black hair away from the baby who was entangling her fingers in it. She stared at Kate with her large dark intense eyes. 'You do. The venue.'

'Tea?'

'Thanks.'

Kate went to the kitchen for another cup and some biscuits for the children. She hadn't any unbreakable cups and she wouldn't risk Simone's children getting their hands on her china.

She returned with the cup of tea for Simone, put it down on the table beside the futon and handed her the biscuits. 'These are for the children.'

The children began to argue and fight over an ornament. Simone stood up, took it from them without a word, put it high up on the mantelshelf, and passed round their biscuits.

'You haven't answered.'

'No.' Kate took a sip of tea. 'It's getting too much.'

'Oh! Is it? Just when we're getting successful.' Simone tickled Cat behind her ears and Cat reached her face upwards to encourage Simone to continue. She kneaded her claws into Simone's leg, the pleasure of being caressed by her almost too much to bear. Kate felt a stab of jealousy. Cat was *her* pet.

'Don't you call it success?' Simone pursued.

'No, I don't. You've been too successful.'

'Can one be *too* successful?'

'You can. It's getting in too deep for me.'

'What's "deep"?'

Kate moved one of the children away from the fire. 'I've no proper fireguard, not having children myself. Can you ask them to keep away?'

Simone ignored her and pressed home her question. 'What's "deep"?'

'I prefer not to do harm.'

'Harm? What harm have we done?'

'You don't need me to spell it out.'

'Only their just deserts.'

'No, not their just deserts. Punishment.'

'Going moral, are we?'

'Yes, if you like to call it that. I've a job to do here and I don't want to jeopardise it.'

'It won't.'

'It will if these last weeks are anything to go by.'

Simone accused her of backing out.

'Perhaps.'

'I'll take Cat then.'

'No, not Cat.'

'I shall. I can.'

'Simone! Leave Cat here with me.'

'On loan.'

'No, not even on loan.'

Simone smiled that slow, deep smile of hers. It was an all-knowing, threatening, wait-and-see smile and Kate didn't like it.

Simone slid Cat off her knee and stood up. 'I'll leave then. I'll let you know when and where. I've a place in mind.'

'I shan't come.'

'You will, or I'll have Cat.'

Kate stood up to emphasise her protest. 'Not Cat; she won't come.'

'Won't she?' Simone raised an eyebrow at Kate and then stared deliberately into Cat's bright green eyes. Cat was looking up at her adoringly.

The children followed their mother out of the house. She didn't tell them she was going, didn't gather them together ready to leave; they were simply expected to follow. Kate watched her crossing the playground. Cat scratched at the outside door wanting to be let out, but Kate ignored her. She had a strong feeling that Cat really would go with Simone and she wasn't having that.

But, later that evening, Cat just had to go out.

'Mummy! Mummy!' Harriet heard the front door slam and the thud of eager footsteps into the kitchen. Why did her children always assume she was in the kitchen? It said something about her that she didn't quite enjoy.

'Flick! I'm upstairs changing Fran.'

The footsteps pounded up the stairs and she heard Flick saying breathlessly as she reached the landing, 'Cat's missing!'

'They're not – they're in the house somewhere.'

'No!' Flick appeared in the bedroom, flung herself down on the bed next to Fran and gasped, 'I mean *Cat*, Ms Pascoe's cat.'

'Oh dear!'

'She's said we must all keep our eyes open and check our sheds and things just in case she's locked in somewhere. Have you checked our shed?'

'No, I didn't know to check it, did I? That's it, Fran, there you are. Off you go.' Fran sat up and began searching Flick's pockets to see if she had brought any treasures home from school. Harriet sighed. 'Can't wait for the day she's trained. Roll on the glorious day!'

'She won't be a baby sister any more then, will she?'

'Not a baby, no. So, about the cat. How long has she been missing?'

'Since last night. We've searched everywhere. Ms Pascoe's so upset she doesn't know what she's doing today, but she did say she's going to get us computers for school. Though I shall have left by then, won't I?

'You will. Lady Wortley's here you come!'

'I'm glad I got in. Celebration night tonight, isn't it? I wish Grandma could have been here. She would have been so pleased for me, wouldn't she?'

'She would indeed, darling. I'm sorry too.'

Flick changed the subject quickly; she didn't want Mummy crying again. 'Can I go round to the Store with my pocket money?'

'Yes. Mind when you cross Shepherd's Hill. Have your drink when you get back, eh?'

Flick marched purposefully to the store, her pound coin held tightly. As she pushed open the door she listened for the ping of the bell, a sound her daddy said he loved, which she knew meant he loved the idea that customers were coming in to spend; it really wasn't just the *sound*. It being going-home-from-school time the Store was crowded. She loved it crowded. It felt like the shops she went to with Grandmama Charter-Plackett when she stayed with her in London in the holidays. It was good going out with her, but she still liked Grandma Sadie best. She was fun! *Had been* fun.

Flick pushed her way to the sweet counter. The Paradise children were there and she saw Dickon Paradise sneak a tube of Love Hearts into his pocket. 'Dickon! I shall tell your mummy. You've to pay for that.'

In reply Dickon kicked her ankle hard, little Valentine added another for good measure, and so did Hansel. Flick hopped about complaining, 'That hurt! Mrs Paradise, Dickon's got sweets in his pocket. He's nicking them!'

Simone gave Dickon a hard look and he pulled the sweets from his pocket and gave them to her. She put them back on the display.

Dickon poked his tongue out at Flick as far as it would go. She put hers out too and they stood within a hair's breadth of each other grimacing fiercely. Flick pulled her very nastiest face at him and turned away.

Then she saw Ms Pascoe. 'Ms Pascoe! Isn't it busy in here?'

'It certainly is. This is quite the wrong time to come, isn't it? What are you here for?'

'Spending my pocket money.'

Simone passed close by. Flick heard Ms Pascoe say quietly, 'Well, where is she?'

Simone Paradise paused and, pretending to be choosing corned beef, said innocently to a tin from Brazil, 'Who?'

'Cat.'

'I don't know where your cat is. I know where *mine* is.'

'You've enticed her away. She wouldn't leave me otherwise.'

'No?'

'You've locked her up.'

'Me? Do that to a defenceless animal? Tut tut!'

Flick stood looking up at the two of them, unable to understand. She could feel the sparks between them though. Almost touch them. How funny, feeling that. Mrs Paradise must have stolen Cat. She hadn't got a cat, she knew that for a fact. Dickon longed for one and his mother said 'no'. Another mouth to feed, she always said and she was right; she had six people to feed already and no daddy working for them. Flick wondered where their daddy was, though there'd be no room for one more in that tiny cottage; they must have to sleep head to toe already.

Ms Pascoe said, her lips tight with anger, 'Let her go!'

'At the next meeting.'

'I'm not coming.'

'You are. I'll tell you when.' Simone sailed to the

till, the children struggling to keep up, and queued to pay.

Flick looked up at Ms Pascoe's face. She wished she hadn't. Ms Pascoe was sad and angry and fearful all at once. She bought herself some chocolate and went home, puzzled by the adult world and glad to get back to Mummy and Fran who made sense. Poor Cat. Perhaps Mrs Paradise was only teasing. That would be it, she was teasing and Ms Pascoe didn't realise she was. She'd tell her in the morning.

But there was Cat asleep as usual on Ms Pascoe's classroom windowsill when Flick got to school the next morning.

'Oh, Ms Pascoe! Cat's back again. I knew Mrs Paradise was teasing. Did she come back all by herself?'

'Last night.'

'I expect you'll be relieved.'

'I am.'

Kate found it hard to lie outright. Cat had indeed come back last night, but only because Kate had gone to get her. She'd waited until half-past eleven and then driven to Little Derehams and parked her car just before she came to the first house in the village. Her torch had flashed onto the name on the first gate. *Keepers Cottage.* Who lived there? Oh, that was it, Gilbert Johns. There was a car parked outside – a little Fiesta. Visitors at this time of night, Gilbert? The village would be talking.

Unlike Turnham Malpas, Little Derehams was one of those spread-out villages. The cottages were dotted here and there along the entire length of what was known as the High Street. The shops and the smithy and the little school and the inn had all been converted into bijou residences and the village lay quietly sleeping, just as it did during the day. Here and there a light shone from a bedroom window but that was the only sign of life.

Kate, having checked the address in the school records, had easily recognised Simone's cottage. The front garden, instead of having lawn and flowers like everyone else's, had a children's swing in one corner and the rest was given over to vegetables. It couldn't be anyone else's but hers. There were no lights showing at Simone's windows, so she could perhaps safely assume they were all in bed, but even so not wishing to risk the gate squeaking Kate had climbed over the collapsing wire fence. She followed the little earth path which ran down the side of the cottage and found the shed. She was sure that was where Cat would be, locked in the shed. There was a padlock, but the door and the shed itself were so worn and rickety that she pulled the padlock off with the bracket with scarcely any effort at all. In a loud whisper she called, 'Cat! Cat!' But Cat wasn't there. Simone must have shut her in the house. Unless she'd k——. Kate shuddered. No, she wouldn't have, because then she'd have no further hold over her. No, Cat must be in the house.

Typical of Simone's relaxed attitude to life, the back door was shut but unlocked. Kate very, very gently turned the knob and slowly opened it. Her heart was pounding and her hands were shaking. She stepped in and shone her torch round the room. At some time the two rooms of the cottage had been converted into one, so the room now ran from the back to the front of the cottage; it was long and narrow and so dreadfully disorganised and untidy that Kate shivered. She recognised that with five children in the house it would be difficult to keep tidy, but this! Heavens above. What a mess! Dried herbs interspersed with small garments belonging to the children hung to dry from a long pole suspended from the ceiling by old rope tied to each end. Dishes stood unattended in the sink. Shoes and socks and clothes lay on the threadbare carpet; discarded toys all over the table, along with a half-full milk bottle and the remains of a loaf of bread, roughly hewn as though one of the children had cut the last slice. Dust and clutter were everywhere.

Kate shuddered again. Cat living in this mess. There was a scratching sound. Kate panicked, someone was coming! Hang on – she knew that scratching sound. She opened the door which concealed the staircase. And there was Cat waiting on the bottom step. Kate picked her up and Cat purred intensely. Terrified that someone upstairs might hear the loud purring, Kate hugged Cat to her and headed for the back door. Just as she reached it she heard noises from the far end of the room. She swung round searching for the source of the noise and her torch shone on Dickon. The poor child must have been sleeping on the sofa. Now he was standing up on it wearing only a short, badly-torn vest, clutching a blanket in his hand. When he caught sight of her face in the beam of the torch he shouted, 'Simone! It's Ms Pascoe. She's pinching Cat. Simone!'

But Kate was gone. Clutching Cat to her she fled down the earth path, stumbled over the wire fencing and set off down the High Street for the safety of her car. Quick! Quick! She wouldn't put it past Simone to come racing after her in her nightgown – that was, if she ever wore anything so normal as a nightgown. There was a long gap between the last cottage and the one belonging to Gilbert Johns, and by the time Kate was nearing the latter she was gasping for breath; it was so awkward walking rapidly with a heavy cat in her arms. The beam of her torch shone directly onto Gilbert Johns. He was standing on the footpath close to the Fiesta, kissing

Louise from the Big House. Then Kate tripped and couldn't save herself. Cat leapt out of her arms, and Kate measured her length on the path. 'Damn and blast! Cat! Cat! Come here.'

Gilbert's clutter was almost as bad as Simone's but his, caused as it was by books and archaeological artefacts, was more acceptable. Louise made her a hot drink, found an old dish and gave Cat some milk, while Gilbert bathed Kate's knees, and tried to scrape the grit from a cut on her hand with a wet tissue.

'My dear Kate, what on earth are you doing in Little Derehams at this time of night with your cat? Nice though it is to see you, it does seem a rather late hour to be about, does it not?'

Kate sipped her tea. To hell with it having cow's milk in it. 'What am I doing here? Searching for Cat, and finding her.'

'Where was she?'

'That doesn't matter.'

'Huge cat,' Louise said. 'Some people say it's descended from a panther.'

'Some people are daft.'

'Sorry!'

'Didn't mean you! But she isn't, she's just grown big that's all. Ouch!'

'Sorry, trying to be gentle. It's a nasty cut. Can you find the first-aid box, darling? I think it's in the boot with the spades and whatnot.'

Kate almost smiled. Somehow the word 'darling' coming from Gilbert's lips seemed out of place, but he obviously thought a great deal of Louise. Lucky girl to have someone like Gilbert. Such a nice man. Louise reappeared carrying an enormous bright green first-aid box.

Kate was amused. 'Overegging the pudding rather?'

Gilbert laughed. 'It's the one I take on digs. Can't be too careful.'

He cleansed her grazes with antiseptic wipes and then put dressings on both knees and on her hand. 'There we are, all done. You can finish your tea in peace. Louise would you give Kate a lift when she's ready?'

Kate answered for her. 'No need, my car's just down the road a bit.'

'I smell a smattering of skulduggery here. Can I give you some advice?'

'About my cuts?'

'No, about the company you keep. Just watch it. You've too much going for you to let it be spoilt by dabbling . . . Well, you know what I mean. Think on it. OK now?'

Kate stood up. 'Come on, Cat. Let's go home. Thanks. Thanks for the tea and the plasters and the advice.'

'Not at all, any time.'

Chapter 20

Kate got the message about the next meeting in a note given her by Simone's daughter, Florentina. Both Dickon and she were in Miss Booth's class. Florentina knocked on her office door just before school began. 'Note from Simone.' She was a child of few words like her brother.

Kate waited until Florentina had left and then she opened the note. It was scribbled on the back of a leaflet advertising the start of a mobile hairdressing service visiting the villages. On the blank side, Simone had written *'Eleven p.m. tonight. Rendezvous to be advised. Come.'*

Well, she wouldn't. Not any more. Gilbert was right: she'd too much going for her. Kate tore the message into little pieces and dropped it in her waste bin. This afternoon after school she was going fund-raising and the first person she was trying was Mr Fitch. The appointment was for four o'clock and she would be going up there full of charm and persuasion. She'd get him to buy the computers if it was the last thing she did. She'd wear her most demure dress because she felt that was what would impress him, being the kind of man he was. Oh yes! Craddock Fitch, here I come! The bell rang so she went out into the hall ready to start the school day.

Louise welcomed her and asked her to take a seat. 'Mr Fitch has someone with him and they're over-running their time, but I'm sure he won't be long. All your injuries doing well?'

'Yes, thanks.'

'Lovely day! Spring is sprung as they say.'

'Quite! Gilbert's nice.'

Louise blushed. 'He is.'

'You should marry him.'

'Didn't think you'd recommend that. Not your style.' The telephone rang and she had to break off. When she'd replaced the receiver and made a note of the caller, Louise finished by saying, 'I might at that.'

'Why not. Men like him are hard to find. He seems besotted.'

'He is. I don't know why.'

Kate nearly said, 'Neither do I' but changed it to, 'Don't do yourself down.'

Mr Fitch's caller suddenly emerged from the library and stormed out through the front door without so much as a good afternoon.

'Whoops! Better watch it. That didn't go too well, did it? Best of luck!'

Louise showed her into the library. Kate loved the room immediately she entered it. It was large and although oak-panelled, wasn't a dark room because of the almost floor-to-ceiling windows. Mr Fitch stood up to greet her. There was a spill-over of anger from his last appointment; his thin lips were pinched into a straight line and his eyes sparking angrily which didn't bode well for Kate, but she ploughed on just the same.

'Good afternoon, Mr Fitch. I'm pleased to meet you. I've heard so much about you.'

'Not all of it good, I've no doubt.'

'Not so. I've heard about you paying for the central heating at the church and rebuilding the cricket pavilion. Both excellent contributions to village life.'

'Thank you. Tea?'

'That would be nice. My voice needs lubricating after a day teaching; a cup of tea would be wonderful.'

Mr Fitch called Louise and asked her for tea. 'Now, young lady, what can I do for you? Not wanting a job, I assume?' He smiled when he said that and she felt warmed by his attitude.

'I'm here in my capacity as head teacher in the school. I may as well come straight to the point; the office won't or can't provide us with computers. Too small a school to make the expenditure worthwhile et cetera, et cetera. But these children need them. They'll go to the comprehensive in Culworth at eleven and they'll have them there and our children will be seriously disadvantaged. I don't like to think of them missing out on modern technology, it's just not right. I'm aiming, you see, to give the children an all-round education. Not just the three Rs, though they are necessary as they are the tools with which they learn about the world and everything in it. So I wondered with your expertise in marketing if you could think up a way of me raising the money to purchase them. I know a computer auction place where I could buy second-hand ones relatively cheaply, so I could probably buy two for the price of one new one if you get my drift.'

Louise brought in the tea and poured out for them. She handed Mr Fitch his cup for which he simply nodded his head and gave Kate hers. 'Thank you. That's lovely.'

'How many were you thinking of buying?'

'Ten.'

'Ten?'

'Oh yes. There's nothing more frustrating than waiting a whole lesson for a turn and the bell going and that's your chance out of the window for that day. Ten definitely. Well, that's my aim to start with.'

'Who'd do the teaching? I mean, I can't see that old biddy Hetty Hardaker having much nous about computers.'

'Me.'

'I see. You've it all worked out then.'

'Yes.'

He sipped his tea and looked speculatively at her over the rim of his cup. He put it down on the saucer without saying a word and fiddled instead with his gold pen on a piece of paper, making calculations.

He clipped the top back on his pen and said, 'In August, while we have no students here, this place is being stripped out and re-equipped with the very latest in computers. As I expect you are aware, as fast as you install computers there are new developments which make yours out of date almost by the time the staff have mastered the use of them. We're having state-of-the-art systems put in – the whole shebang. If you wait till then, I'll let you have fifteen computers and some printers for an absolute song. They're worth next to nothing on the market; they were old hat when they came here, but for what you want them for, they will be ideal. It would be a start, wouldn't it? What do you say?'

Kate was overwhelmed with gratitude. She stood up, then sat down again, hardly able to contain herself.

'I can't believe it. I am so grateful – you've no idea. I only came to pick your brains for some fund-raising ideas! Wait till I tell the children. They'll be thrilled. I am too – absolutely thrilled. Thank you very much indeed. Such generosity.'

Mr Fitch was obviously very well-suited with her response. 'Not at all. Got to help the children along. Couldn't talk to that stuffy dyed-in-the-wool Mr Palmer, but you're different.' He stood up and wandered over to the windows, his hands in his pockets. 'I've been meaning to set up an educational trust. The kind of trust which would help bright children to get the best from life. The sort of thing I have in mind is paying for someone to go to Prince Henry's or the girls' one, Lady whatever . . .'

'Wortley's.'

'That's right, Lady Wortley's – someone who's clever enough to go but can't afford the fees. What do you think?'

'I have to be honest with you. I don't agree with private education.'

'Why the blazes not? What's wrong with children being clever?'

'They can be clever at the comprehensive.'

'Well, I'm disappointed. Very disappointed. Maybe I misjudged Mr Palmer. He would have jumped at the chance, him being an old stick in the mud.' Kate couldn't see his smile nor the twinkle in his eyes as he said this.

Kate felt lashed by the assumption that Mr Palmer would have been more open to new ideas than she. Perhaps Mr Fitch was right. Why shouldn't children from poorer homes have the benefits? 'Could I give this my consideration and get back to you?' she asked. 'We've three children going in September, but all their parents can pay, no problem. I'll think about the children who'll be leaving in July next year. I'll let you know.'

'It would be called the Beauchamp Educational Trust.'

For a moment Kate couldn't think what the Beauchamp bit was, and then she remembered Flick's grandmother. 'Right. I see. Yes. Well, Mr Fitch, I mustn't take up any more of your time, but I will say this – I can never thank you enough for your promise of the computers. Never. I shall be indebted to you for ever. As for your idea of the Trust, I shall put my mind to it forthwith. This village should appreciate all you do for them. The cricket club especially, this year. I'm so excited. I'm a fanatical cricket fan.'

'Do you play?'

'I did with my brothers, but I'm in the tea-making department this year. The pavilion is looking marvellous.'

'You've been to see it?'

'I have. Thank you again. I shall be in touch.' She shook hands with Mr Fitch and went out. Louise looked speculatively at her as she shut the library door. 'Your interview went well by the looks of it.'

'It did. All due to the Pascoe charm. He's promised to let me have the old computers he's throwing out in the summer for the school! I just can't believe my good luck.'

'Wow! You must have made an impression! He's had a really bad day today, poor man. I wonder he didn't bite your head off.' Kate winked at Louise and left, her heart full to bursting with pleasure. Fifteen computers for virtually nothing. She couldn't believe it. All she had to do now was sever her connections with Simone as carefully as possible. That part would have to be stopped. She had never meant it to go so far.

When she got back to school Hetty Hardaker's car was still there.

Kate put her head round Hetty's classroom door. 'Hello, Hetty, still here? Everything all right?'

'It is. I can't stand these walls any longer so I've ripped everything off and I'm making a fresh start. New notices, new pictures, new charts.'

'Spring must have got to you!'

'Indeed it has.'

Not relishing Hetty's response to her computer idea, Kate said speculatively, 'I've got good news.'

Hetty paused. 'Yes?'

'In the summer Mr Fitch is having his computers replaced and he's promised us the old ones for the school.'

'I don't believe it. Great minds think alike!'

'What do you mean?'

'I've been thinking about computers and wondering how we could lay our hands on some, and there you've come up with the answer. Brilliant!'

'Brilliant?'

'Oh, yes. We need them so badly.'

'Do we?'

'Oh, yes. I wanted Mr Palmer to get some but he wouldn't. The dear man was such a love but he could be quite narrow-minded.' Hetty rolled her eyes heavenwards.

Kate was amazed. 'I didn't think you would agree. Are you at home with computers then?'

'Oh yes! Theo and I spend many a merry hour with our computer. It's Theo's hobby.'

'So you would be able to teach the children then?'

'Oh yes, I'm sure I could.'

'Well, that's wonderful. I thought you wouldn't want them.'

'I most certainly do.' Hetty rolled up a heap of old paintings and stuffed them into a bin bag. 'I'm sure Theo would give a hand to set them up, if you like. Right – I'll just get rid of these and then I'll be off. We'll have to persuade Margaret, she's not computer friendly at all, but leave her to me.'

And Hetty bustled off to the bins leaving Kate non-plussed. How surprising people could be. She'd have laid a bet on Hetty being antagonistic to modern technology and here she was, probably more knowledge-able than herself. Kate raised her clenched fist and shook it at nothing in particular. Great! At last Hetty was coming over to her side.

The following morning Pat Duckett was banging on Kate's door by five minutes past eight. Kate was already dressed and hurried to the door, toast in hand.

'Ms Pascoe, you'll have to come – the school's been vandalised! Such a mess you never did see.'

Kate stood for a moment trying to take in what Pat was saying. 'Vandalised? What do you mean?'

'Everywhere's had paint thrown over it, the piano music's been torn to shreds, the books in the library corner 'ave all been torn up, and . . . Oh, it's terrible – it's as if a bomb's dropped on it. They got in through the kitchen window – all the glass is in the sink. I'm so upset.' Pat got her handkerchief out and blew her nose. 'I've never seen such a mess in all my born days. If I'd known they were going to do it, I wouldn't have wasted my time cleaning last night. I'll call the police, shall I?'

'Not yet. Let me see it first. I'll just get my things.'

Pat waited for her and the two of them crossed the playground together and went in through the main door. One of the children had left his coat the previous night; the sleeves had been cut off and they lay on the floor of the passage.

The library corner was devastated. Some of the books had been thrown right the way to the other end of the hall, some had been dropped where they'd been torn up. The Maypole ribbons had been cut close to the top and what was left of them hung in silent condemnation. Chairs were overturned, and the piano stool had had its lid almost wrenched off; its contents were in shreds, strewn all over the floor. And over everything were huge splashes of the paint the children used for their artwork. Red. Blue. Green. Yellow. Black. Orange. Purple. Great vivid streaks of it thrown at random straight from the jars. The jars themselves had been smashed against the wall between the doors to Classes One and Two.

The glass window in Kate's office door had been broken as though punched by a great fist. Kate stepped carefully through, broken glass littered the floor. Her filing cabinets hadn't been touched, thank goodness. All those school records!

She came back out into the hall again to speak to Pat. 'Don't touch anything. I'll ring the sergeant, though what he can do about it I don't know. They haven't exactly left their calling card, have they?'

Then, for some reason she didn't know, Kate looked up at one of the hall windows. The windows were set so high that the children and the teachers could only see the tops of the trees at the edge of the playground. Whoever had painted on the window must have had a ladder or managed to climb up on top of the piano and reached from there. In each pane of glass except for the topmost ones, there was a crucifix, painted in black. But each and every one was upside down.

Pat drew in a deep breath which was audible all over the hall. 'Oh, Good Lord! Ms Pascoe, what does that mean?'

Kate tried hard to disguise the fact that she was trembling. She cleared her throat. 'We won't call the police, I think. Better not.'

'Oh, but we must! If you don't, I shall. These children need protecting. Whatever would the parents say if we didn't? There might be something here the police can detect that we can't. Well? Shall I or will you?'

'I think the thing to do is for us to clear up as best we can, and say nothing at all.'

'The office won't like that. What about the insurance? They can't replace all this stuff without the insurance knowing the police have been. No, I'm phoning them now and then we'll get in touch with the office when it opens. Better make it ten past nine as they won't be there dead on time, I don't expect – the lazy, idle beggars. Do 'em good to be at the sharp end for a while, then they'd know what life's about. Come on, Ms Pascoe, don't take on so. Once the police have been we'll soon get this lot cleared up.' Pat put her arm round Kate and gave her a hug. Kate was white and shaking and unable to speak. She seemed rooted to the spot staring up at the upturned crosses.

'I'm right, yer know, we've got to phone the sergeant.'

Kate nodded and Pat tiptoed amongst the broken glass in the office to look up the village policeman's number in Mr Palmer's old address book.

The sergeant was there within ten minutes. 'Now then, what have we here?' He was as appalled as Pat and Kate had been.

'Well, this is a first, and not half. I've been 'ere fifteen years and this has never happened before. *Never*. They get it in Culworth but not here. That right, Pat?'

Pat nodded. She heard the sound of children's voices. 'Ms Pascoe, the children are arriving, and it's raining now. What shall we do?'

Kate visibly pulled herself together. 'I haven't looked in the classrooms. Are they all right, Pat?'

'Seem to be. Shall I put the first ones in your classroom then?'

'Yes, please.' Pat went off to see to the children.

'Anything missing, Miss Pascoe?'

'Difficult to tell, but I don't think so. It's just pure vandalism. Children, I expect.'

'Them crosses upside down on the window – that's not kids. No, them's ominous they are.'

Chapter 21

'Just what is going on, Ms Pascoe? The welfare of these children and of the school is of the deepest concern to me. I want answers, please. Now what have you to say?'

Peter was sitting in the head teacher's chair and Kate was perched on the edge of the washbasin. He folded his arms and waited. She hadn't noticed before just how penetrating his eyes could be – a rich blue, not an icy Scandinavian blue, and they were looking straight into her soul, or so she felt. Kate had intended having the crosses washed off the windows before he saw them or, better still, before the news leaked out all round the village, but the pressure of keeping the children under restraint while Pat and she made everything safe had prevented her from climbing up to wipe them off. So now he'd seen them and he was utterly determined to find out what she knew.

Did she know, or was it only surmise? She knew all right. But just how little could she get away with telling him?

'I really have no idea who's done this. Just mindless vandalism, and it happened by chance to be our school.'

Peter looked reproachfully at her. 'Please don't take

me for a pathetic nincompoop just because I wear a clerical collar. The two are not synonymous, believe me. It is not vandalism quite by chance at all. You know as well as I do that what has happened is *significant*. Crosses upside down have a special symbolic meaning, don't they?'

'Do they?'

'Whoever did this has connections with black magic or witchcraft, or alternatively is trying to give that impression.'

Kate didn't reply.

'I am well aware you know far more than you are willing to tell me, Kate. I'm sorry, but you've made me very disappointed in you. As you are not willing to tell the truth, then I can only assume you are implicated in some way and I shall have to take steps. Quite what I don't know, but something will be done about it, and don't think I shall brush it all under the carpet and play a wait-and-see policy because I shan't. Now get me a bucket of warm soapy water and a cloth and I'll climb up and clean off the crosses. Being tall, I can easily do it from the top of the piano.'

Peter stripped off his cassock and, wearing only his shirt and trousers, climbed onto the piano with the bucket and cloth. The children leaving their classrooms to go out to play giggled when they saw him.

'Give us a tune, Rector!' Brian couldn't resist saying.

'Oooh, mind out, Rector. Don't fall off!'

'When I'm cleaning winders:' Stacey thrummed an imaginary banjo.

Peter grinned down at them and pretended to flick water on them out of the bucket, then he grimly carried on wiping. Fortunately it was only the school water paint the vandals had used, so with only a small amount of energetic rubbing the windows quickly came clean.

Pat called up. 'You shouldn't be doing that, Rector. I

was going to get Barry to do it in his lunch-hour.'

'Don't you worry about that. Have you some window-cleaning stuff, Pat, then I can give them a good polish while I'm up here?'

'That's not for you to do, sir. The window cleaner's due next week.'

'I'd like to do it.'

'Very well then, hold on a minute.'

By the time he'd got down from the top of the piano, the children were coming back into school from the playground. Kate was standing in the hall holding a mug of coffee for him. Peter took the mug from her and just before he drank from it, he said, 'Well?'

'Will you give me forty-eight hours?'

'Then you'll have something to say to me?'

Kate nodded. 'Yes.'

'Very well. In the meantime I shall make my own enquiries.'

'Thank you.' Kate half-turned away and then turned back and said quietly, 'Be careful.'

Peter raised his eyebrows at her but she had gone.

'So there he is up on top of the piano cleaning the windows.' Pat took another sip of her drink and then nudged Vera. 'Tell yer what, he strips well. Can't see nothing under that cassock he wears, but by jove, yer should have seen 'im! He looked great, he did. Muscles the size of cannon balls he has and such a broad back. Must be all that squash he plays.'

Willie disapproved. 'That's enough. It's not decent to speak of the rector like that.'

'Come on, Willie. He's a man isn't he, as he has well proved.' Pat winked at Vera.

Vera giggled and gave Pat a dig in the ribs. 'Shut up, Pat, show some respect!'

'I 'ave a lot o' respect for him. Can't think of a worse

job for a man to be doing. You 'ave to be devoted and not 'alf, to do what he has to do. He's a wonderful chap, and I'd be the first to say so. He was lovely when Barry and me went to see him about fixing the wedding date. All I was saying was he looks great when he isn't togged up.'

'Tell us what happened then.'

'Well . . .' Pat launched herself on a description of the hall as she'd found it that morning. Vera and Willie were appalled. 'But the worst was, the crosses were upside down. Before she saw that, she was all set for phoning for the sergeant, then she claps 'er eyes on them crosses and Bob's yer uncle she changed her mind. Now why, I ask yer? Why should that be?'

Willie said, 'I reckon she knows a thing or two and she's protecting someone.'

Pat leaned forward across the table, pushed her glass aside and said in a low voice, 'No, yer wrong there. Not *protecting* someone, *frightened* of someone 'd be nearer the mark.'

'Frightened?' Vera said loudly.

Pat gave her another sharp nudge. 'Don't shout. All the bar'll know.'

'It must mean something nasty-like, putting 'em upside down.'

Willie nodded sagely. 'Something evil, I'll be bound.'

They all three turned to look at the bar counter when they heard Ralph's deep voice. 'Good evening, Bryn. A double whisky if you please.'

'Good evening, Sir Ralph. Still keeps cold, doesn't it?'

'It certainly does.'

'Lady Templeton well?'

'Yes, thank you, very well. She's gone into Culworth with Celia Prior to an exhibition of quilting so I thought I'd come in here and catch up with the gossip.'

Bryn smiled and nodded his head in the direction of Pat's table. 'I'd sit over there then, if I were you. Pat's in the thick of it about the vandalism at the school last night.'

Ralph paid for his drink and acknowledging Bryn's advice, went across to join them.

'Good evening. May I join you or would it be an intrusion?'

Willie moved along the settle and patted the seat next to him. 'Sit 'ere, you're more than welcome.'

'Good evening, Vera, good evening, Pat.' They both chorused together, 'Good evening, Sir Ralph.'

His presence put rather a damper on Pat's story and she found it difficult to carry on.

'Your very good health.' Ralph drank from his glass and then prompted her to expand on her story. 'Bad news about the school today. I'm sorry.'

'So was I. Took us two hours to clear up and all the children there and everything. All the piano music will have to go in the bin when the insurance has seen it, and most of the books in the library corner. Her on the mobile library 'll have something say, I've no doubt. She swops our books over for us from time to time, yer see. It'll have right depleted her stocks.'

'Any idea who it was?'

'No, none at all. The rector's very upset. He cleaned the windows for us. Do you know what it means, Sir Ralph – crosses upside down?'

'Work of the devil, I should think.'

Vera eagerly took him up on this. 'Well, our Rhett said just the same. It's upset him, it has. Thought he was going to start being all funny again, but he's managed to master it.'

'He thought so too, did he? Ever get to the bottom of what it was that upset him?'

'No, all he'll say is that it was the devil after him. He still keeps the cross round his neck that I bought him and he's been real quiet since it all happened, not going out and that. Mind you, he's that jiggered when he gets home after working outside and that in the gardens, he's no energy for anything. Eating like a horse he is now. He'll eat anything at all. Best day's work the rector did, getting him that job. Doing him no end of good.'

'Would Rhett talk to me?'

Vera fidgeted with her glass for a moment and then said, 'Well, I don't rightly know. He can be a bit odd if yer try to talk to him about it. Shuts up, like.'

'I can be very persuasive. Is he in now?'

'Well, yes, he is. Don's at work and I just came across for an hour.'

'Drink up and we'll go across together, but you'll have to leave us to talk. He probably wouldn't open up if his grandmother was there.'

Vera eyed him speculatively. 'Are you thinking he can throw some light on this trouble at the school?'

'Yes, I am.'

'He didn't do it, Sir Ralph. It really wasn't him, he's not like that.'

'Not for one moment was I thinking on those lines. No, no, not at all. I simply want to talk to him about his experiences. Now, will you let me?' He smiled that famous Templeton smile, the one Muriel always found so irresistible, and it worked the same magic on Vera.

'Well, of course. Yes, of course.' Rapidly she ran through in her mind just how tidy she had left her living room. She hadn't expected to be taking aristocracy home with her when she'd set out.

'Finished then? No time like the present.'

'Oh yes, of course, yes.' She got up to go. Vera gave Pat a nervous smile and went ahead of Ralph who had stood waiting for her to go in front of him. He held open the door for her and she scuttled out.

★

As Vera put her key in the latch they heard footsteps behind them and, while she struggled with the door which was stiff after the rain, she heard Ralph saying, 'Oh good evening, Peter.' And there he was, dressed in jeans and a thick bright pullover.

'Ah! Good evening. I've come hoping to see Rhett. I didn't know you had company, Vera. I'll come another evening, shall I?'

Ralph asked Vera if she would mind being invaded by not one but two visitors. Vera swallowed hard. 'No, not at all. That's quite all right, I'll go in the kitchen and keep out of the way. Rhett's in 'ere.'

He was laid full-length on the sofa watching television, his boots resting on one arm, his hands behind his head on the other, an empty beer can lay on its side on a table by his elbow. Vera said loudly, 'Our Rhett, you've got visitors.' Ralph blinked when he saw the picture on the screen. Rhett shot into a sitting position; his finger went straight on the video remote control and the screen went blank, for which Ralph was grateful. Never in all his days . . .

But Peter was speaking. 'Quite by chance, Rhett, you've got two visitors and I have an idea we're both here on the same errand. Would you have some time to spare to talk to us?'

By this time Rhett was on his feet. 'Yes, yes of course.'

Without waiting to be asked Ralph chose a chair and sat in it. Peter went to sit on the sofa and Rhett stood on the hearth-rug.

'As you were the first on the doorstep, Ralph, would you like to begin?'

'Very well. I know this is a very delicate subject for you, Rhett, and you've been quite ill with the worry of it all, but it's reached a time when we've got to talk. By the way, I should have asked you first how's the job going.'

'All right, thanks. I like working with Mr Stubbs. He's good. Says I can go on a day-release course at the horticultural college if I show I'm taking an interest.'

'And are you?'

'What?'

'Taking an interest.'

'Oh yes. It's great. Can't wait to get going in them greenhouses. You should see what Mr Stubbs grows in there.'

'I know, it's quite wonderful, isn't it?'

'Yes, it is. Them greenhouses is over a hundred and fifty years old. Growing grapes for one hundred and fifty years —can you imagine that?'

'Well, yes I can.'

Rhett flushed and looked embarrassed. 'Oh, of course. I'd forgotten.'

'That's all right. Let's get down to business. Now you're feeling so much better, can you tell us why it was you were so frightened by seeing this dog Jimmy's adopted?'

Rhett's hand went inside the neck of his shirt and out came the cross his grandma had bought; he wrapped his fingers tightly around it. He looked at Peter, then back to Ralph. He stared at the floor, he gazed at the blank screen and then eventually muttered, 'I thought I'd seen a ghost.'

'There was more to it than that, wasn't there?'

Rhett stared at Ralph. 'The devil. I could see the devil in him.'

'He's a harmless, bright little dog. Got lost and happened by pure chance to turn up here.'

'Not chance.'

'No?'

Peter said, 'If it wasn't chance, then what was it?'

Rhett hesitated and then gazing anywhere but at the two of them, he said, 'He'd been called up.'

Ralph, making military connections with the words Rhett had used, was puzzled. 'Called up?'

'By . . .'

Peter prompted him. 'Yes?'

'The devil.'

Wishing to clarify things and move the story on, Peter said, 'You believe Sykes was brought back to life by the devil?'

Rhett nodded. 'We was in the wood doing these incantation things and . . . they said they knew Sykes was buried there and we'd practise on him. Prove just how powerful we were. Like an experiment what wouldn't harm nobody and we'd see if we could do it.' Rhett had difficulty continuing. He took in a deep breath and started again. 'Course, I thought it was daft but then it seemed to get serious and what with the dark and the fire and the candles and that, and all these strange words and them speaking like being in church kind of – I began to believe we could do it. Then next morning in daylight–like, I thought how daft can you get? He's dead and buried like, isn't he? Dead as a doornail. Then I saw him in Jimmy's garden and . . .' Rhett shuddered at the thought of that terrible encounter.

Peter, looking straight into Rhett's eyes, said, 'You mean you really believe this new Sykes *is* the old Sykes?'

'Well, I did at the time. Absolutely convinced, I was. Now I'm not so sure – not after I'd talked to you. But it does make yer think, doesn't it?'

Peter reassured him. 'Well, it isn't the real Sykes, I can assure you of that. You mention other people. Who leads this "meeting"? We need to know.'

Rhett shut up like a clam.

Ralph tried another tack. 'After you'd been taken ill I went to investigate for myself and I saw five people in the wood, with the altar and the black candles, but they all ran away before I could identify them. Who were they?'

Rhett began pacing up and down the room. Finally, he appeared to come to a decision and stood in front of

Peter. 'I won't give any names,' he blurted out. 'Definitely daren't give names. I've never been again, not since that night. I was too scared of what we were doing.'

Peter said, 'You weren't successful, though it must have looked like that to you at the time. It was coincidence that the dog turned up when he did.'

'Are you sure? Just a great big coincidence?'

'I'm sure.'

'Thank God for that. Beg yer pardon, Rector.'

'No need to beg my pardon, I'm glad you've got it sorted out once and for all. Thank you for telling us that, Rhett. All this damage at the school is connected with it, too. It's got to be stopped.' As an afterthought he asked, 'You're not being threatened, are you?'

'No, not really.'

'I want you to know that if you need help, you can ring me or come to see me at the rectory any time, day or night. We can't have people like you and the sergeant's wife,' Rhett looked uncomfortable and cast shifty glances at Ralph and Peter, 'scared out of their wits. These things can escalate and cause terrible trouble, which indeed they already have. If you feel one day that you are able to name names to me or to Sir Ralph, your information will be treated in the strictest confidence. We shall never and I mean *never* divulge who told us. You're not a fool, Rhett, you've a good job with prospects and you can't let wicked, evil people ruin your life. I forbid it. So you and I together will conquer this. Right?'

Rhett looked pleased that he had an ally. 'Yes, sir. Right.'

'I must know who else is involved. If you can't speak the unspeakable then put a note through my letterbox. I shan't know who's put it there, shall I, when you haven't signed it?'

Rhett managed a slight smile. 'I'm not going any more. I daren't. But I might write that note.'

Ralph stood up. 'I won't have the life of this village torn apart. People can't look each other in the eye any longer.

It's never been like that before. You and the rector and I shall put a stop to it.' Ralph changed the tone of his voice. 'By the way, I see you're down for the cricket team, Rhett. Delighted. We need young chaps like you, and with all that hard work up at the Big House you'll be building good muscle. We'll make a batsman out of you yet!'

'Bowling's my thing.' He imitated a bowling action and Ralph was impressed.

'By jove! Very good. Yes. Mr Fitch is providing us with practice nets and I shall be interested to see how you develop. We'll be off now.'

Peter said as he left, 'Good night, Rhett.' He shook Rhett's hand and smiled encouragingly. 'Thank you for all your help. You're a grand chap with a lot going for you. Remember, I'm on your side in this. God bless you. Sleep well.'

Ralph and Peter crossed the road together and stood talking in the light of the lamp above Ralph's door. 'So now we know why the sergeant's wife has gone so peculiar. She was obviously there that night too. That's two names anyway.'

Ralph nodded. 'Let's hope he takes the hint and gives us the other names.'

'He's been dreadfully frightened. The shock of seeing the dog! No wonder he went berserk.'

'Is there any wonder that he snatched at some kind of excitement? Things aren't what they were when I was a boy, are they? I feel sorry for teenagers nowadays. When they're too young to have their own transport what on earth do they do every night stuck here?'

'Watch appalling videos?' Peter asked.

Ralph groaned. 'My goodness me. No wonder his mind worked overtime, no wonder at all. Any more ideas yourself about who's involved?'

'Might have. Good night.'

Chapter 22

The forty-eight hours were up and Peter had heard nothing from Kate, so when he took the twins to playgroup he made his way to Kate's little office and tapped on the door.

'No good knocking there, Rector. Ms Pascoe's not in this morning. She's in bed with a sore throat. We've a supply teacher coming any minute.' Pat folded the duster she'd been using to get the early-morning dust from the piano keys and shook her head. 'Oh yes, sore throat it is. She sounded really ill – could hardly speak. I've offered to go in and get her anything she needs but she said no, thanks.'

'Oh dear, I am sorry.'

'Hopes to be back in tomorrow, though I can't see that, 'cos she sounded so dreadful. Didn't seem quite right in the head, yer know. Her mind was wandering, kind of. If it's urgent you could pop a note through her door. I know where she keeps her scrap paper.'

'It's not urgent, it can wait. Only six weeks to go to your wedding, Pat. Got everything organised?'

'We have. We've not invited loads of guests, only from Barry's side. Dad and me's not got many relatives.

I'm glad you and Dr Harris and the twins have accepted. Jimbo's doing the food, so we know that'll be good.'

'Barry got the honeymoon arranged? He seemed very secretive about it when I spoke to him last.'

'All I know is, it involves an aeroplane and hot weather and I've to pack a swimsuit and some suntan lotion and I've to have smart dresses for the evening. That's why we've had such a long engagement – well, ten months – he's been saving up for it. Says he wants the honeymoon of a lifetime as he won't be going on another.'

Peter was about to relate to her the story of his own honeymoon when Hetty Hardaker brought her class in ready for prayers. Pat dashed off towards the kitchen.

'Mrs Hardaker, would you like me to take prayers as Ms Pascoe is ill?' Peter offered.

'I would indeed, Rector, that would be a help. I'll leave it to you and Miss Booth then, if I may.'

When prayers were finished, Peter went to stand in the school playground and look at the school-house. The bedroom curtains were drawn, and there were no signs of life at all, apart from the living-room windowsill where Cat lay sleeping.

As he set off back to the rectory he glanced towards the Store, and by chance sitting outside on the seat so thoughtfully provided by Jimbo, was someone with whom he wanted to have a word.

'Good morning, Ellie.'

The sergeant's wife looked up, startled, her lacklustre brown eyes showing no recognition. Her hair, never more than an orderly bird's nest, was now quite awry, and her face, paler than ever, gave the impression the blood had been drained out of her. Her squashy nose sat like a lump of blanched dough on her face. Ellie could never have claimed to dress in the height of fashion, and she certainly wasn't dressed in it now. Her coat was buttoned up wrongly, leaving the top edge on one side rubbing against her chin. Her tights were wrinkled, her shoes grubby and she had odd gloves on.

So that his height did not intimidate her, Peter sat down on the seat. It held four comfortably so he didn't overcrowd her.

'I haven't seen you for a while. How are you?'

Ellie finally recognised who he was. 'Don't you 'ave nothin' to do with me, Rector. You buzz orf. I ain't your kind.'

'Why's that?'

'I be evil, I be.'

'Anyone less evil than you, Ellie, I couldn't imagine.'

'Oh, yes, I be.'

'Why? What have you done? Robbed a bank?'

She looked puzzled. 'Robbed a bank? That'd be nothin', no, nothin' that'd be.'

Peter sat silently waiting. Ellie eyed him furtively. She fidgeted with her gloves and looked at them with surprise as though realising for the first time that they were odd. She shuffled around in a coat pocket and came out with what was obviously one of her husband's handkerchiefs. She blew her nose, wiped her eyes and then said, 'If I went to church, would that get me out of it?'

'Very likely.'

'It gets a hold, yer see. Gets a hold. I'm frightened to sleep.'

'Nightmares?'

She seemed relieved he'd got to the root of her problem. Her head nodded vigorously. 'That's right.' Ellie shuddered. 'Terrible.'

Peter sat companionably beside her.

Two people, one of them Mrs Jones, Pat's future mother-in-law, came by the seat.

'Good morning, Rector. Nice fresh day.' She looked at Ellie then at Peter and strode inside eager to get on with her work, for the temporary takeover of Sadie's mail-order business had changed to permanent and she loved it.

Ellie sat lost in thought. Jimbo came out with two coffees.

'Chilly sitting out here. Mrs Jones thought a coffee might be welcome.' He winked at Peter and went back inside to deal with his customers.

Ellie found the coffee too hot. 'There's no sugar in it either.' Peter didn't offer to go inside to get her any. He had the distinct feeling that if he left she would disappear. Then she gave a huge sigh. 'I can't go on no longer. Got to talk.'

'I'm listening.'

She stared into the distance watching Jimmy's geese chasing a dog away from their pond. 'Life gets terrible boring living hereabouts. I'm a town girl myself, you know. Hustle and bustle I likes, really. That's me. Markets and people and cinemas and things. Can't stand all this quiet. Stood it fifteen years, then this happened and it pepped things up no end – at first. Really looked forward to it. Like a whole new world, it was. But, Rector, things is bad. That bad, I don't knows which way to turn, I don't.' Tears straggled untidily down her cheeks and settled in the grooves beside her mouth.

'Fun it was, exciting. 'Tain't exciting being married to the sergeant. He's that predictable. Nothin' different, always the same. Black treacle on his porridge summer and winter. He even stirs it just the same way every morning. Always says, "Isn't this grand? Why don't you 'ave some?" *Every blessed mornin'*. But the bonfire and the chantin', like. Now that was thrillin'. But now I'm terrified.'

'You don't have to stay terrified.'

'Don't I?' For the first time she stared directly into his eyes. 'Look at what 'appens to them that defy her.'

'What?'

'School gets done over, don't it?'

'You mean Ms Pascoe defied her?'

Ellie nodded. 'We 'as to attend, yer see. She's got a grip. Be makin' a doll like Ms Pascoe, she will, sticking pins in it. Oh yes, it'll be the end of her.'

'Who'll be making the doll?' As soon as he'd asked the question he knew he'd gone on ahead too far, too fast. Ellie leapt up from the seat, the coffee in its paper cup spewing out all over her coat. To delay her, Peter took out his handkerchief and, gripping her arm, sympathised over the spill and began to wipe it away. 'There we are, Ellie, got you all clean and smart again. Now, where were we?'

Ellie sat down again. She gave the village green a full inspection and answered, 'I don't know where you are, Rector, but I'm in hell. Hell on earth.'

'Look Ellie, tell me everything, get it off your chest so to speak. I shan't tell *her* what you tell me. Believe me. As God is my judge, I shan't say a word.'

She looked at him, assessing his trustworthiness. '*She's* a witch, there's no two ways about it. *She* put the evil eye on Mrs Beauchamp and she died. Then *she* had a go at bringing Sykes back to life, and she did. It was then I knew she really had killed Sadie Beauchamp. We couldn't stop. Now *she's* going to get rid of anyone who crosses her. Full of power now, yer see. Evil that's what she be, and her with all them kiddies. Success has gone to her head. You've got to stop it, Rector. Something's got to be done.'

'I find it hard to believe that this mysterious "she" could actually kill someone.'

'Oh, but *she* did. Oh yes. There weren't no proper verdict, were there? Not heart attack nor nothing. It be very peculiar. We're all joined to her in sisterhood, so we's all guilty of murder.' Ellie clutched his hand. 'Help me, Rector.'

'I can't help unless I know who's the witch.'

Ellie stood up. 'If I tell you I'll be dead in the mornin'. That's the threat – death. I sometimes think it would be for the best.' She looked vaguely about her and then said, 'The sergeant wants steak for his dinner. I'll have to go and see to that.' And Ellie trailed off into the Store leaving Peter studying the geese.

So it wasn't Kate. Unwittingly Ellie had told him who the witch was – Simone Paradise. She always had been strange. Her lifestyle told one that, even if one didn't know about the evil eye and such-like. Kate had said 'be careful'. Even though he never acknowledged it to Caroline, for the logical part of his brain denied the truth of it, he still felt shudders down his spine when he recalled the two near-brushes with death he'd had over the church charity fund a while back. And now this, too, was evil and menacing.

Witchcraft. *Was* it witchcraft or someone pretending it was? Whatever, people were believing it. What he had to do was witness what went on. But now he didn't know where they met. And there was this business of making a doll . . . and Kate *was* ill. He shot to his feet. Caroline was the answer. As soon as she came back from the surgery he'd get her on to it.

He got home about half-past one, hoping that she would be able to have a late lunch with him. 'Caroline! Caroline!'

She came running down the stairs. She'd changed from her surgery suit and was wearing a hyacinth-blue

jumper with black trousers and she looked lovely. He
desired her, but that would have to wait.

He bent down and kissed her lips. 'I'm late. Had
lunch?'

'No. Waited for you.'

'Good. Need a word.'

Sylvia had made their lunch for them and it was
waiting under wraps on the kitchen table.

'Thank you, Sylvia. We need a quiet moment, if you
don't mind.'

'Not at all, Rector. Coffee's ready in the pot. I'll go
and sit with the children. It's *Sesame Street* time.'

As Sylvia closed the door behind her, Caroline said,
'What's so private that Sylvia can't hear?'

'I want you to go across to the school-house and see if
Kate is ill.'

Caroline raised an eyebrow. 'What are you up to,
Peter?'

Peter explained his conversation with Ellie.

With her sandwich halfway to her mouth, Caroline
said, 'Oh my God! Really!'

'That's why she was so frightened when Sykes turned
up – well, not Sykes, as you know, but she thought it
was. She thought then she knew that Simone really had
done Sadie in.'

'Oh my God! I can't believe this.'

'Exactly.'

'But it can't be *proved*, can it?'

'Well, she didn't do it really, did she? Now come on,
darling, you know it's not possible.'

Caroline looked doubtful. 'Isn't it?'

'No, definitely not. It's all in the mind.'

'Yes, it is. But it's like witch-doctors in Africa – they
can have a powerful influence on the mind.'

'For heaven's sake, Caroline, you're a scientist, a

person with a trained mind. You are not allowed to believe it.'

'No, of course not, but . . .'

'So will you go? Pretend you're concerned and can you help in your capacity as—'

'A nosy-parker?'

Peter laughed. 'If you like.'

She finished her sandwich, took a long drink of her coffee, and said, 'I'm off then. To do the rector's dirty work.'

'I can hardly go myself, can I?'

'Certainly not. Don't eat my fruit pie. I'll have it when I get back.'

Caroline knocked on the front door of the school-house knowing she wouldn't get an answer, but she had to knock first. She went round the side and looked in through the kitchen window. There was a mug and a plate on the drainer by the sink, but nothing else. So presumably Kate had had something to eat at some time. As Caroline peered in, Cat came into the kitchen. She jumped up onto the draining board and licked the plate, jumped down again and prowled about and cried.

Caroline went to stand below the bedroom window. 'Kate! Kate! It's Caroline Harris. Let me in.' There was no reply. Caroline could hear the children having a singing lesson. She checked that Kate's car was there. It was, so she must be either in school or in the house.

In school there was no sign of Kate. A teacher Caroline didn't recognise was taking the singing. She went to tap on Hetty Hardaker's door. 'Ms Pascoe not here?'

'No, Dr Harris. She's in bed with a sore throat. Sorry.'

Caroline acknowledged the information by nodding her head and smiling. So she was in the house.

Pat was leaving after clearing up from school lunch. 'Hello, Dr Harris. Long time no see.'

'It is. How are things, Pat?'

'Fine, thanks.'

'Not long now.'

'No, that's right.'

'Got your suntan lotion ready?'

'So you know about it too.'

'Oh yes, but my lips are sealed! I wish I could get into the school-house. I'm worried about Kate.'

Pat went to a drawer below the kitchen draining board. She pushed her hand right to the back, behind the tea towels she kept in there, and came out with a huge key. 'Here we are. Spare key she doesn't know I've got.'

'But how shall I explain that?'

'If she's dead you won't have to.'

'Dead?!'

'You don't know these days, do yer, with all these strange things going on hereabouts. Anything could have 'appened.'

'Now I really am feeling spooky. Come with me?'

'Sorry, no. Not again.'

'You've been in before then?' Pat nodded. 'What have you seen that makes you not want to go again?'

Pat shook her head. 'Nothing. Time I was off. Good luck.'

'Won't you wait to see?'

'I'll know soon enough. Sorry.'

The key turned readily in the lock. 'Kate! Kate!' Caroline called. There was no reply.

Caroline went cautiously up the stairs. She was being ridiculous. She'd seen plenty of dead people before now – had dissected them, in fact. But she really didn't want to see Kate dead, still less contemplate all the conclusions the village would draw if she were.

She wasn't dead. But she was dreadfully ill. Caroline could immediately see that she had a raging temperature and was quite oblivious to her surroundings. She'd thrown off her duvet at some stage and lay haphazardly on the mattress like a doll carelessly flung down in a temper. Sweat poured from her face, and her body glistened with it. Her nightgown, which Caroline couldn't help noticing was deep purple satin, was soaking. Her long dark hair lay like damp ropes on the pillow and around her shoulders.

'Kate? Kate?' But she couldn't be wakened.

Caroline ran downstairs and dialled Emergency. 'This is Dr Harris speaking. I need an ambulance.'

Caroline went with Kate to the hospital and gave the duty officer in Casualty as much information as she could. When the doctors heard Kate had worked in Africa for several years they said that might be a possible area to look at when diagnosing what the matter was.

Caroline went to see her each day, but it wasn't until the fourth day that she was able to speak.

'Kate – at last! I thought you would never wake up. How do you feel?'

'Terrible!' Her voice was slight and very husky.

'Better than when I first found you, anyway. You've been getting the full treatment. Everyone's been so worried about you.'

'Sorry.'

'I've been worried that there might be someone I should have contacted, but I didn't know who.'

'There isn't anyone really. My brothers are all abroad. I have an uncle but he wouldn't come to see me anyway.' A tear slid from the corner of her eye.

'I've brought flowers from the children at school.'

'How lovely. They are great, my children are.' Her

voice croaked as she asked, 'Could you possibly help me to a drink of water?'

'Of course. Gladly.'

Caroline settled her back onto the pillows again and said, 'You must be exhausted. Shall I leave you to sleep now?'

'Yes, please,' Kate whispered. 'There really isn't any need to come to see me again. I know how busy you are.' Another tear slid down her cheek.

'It's Peter's hospital day tomorrow so he'll come if that's all right.'

Kate turned her head away. 'Peter gave me forty-eight hours.'

'Did he?

'You don't know, do you?'

'A bit. He doesn't tell me everything.'

'I've been such a fool.'

'It's never too late.'

'It nearly was. If it hadn't been for you . . . How did you get into the house?'

Caroline couldn't lie. 'Pat has a spare key she's been meaning to give you. Mr Palmer gave it to her in case he lost his.'

'I see. Well, there we are then. Saved by Mr Palmer.'

'Sleep yourself better. Peter will be in tomorrow. I'll ring the day after and see what the position is.'

Kate gave a half-smile and her eyes began to close. 'The trouble with Peter is you can't withhold the truth from him for long, can you?'

'I know who's at the bottom of all this. Altogether, I have four names now.'

Kate eyed him warily. 'You do?'

'Inadvertently, someone gave the game away. If you're feeling well enough you can fill in the rest of the story, starting with Simone.'

'The one thing I dread doing is anything which will leave those children without their mother. There are five of them – all dear children, but hopeless in school. Too tired, undernourished, badly clothed, badly housed . . . I mean, have you ever been inside their cottage? It's terrible. Just awful. I wouldn't allow Cat to live in the conditions those children have to endure. Poor Dickon sleeps under a blanket on the sofa and his night-clothes are a torn vest. But they adore their mother, and she them in her own way.'

'Well, perhaps I can do something about that. You tell me your story.'

Kate reached for the glass of water on her locker. She sipped it slowly, using it as a delay while she assembled her thoughts. She put down the glass, drew in a deep breath and said, 'I've been thinking long and hard since I became conscious.'

'What has been the matter, by the way?'

'The tests aren't completed yet but they think it's one of these recurring things I picked up in Africa. Gradually, let's hope, the attacks will become less frequent.'

'I'm glad about that. Everyone thought Simone had stuck pins in a doll and your illness was the result.'

Kate gave a small smile. 'It could very well be. She was very angry because I'd decided not to attend any more meetings. Saw me as a kindred spirit, you see. She thought the others only came for the excitement – which they probably did. I was the real convert, she thought.'

'Which to a certain extent you were.'

Kate looked straight at him. It was now or never. She had to decide. Did she tell the truth or mask it in generalities? She studied his face, his red-blond thatch of hair, the startlingly blue eyes emphasised by the contrast of the deep black of his cassock. His silver chain on which his cross hung, tucked as always into his leather belt. An ancient garb which didn't manage to disguise the astute, up-to-the-minute man beneath. Confronted by Peter there was no place to hide.

'When I was in Africa, I met a modern version of a witch-doctor while I was visiting a mission school in the hills. I came under his spell. I couldn't stay away. That particular school came in for a great deal of my attention. He taught me such a lot.'

'About *what*, though?'

'Herbal medicines, spells, witchcraft. About the language to use – everything. He gave me Cat. Said she was my familiar. I fell in love with him. "Obsessed" is the only word to describe my state of mind. In his own way he loved me too, though I knew it was partly pride that his knowledge was superior to mine – I was the pupil and he the teacher. I had it all worked out. I was going to stay in Africa for ever and live with him. Then one day there was one of those sudden inexplicable risings which are a feature of a country where a tinpot despot, with the army in his pocket, rules supreme. Jacob unwittingly came across a group of the terrorists and . . . well, I hope they killed him quickly. I knew nothing for days, had no news at all. Then some refugees from one of the schools I visited, recognised me and told me what they'd found in the bush.'

Kate paused for a moment to control her tears. 'It doesn't bear talking about. Africa held no more fascination for me after that. I had a slight bout of this illness, though medicine being what it is in remote parts of Africa no one knew what I had, and I made that my excuse for leaving. Said my health couldn't stand the climate, et cetera.'

At last Kate wept. Peter handed her a tissue from the box in her locker. He held her hand whilst the storm raged. A nurse smiled round the door and quietly pulled it shut. The clatter of the busy ward next door was shut away and the two of them were left together in the silence.

Slowly Kate's tears subsided. 'I'm so sorry.'

'Not at all. It will have done you good.'

'How embarrassing.'

'Don't fret. I've watched healing tears many times before.'

'I expect you have. But I'm sorry for breaking down like that. It's this dratted illness, it's left me feeling so weak.'

'Look, if you feel you've said enough for today . . .'

'No, don't go. I must tell you everything. Right now. You need to know. The people involved are Ellie, Valda and Thelma Senior, Venetia Mayer from the Big House – you know, Jeremy's wife . . .'

'Venetia Mayer? I don't believe it!'

'Oh yes, she's a fervent participant. Simone, of course, Rhett Wright but he refused to come after the dog turned up, and that's about it. Two of the weekenders came a couple of times but then they stopped.'

'About this business of Sadie Beauchamp . . .'

'We had nothing to do with that at all. That was Simone and only Simone.'

'The way you say that, you seem to really believe she could be responsible for someone's death.'

'Do I? That's stupid of me. She can't, of course.' But Kate didn't speak convincingly.

'And Simone – how about her?'

'Somehow she guessed the very first time she saw me with Cat how things were. Foolishly, I acknowledged she was right. I got embroiled but drew the line when things got too deep. She behaves like, and considers herself to be, some kind of witch. There is no doubt in my mind about that. She happens to be evil, unfortunately. I'm sorry. I'm so tired now.' Kate lay back against the pillows and closed her eyes.

'I'll leave. May I say a prayer?'

Kate nodded. Peter held her hand, asked for God's blessing on her, and made the sign of the cross on her forehead with his thumb. This time she didn't shudder.

As he left she said, 'Take care. Please, take care. Never underestimate her power. She's so full of her success she is on the verge of being evil just for the sake of it.'

Chapter 23

That night the twins had feverish colds and Caroline knew when she put them to bed that she was in for a bad time. Alex couldn't stop coughing and Beth had a vicious sore throat and a runny nose which, despite Caroline's anxious care, had already made her nose bright red.

'It's no good, Peter, I'm going to put the camp bed up in the children's bedroom and sleep in there. Otherwise I shall be back and forth all night, and you'll not get any sleep either.'

'Let me help.'

'Certainly not. I've no surgery tomorrow and you have a day's work to do. I insist.'

'Well, if you're sure, but do wake me up if things get serious, won't you?'

'Of course.'

'I'll get the bed out and make it up for you – it's the least I can do.' He turned to go then came back into the kitchen. 'They are going to be all right, aren't they?'

Caroline studied his face. 'It's this witchcraft thing, isn't it?'

'Kind of.'

'Of course they are. They've both got a cold, that's all. Children do get them all the time.'

'I suppose they do. It's Kate, you see. She's an intelligent woman and yet . . .'

'And yet?'

'And yet she's quite alarmed about Simone Paradise. She doesn't believe Simone killed Sadie, but at the same time . . .'

'Yes?'

'At the same time she's terribly wary of what Simone will do next. She warned me to be careful.'

'I think you should do something tomorrow, before it's too late. I'll give it some thought in the dark hours of the night when I'm awake with our best beloved.' She shooed him out of the kitchen and made up a flask of cold orange juice to take upstairs for when the children woke.

Before she left the kitchen, Caroline stood looking out at the garden. A strong wind was getting up, the bushes at the bottom by the boundary wall were already swaying back and forth, and the wind seemed to be rustling through the thatch in an insidious kind of way. She was glad she lived in a solid well-built old house and not some flibberty-gibbet jerry-built construction. As she watched, the rain began − heavy slow blobs which dripped steadily onto the terrace. What should have been a moonlit night was dark and foreboding. A huge flash of lightning lit the garden and thunder cracked loudly right overhead.

'Mummy!'

Caroline picked up the flask and ran upstairs. 'All right, darlings, Mummy's coming.'

The storm was the worst in living memory. When the villagers opened their curtains the next morning and saw the damage, there were quite a few who trembled.

Indeed, they'd trembled during the night too, for the storm had raged for three hours, whistling down chimneys, slamming doors, and waking children who'd rushed to huddle in their parents' beds. Jimmy's chickens had squawked and screeched until he'd been driven into going outside to check on them. Sykes, well aware it was forbidden, had crept into Jimmy's bed and when Jimmy got back in, they'd clung to each other through the worst of it. Cats had fled into wardrobes, dogs had howled and debris blowing about had smashed a window at the Store.

But what really struck terror into their hearts was the sight of a huge branch of the royal oak tree lying on the ground. Almost one third of the tree had crashed down. Old villagers and newcomers alike knew the legend – when the oak tree dies, so will the village.

Peter had gone to the church at half-past six to pray. He'd been awake a large part of the night despite Caroline's solicitude; no one could have slept through that storm. So much water had run away down the church path that his trainers squelched as he walked. Before unlocking the door he'd decided he would walk round the building to inspect it for damage just in case. There might be tiles off the roof or hanging dangerously. He'd found that lightning had struck the church tower. The spire was fine but the square tower, where the lightning conductor should have saved it, had a long blackened streak down one side and several stones had been dislodged.

Willie appeared with his raincoat on over his pyjamas. 'Well now, Rector, this is a pretty kettle of fish. What a night! See what's happened? That daft builder's taken down the conductor while he pointed them stones and never put it back. Look, yer can see.'

'I can. Never noticed that when I came round to inspect it yesterday.'

'Better get on to 'im then, the lazy idle . . .'

'He wasn't to know we were going to have the storm of the century, was he?'

'No, I guess you're right, but he'll have to bring his scaffolding back and start again. You can see there's been a long line of stones dislodged right from the top. Any damage to the rectory, sir?'

'No. You all right?'

'Yes, we's fine thanks. Couldn't sleep mind, but who could? Mr Charter-Plackett's hammering some wood onto his window, can yer hear him? Be ages before he gets a glass firm to come right out here. They'll be too busy in Culworth.'

The window was in fact replaced before lunchtime. The men from the glass firm were enjoying a coffee from the customers' machine when Peter, in response to a telephone call from Jimbo, went into the Store to speak to him.

The two men touched their caps to him. 'Morning, Reverend. Bad night last night you 'ad 'ere.'

'It was, indeed. I'm surprised you're here. Thought there'd have been more than enough work for you in Culworth.'

'No, not there, Reverend. It's bin windy an' tha', but no broken windows. Seems Turnham Malpas caught the worst of it. The eye of the storm, I think they calls it. Well, we'll be off now. Thanks for the coffee, Mr Charter-P. Would you sign for us, please?'

Jimbo did as he was asked and when they'd left he looked at Peter and nodded his head in the direction of his storeroom. Peter followed him in. Jimbo took off his boater, smoothed his bald head, folded his arms and said, 'Well?'

'Well?'

'What about it?'

'I'm sorry?'

'Isn't it time something was done?'

'I've got the men coming this afternoon. They're putting the scaffolding up again and then—'

'I'm talking about this witchcraft thing.'

There was a tap at the door. It was Linda. 'Excuse me, Mr Charter-Plackett, sorry to disturb, but Sir Ralph's wanting a word.'

'Show him through here, if you please.' They paused for a moment awaiting Ralph's arrival.

'Good morning, Ralph.'

'Good morning, Peter, Jimbo. Top-level conference, what?' Ralph smiled at the two of them.

'Sort of.' Jimbo looked at Peter again. 'Well?'

'If either of you is going to stand here and tell me that the storm last night was anything at all to do with witchcraft . . .'

Ralph retorted, 'We're not, but—'

'*But*,' said Jimbo, 'the whole village is frightened. They've been coming in here this morning exchanging news about the damage that's been done and uppermost in their minds is the damage to the church – where else would the devil aim for, they say – and the damage to the royal oak. Some of them have blenched when they've seen the old tree. They are truly scared. There's nothing in it, I know, but it is all getting very sinister.'

'I know all their names.'

Ralph looked surprised; his bushy white eyebrows shot up. 'You do? Excellent! Give them to me and I'll pay them all a visit. Tell them where to get off. I'm not afraid.'

'Neither am I, but what does one say? "Please stop consorting with the devil?" Or: "I shall report you to the police?" And: "Was it you who brought this storm down on us?" The more we say, the more credibility we are giving them. But somehow it must be stopped because I, as a man of the church, will not allow it to go on. I can feel evil in the air. But how?'

'Tell them to damn-well give it all up; they're endangering their immortal souls. How about that?'

Peter nodded his head. 'They are, but they won't listen to that. On the other hand, I think I may have found out where they're holding their meetings now.'

Ralph's head came up with a jerk. 'Where?'

'Caroline was up with the children most of the night, as they've got heavy colds. They sleep in the bedroom overlooking Rector's Meadow and before the storm really got going she saw lights in the old hay barn.'

'Right! I shall watch every night from our bedroom window and when I see lights again I shall telephone you and we'll surprise them, the three of us – agreed?'

Peter and Jimbo looked at each other and then they both said, 'Very well.'

On Sunday morning when Peter went into St Thomas à Becket's for the ten o'clock service he found that almost every seat was taken. The congregation had been growing steadily since he'd first come to Turnham Malpas, but for an ordinary morning service the numbers were phenomenal. He knew enough not to congratulate himself on making a breakthrough. These people were in church because they were scared; it was a clustering together for mutual support. As he took his place and was about to say his opening prayer, his eye caught Ralph's.

Peter was surprised to find himself recognising a Lord of the Manor look in Ralph's eyes. A look which said, 'This morning you will preach the sermon these people, *my* people, need.' The incumbent, long ago at the mercy of the Templeton family to be dictated to as they wished, was under no obligation to the Templetons any longer, but Peter felt compelled to acknowledge Ralph's request. As they sang the first hymn, he battled with himself. Ralph had no authority to be instructing him in what he should say from his own pulpit, none at all. But he was right. Peter's theme of 'Go out into all the world and preach the Gospel' had no place here this morning. The congregation needed a strengthening sermon with a message of comfort – and that was what they would get.

After the service, Ralph came to stand beside Peter as he shook hands with his flock. 'Mind if I shake hands, too? I'll stand further down the path.'

'Not at all. Of course you may.'

Many of the congregation thanked him for his sermon; many of them also looked to Ralph for support.

That night, Ralph keeping watch yet again from his upstairs window, saw the lights and telephoned Peter and Jimbo.

Chapter 24

Muriel was scared. Going by chance to seek out the witches' coven had been exciting, but the enterprise Ralph had initiated tonight was quite another matter.

Ralph kissed her cheek. 'My dear, please don't worry yourself. Three grown men going to rout out some silly women with turnips for heads is nothing for you to get scared about. Now go to bed—'

'Go to bed – how can I? I shan't sleep a wink.'

'Of course you will.' He kissed her cheek again, his face full of excitement.

'I think I'll come with you. I shall be dressed in a trice.'

'Absolutely not, my dear. I cannot allow it.'

Reluctantly, Muriel acquiesced. 'Very well then, but take care, Ralph, you're all I've got.'

'Muriel! But someone has to get rid of these people, haven't they – and who better than me?'

'No one better than you.' They heard a knock at the door. 'Off you go.'

'I'll try not to wake you when I get back.'

Muriel couldn't help smiling. How on earth did he think she was going to sleep with all this going on? As he left to go downstairs to answer the door she called over the banister, 'And they haven't got turnips for heads! Remember!'

Ralph chuckled as he opened the front door to Peter and Jimbo.

The three of them walked through Ralph's house into the garden and then via his back gate into Pipe and Nook Lane. They climbed over the stone wall and stood quietly conferring.

'There's no cover at all. I think the best thing is to walk round the perimeter anti-clockwise, don't you?' whispered Jimbo.

'And come up on the lee-side of the door, so to speak? Yes, I agree. Let's keep well into the hedge.' Ralph led the way. He had his walking stick with him and he noticed Jimbo had one too. Peter had come unarmed.

The sky, still sombre and looming after the storm, afforded little light for their walk. Ralph set a steady pace and Peter remembered his heart attack and wondered whether it was wise for Ralph to have come. But there was no stopping him once he'd made up his mind. Above the heads of Jimbo and Ralph he could see the barn. There was a glimmer of light through the opening at the top of the roof. They must surely be there then. In his heart, Peter was dreading the confrontation. Who would they find? A few women in need of excitement like Ellie had said, or an evil woman set on devilry? A few sad teenagers lulled into believing like Rhett had been, or serious opposition? Real danger from a handful of fanatics, or two illicit lovers having found a safe place to meet? Then they really *would* feel foolish.

They arrived at the barn rather sooner than Peter would have wished. Listening below the opening at the apex of the roof they could hear very little: the murmur of voices, rustling of feet, nothing more.

Ralph went quietly round the end of the barn to the

huge door set midway in the long wall. He couldn't get it open. The three of them stood holding their breath but no one inside appeared to have noticed they were trying to get in. The door was made to open outwards and it took all Peter's strength to budge it. He did it slowly, slowly, daring it to creak. He slipped inside first, followed by Ralph and then Jimbo.

At the far end, an altar had been made from an upended bale of hay. Glowing black candles were balanced precariously on it. On top of the bales which were stacked two and three high against the walls, about twenty more candles had been lit to illuminate the great barn. Six people, all dressed in black, were standing within a circle drawn on the floor of the barn. In the light of the candle-flames Peter could recognise Simone, Venetia, Valda and Thelma Senior, Ellie and . . . *he couldn't believe it* . . . Kate. He wiped the sweat from his top lip and glanced at Ralph and then at Jimbo. They were quite motionless. Eyes wide. Staring.

The candles cast wavering shadows on the walls of the barn and on the bales of hay. The air was filled by the smell of the burning wax and, overlaying that, the reek of old dry-as-dust hay. The combined stench was suffocating. Peter shuddered. The group was chanting. There was a strange feeling in the air – a menacing atmosphere by which a man of his calibre and outlook should not be affected. But he couldn't help it. It was like being in church yet not, just as Rhett had said. The hairs on the back of his neck stood up and Peter could feel his spine begin to tingle. He and Jimbo and Ralph were still undetected. The figures in black were too intensely involved in their chanting, to be aware of the three men standing in the shadows by the door.

There was a movement just beyond him on his left. Instinctively, he flicked his head to see what the threat was. There was Cat crouching high up on a bale. Her tail wagged furiously from side to side, the movement of it playing a sinister dancing pattern on the wall behind her. Suddenly Cat leapt down to the earth floor, and covered the distance between herself and Peter in less time than he believed possible. She sprang and yowled at the same moment. Her claws, like a dozen fine needles, sank into his leg. He bit his lip to stop himself from shouting out and alerting the worshippers, but it wouldn't have mattered. Cat's spiteful howl had broken the absorption of the group swaying in the circle. It took them a moment to focus, for their minds were so completely out of this world, that they couldn't take in what had happened. When they did, their reaction was like that of Cat's.

None of the three men had fought with a woman before but they were doing it now. Only Kate stood back; the other five were clawing, biting, kicking, clutching, grabbing, screeching. As they struggled and fought, they cannoned into the bales of hay and the candles wobbled dangerously. Some fell to the floor. Small fires began here and there but no one noticed.

'Stop it! Stop it!' Kate screamed. She rushed forward to try to pull the women away, first one and then another. But her meagre strength could do nothing with these maniacal figures. Ralph in desperation began hitting out with his walking stick, threatening rather than striking. Cat clawed and bit whenever the opportunity arose, and the pain of that, combined with the utter surprise of these wild women attacking them, almost overwhelmed the men.

Jimbo, who was nearest to the door, managed to push it open again and get out into the field. 'Come on! Come on!' he shouted.

The rush of cold air sharpened Peter's wits. 'THAT WILL DO! STOP IT THIS INSTANT,' he bellowed.

He gained a moment's respite and he used it to say again: 'THAT WILL DO. STOP NOW!'

But Simone wouldn't stop. She was the one least influenced by him. Howling like a banshee, she went behind the altar with the candles still burning on it, came out with a knife in her hand and lunged straight towards Peter, her eyes wild with hate.

Kate saw her intention and darted at Simone. She pushed her back; Simone ricocheted against the altar and more candles fell over. In a second the loose hay scattered on the floor flared up.

Ralph, looking round and realising that the fire was catching hold, saw their danger. 'Get out, everyone! Get out!' he shouted. But the foot-wide gap afforded by the open door impeded their escape.

Jimbo tried to open it further from the outside but couldn't. One by one, the women struggled out. Then Ralph. Then last of all Peter. They stood gasping for air, their struggle forgotten in the fear of being burned alive. Peter was standing bent over, his hands gripping his thighs trying to get his breath back so he could speak.

'Who's missing?' Ralph shouted. 'There's someone missing!'

No one answered him, for just then a column of rats streaked through the gap of the door and squeezed out through the rotting places at the bottom, young and old, large and small, tumbling over each other in their rush to escape. The women screamed and they all hastily leapt about to avoid the rats running over their feet. They could hear the scrabbling of their feet and the rush of their bodies through the grass as they fled certain death.

When their panic had subsided, Ralph looked around. 'Simone's not here,' he said.

Peter rapidly counted heads. 'You're right. Stay there – I'll go in!' Jimbo went ahead of him but neither of them could see anything at all. The barn was filled with acrid smoke and scorching flames.

'We can't leave her.'

'We can't see.' Jimbo began coughing.

'She was by the altar.'

Jimbo grabbed Peter's arm. 'Get out, come on – *out!*'

The smoke made Peter's eyes stream with tears. 'We can't leave her,' he said again.

'Get out! And that's an order!' he grabbed Peter's arm and hauled him through the door. 'Ralph – tell him he's not going back in!'

Kate was weeping. Venetia cried too, thick rivulets of mascara running down her cheeks. Valda and Thelma stood rigid with shock. Ellie was retching into the long grass. Of Cat there was no sign. The flames were leaping at the barn door and licking at the openings at each end. It was an inferno. No one could be alive in there now.

'The fire brigade!' Peter shouted. 'We need the fire brigade!' Jimbo dragged his mobile phone out of his pocket and was punching in 999 when they heard shouting.

Across the field from the direction of the Big House they could see someone. It was Jeremy, lumbering along as fast as he could.

'Are you all right?' he called out. 'What on earth's happened? Have you seen Venetia?'

Jimbo waved his mobile phone. 'She's over there. I'm just phoning the fire brigade.'

'God! What the hell is going on? How did it start?' Venetia ran into Jeremy's arms. 'Steady on, old girl. I say, steady on. You're all right now.' He clumsily rubbed her back as he comforted her.

Venetia moaned, 'Take me home, take me home.'

233

Peter was too distraught at the thought of Simone's death to take Jeremy aside and explain. He had to leave that to Ralph.

Jeremy shuddered. 'Simone? Oh no! Can't we get her out? Surely we can.'

Jimbo told him hoarsely: 'We can't get in, it's a wall of fire in there. Believe me, we've tried.'

They stood stricken as the flames roared. The huge wooden beams of the roof withstood the heat for a while but there was a sudden deafening roar and the roof began collapsing. Instinctively they retreated and helplessly watched Simone's funeral pyre.

Peter caught Jeremy's eye and looked questioningly at him, but the other man, shamefaced, avoided his eyes. Peter guessed he'd known all the time what Venetia was doing.

'I'll go and open the field gate for the engine,' Peter said and sprinted across the field towards the gate which was further down Pipe and Nook Lane beyond the rectory. As he rushed past, he saw Caroline standing at the end of their garden. He waved and shouted, 'Don't worry, we're all fine! Just opening the gate for the fire brigade.' The gate was held shut by a complication of chains but thankfully no padlock. On his way back, Peter stopped to speak to her. 'We can't do anything – the fire engine's going to be far too late. The roof's already going. Can't stop.' He embraced her briefly.

'Peter, for God's sake be careful,' she pleaded.

'Of course!'

Five minutes afterwards the engine carefully negotiated the open gate and humped and bumped its way across the field, the large crowd which had gathered in the last few minutes separating to make way for it.

'Heaven help us, whatever next!'

'Thank God nobody's inside!'

'But Sir Ralph said . . .'

'Simone? No!!'

'Them poor kids!'

'Oooh! They'll be all on their own. Poor little devils!'

Peter was devastated. If they hadn't interfered, Simone would be alive still, and some harmless tampering with the devil would have, in all likelihood, soon fizzled out. Jeremy had taken Venetia home. Valda and Thelma still stood in silent shock. Ellie was clinging to the sergeant's arm and impeding his activities. Kate stood watching alone. He went across to speak with her.

It was difficult to talk. The noise of the fire-engine pump, the shouts of the men and the sound of the water pulsating onto the flames made conversation almost impossible. They'd put up the ladder from the engine now and were pumping water into the barn through one of the openings. Peter drew her to one side away from the noise and the ears of the crowd.

'Kate!' His reproachful tone brought tears to her eyes. She looked up at him, her face illuminated by the searchlight on the engine.

'I came to ask her to stop, but somehow . . .'

'Well, she's gone now, God rest her soul, so it can all stop. For good.'

'I've been punished for it, haven't I?'

'You have?'

'Cat's not come out.'

'Ah! Cat.' Peter rubbed his leg where Cat's claws had struck. 'I deeply regret what's happened tonight, but it does put an end to Simone's bizarre influence, doesn't it? If the sergeant's finished with you, I'll see you home. I've already spoken with him. He'll be taking proper statements in the morning when they've . . . you know.'

Kate's face looked girm. 'Found the body, you mean.' Something occurred to her. 'Peter! The children! She left them on their own when she came to the meetings.'

Before he could answer, Caroline was at his elbow. Startled to find her there, his immediate thought was for his own children. 'The twins – what have you done with them?' he asked brusquely.

'Calm down, calm down, Sylvia's with them. I just had to come. Kate, you OK?'

'Yes, thanks.'

Caroline looked devastated. 'Dreadful thing to have happened, really dreadful.'

Peter said, 'Kate's just reminded me of Simone's children. She left them in the cottage on their own.'

'I'll go to Little Derehams straight away and check on the poor things. I'll just fetch the car.'

'We'll come too. You mustn't go by yourself – heaven alone knows what you might find. Come on, Kate. Sergeant! We're going to see to Simone's children. Will you take Ms Pascoe's statement tomorrow?'

'Certainly, sir. We can do no more here tonight.'

Peter drove the car to Little Derehams, Caroline beside him, Kate in the back. He caught the occasional sound of her weeping but he didn't comment. She had more than enough to weep about, and he blamed her for a lot of what had happened. His leg was stinging and he'd be glad to get a chance to look at it. But first things first.

The back door was shut but unlocked. Kate went in first and her fingers searched the wall for the light switch. When she pressed it, no light came on.

'The electricity's been cut off!'

Caroline went back to the car for a torch. The beam showed them the utter chaos of the cottage. Caroline was speechless. She shone the torch along the walls to find another switch and picked her way carefully towards it. But nothing happened when she turned it on. 'You're right, there's no power. How could they do it when there's five small children in the house? It's unbelievable.'

At this moment Dickon piped up: 'Simone? Simone?'

Kate said 'It's all right, Dickon, it's only me. Ms Pascoe from the school.'

He stood up on the sofa cushions, his blanket in his hand. Tonight he didn't even have a vest to wear.

Kate went towards him. 'Where's the light, Dickon? We can't see.'

'Oil-lamp. Got no matches.'

Caroline ran her fingers despairingly through her hair. 'Dear Lord. What are we going to do?'

As they stood motionless trying to take in the deprivations the children had been forced to tolerate, they heard a hesitant fumbling on the staircase. Caroline turned the beam of the torch towards the sound.

Florentina, Valentine and Hansel were creeping quietly down. They were dressed in an odd assortment of clothes – not quite nightclothes and not quite dayclothes. The moment Valentine saw them he began screaming. He struggled down the last three steps, stumbled his way over to Dickon and, pulling him down from the sofa, flung his arms around him and howled.

Florentina, rubbing her eyes, said, 'Go away.'

'The baby. Where's the baby?'

She nodded her head in the direction of the bedroom. Caroline found the baby sound asleep in a large drawer on the floor; it smelt as though its nappy hadn't been changed all day. The bedroom stank of unwashed bodies, of bed-wetting and sheer neglect. Caroline retched.

★

'They've found her body. She and Cat were together. We think she stayed behind to rescue Cat and then—'

'Peter, *please*! I can't bear it. We're all to blame – us, the school, social services. Every manjack of us.'

'We weren't to blame for this witchcraft business. That was her decision entirely. That's when everything began to go wrong.'

'They never appeared desperately neglected before all this, did they? They *used* to be clean and reasonably well fed, but as Kate said, this last few months Dickon and Florentina were useless where school was concerned. Too tired, too hungry, never there. Where are they now?'

'A temporary foster home has been found for them all in Culworth. At least they'll be clean and well-fed and cared for there.'

'And Kate – what was her explanation for being at the barn?'

'She'd gone to ask Simone to stop, and then kind of couldn't resist her influence.'

'I shouldn't say this, but we're well rid of her *and* that bloody cat.'

'Caroline!'

'It's true. Not even you could have brought her to her senses.'

Peter drew back the curtains and looked out at the fading light. 'What a night! What a day!'

'It was hell this morning in the surgery. I don't mind telling you, if I made a correct diagnosis it was only by sheer chance. I *felt* and I'm told *looked* dreadful.'

'You were brave to go. I've had a dreadful day too, full of recrimination and despair.'

He was totally drained, his inner resources leached from him by the flood of people seeking his comfort and reassurance wherever he went.

His early-morning prayers in church had been interrupted by a remorseful Venetia. She had come in and knelt beside him in the war memorial chapel and wept bitter tears. 'Can I come to confession? Do you do that sort of thing?'

'No. You have a direct line to God, Venetia. You don't need me like some kind of holy telephone exchange.'

'Well, will you listen and sort me out? Please, Peter?'

'Of course.' And he had. And he'd listened sadly to her promises to come to church every Sunday, now she had reformed. And he'd wished he could believe her, and had pretended he did.

His regular Monday visit to Penny Fawcett had been delayed an hour by Valda and Thelma Senior begging forgiveness and wanting to take communion, something they hadn't done in years. He'd put them off, said they needed to think some more before they did that. Ralph and Jimbo had both come to see him, to seek assurance in their own way. Ralph had said he was sorry about Simone, but Peter knew full well that underneath Ralph was glad the whole matter had been resolved and if it took a death to do it, so what? The village had been saved from destruction and that was what counted. Peter had visited Kate in school to check on how she was coping, and of course the children were eager to embellish the story of the fire, and request his version of it.

Brian wanted to know where had Mrs Paradise stabbed him?

Flick asked about Cat and had she gone to heaven like her poor old Orlando? Stacey had said, 'My dad says good riddance to bad rubbish.'

A comment Peter felt compelled to explore for his own sake as much as hers.

Altogether he felt trampled. It wasn't just Simone's death, it was the ramifications of it which he found so difficult. And those children. Fatherless all their lives and now motherless. At least the baby, Opal, was too young to know the pain of grief.

He felt Caroline beside him. She put her hand in his and said, 'You've got to hold on in there. You've so much to achieve, so much waiting to be done which can only be done by you. If it's any help, you are my best beloved. I adore you, and I adore your children; they're like my own flesh and blood. They *are* mine, I think, sometimes.'

Peter gripped her hand tightly. 'Thank you. Two such inadequate words, but believe me they are from my heart. Without you I couldn't carry on.'

Chapter 25

Kate had gone to bed early the night after Simone's death. She'd hoped to sleep for hours, she was so exhausted. Up all night and then school all day with the children hyped-up by the night's events, her nerves and her body were strung to breaking point, but she couldn't get to sleep. Kate half-remembered that line from *Macbeth*: '*Sleep that knits up the ravell'd sleave of care.*' If only!

She got up and went to the window. The sky was clear, the village at rest. The moon came out from behind a cloud and lit the houses with a caressing silvery light. English nights weren't like African nights. English nights were gentle and comforting. African nights, dramatic and challenging; there were times when the blood ran cold at the triumphant howl of an animal or the death screams of tortured prey. Turnham Malpas nights were mild, reassuring, and tranquil by comparison. Kate shook herself. *Tranquil?* Anything but, of late.

She should have gone in herself to rescue Simone, but the heat! The flames – and Cat! Simone . . . Jacob . . . Africa! All in ashes. Her head spun. Well, she'd have to allow the flames to cleanse her of everything evil. She'd been possessed. Absolutely possessed! She'd have to go to Peter soon and tell him how she felt and what she was going to do, now it was all over. What *was* she going to do?

Her fingers trailed a pattern on the windowsill. Around the carving of a black child, around a ceremonial knife, around a carved wooden necklace Jacob had given her. Part of the cleansing would be getting rid of anything and everything which reminded her of Africa. Cat had gone – she paused for a moment and grieved – now all the things which hitherto had been such precious mementos must go, too.

Kate resolutely swept the carvings from the windowsill, then rushed to that awkward corner under the eaves and swung angrily at the crystal ball and the candles. The ball fell with an enormous crash, the candles rolled silently across the carpet. She put her slippers on and stamped on the candles, breaking them into a hundred pieces and grinding them into the carpet. She dragged the picture from the wall above the altar and tore it to shreds.

From her wardrobe she took every item of black clothing she could find and stuffed them all into binbags. What she'd wear tomorrow for school she didn't know, but they had to go.

In the kitchen she took her cook's scissors and chopped great lengths from her hair. Then she ran a bath and scrubbed herself, every inch of her body until her flesh stung.

At two o'clock she fell into bed and slept.

'Mummy! Mummy! You'll never guess what! Not in a million years will you guess.'

'Tell me then,' Harriet called out.

'Ms Pascoe's cut her hair. It's so short you wouldn't

believe. We didn't recognise her.' Flick held her finger and thumb three centimetres away from each other and said, 'That long, that's all. And you'll never guess something else.'

'What?'

'She was wearing a funny old red shirt and a blue skirt. They didn't match at all, but it did make a change. She's not wearing black any more, she says. She's going into Culworth this minute to buy clothes, she says.'

'Well, well.'

'And,' Flick took a deep breath, 'and she's going to have two of Mrs Biggs' kittens.'

'No!'

'Yes, she is, *and* . . .' Flick paused for dramatic effect.

'Yes?'

'And she's calling them Beano and Dandy!'

'What sensible names.'

'I told her they'd have to have names or they'd have an identity crisis, being two of them. You couldn't call both of them Cat, could you?'

'Certainly not.'

'And she's organising a holiday for anyone who wants to go – a five-day geography field trip.'

'Really?'

'Yes, it's only for the leavers, though. Not absolutely everyone.'

'Of course not, they're not old enough.'

'Exactly. Mummy, can I go?'

'We'll ask Daddy about it.'

'Daddy will say yes. He always does for me. That's because I'm going to work in the Store when I've qualified.'

'Qualified?'

'Got a degree in something, and I shall work up from the bottom in the business in the holidays.'

'Is that really what you want to do?'

'Well, the boys aren't interested, are they? And I am, so I shall. We shall have lots of Stores when I'm helping Daddy, and you can be rich and do nothing all day like you do now.'

'Thanks. I shall look forward to that.'

'I'm to be Queen of the May. You've to go and see Ms Pascoe about my dress, please, she says.' Flick sat herself down at the kitchen table.

'Darling, how lovely.' Harriet kissed the top of her head. 'You've kept the best till last. Daddy will be thrilled.'

'Where's my biscuit? Oh, home-made – lovely!'

'That's just one of the thousand things I've done today. I shall go and see Ms Pascoe tomorrow about your dress. How exciting. That's wonderful!'

'And my milk, please. Where's Fran? Thanks.'

'Playing with the twins.'

'I wish she wouldn't. I like her to be at home when I get in. She *is* my sister. She likes the twins too much.'

'Well, they are more her age, aren't they? And they are good fun. It gets lonely for her here on her own when you're at school. They love looking after her.'

Flick sipped her milk thoughtfully and then, not looking at her mother, said, 'I shall be glad to leave school. You outgrow things, don't you? Sometimes they seem to talk such nonsense. It happens and you don't know it till they say something and you think that was stupid.'

'I know just what you mean. Geography field trips can be very uncomfortable – tents and things. Are you sure you'd like that?'

'Oh, we wouldn't be in tents. We'd be in a big house. I'd like that.' Flick stopped at the door for a moment. 'Ms Pascoe's quite different today. She took prayers herself, and we didn't meditate.'

'I am glad.'

'So am I. It was a bit silly, wasn't it?' Flick trailed away upstairs leaving Harriet feeling that her little girl had suddenly grown up overnight. Thank God Kate had decided to join the rest of the human race, and not before time.

Kate rang the rectory bell at eight o'clock that night. She'd come to talk to Peter. Make a clean breast of everything and tell him she'd done with voodoo and black magic. All it had brought was tragedy – to Jacob; to Cat, to Simone. It was a moment before her ring was answered. When the door opened, it was Caroline standing there.

'Why, Kate! How lovely to see you. You look so different – it's your hair. Do come in.'

'Thank you. Is Peter in?'

'Out, I'm afraid. Can I help?'

'Oh well, I'll leave it then, come another night.'

'Please don't. I'm all by myself, the children are in bed and I'd enjoy some company.' She didn't want Kate to leave; this could be her chance to find out.

Kate stepped back out again on to the stone step. 'No – no, thanks.'

'Please!' Caroline pleaded with her.

Kate smiled. 'Very well then. Yes, I will – why not?'

'Good. I'll take your coat.' She held out her hands for it and then gasped when she saw what Kate had on underneath. 'Oh, what a lovely suit, such a gorgeous red. I've only seen you in black before. And your hair – turn round, let me see. Oh, it really suits you.'

Kate looked embarrassed. 'I've been into Culworth and put all my black clothes in the bin.'

Caroline studied her face. 'New start?'

'Something like that.'

'Good, I'm glad.' Caroline showed her into their sitting room. 'Do sit down.'

Kate took an easy chair. 'I think I said this the last time I was in this room, but I'll say it again. I do like it very much.' She looked round appreciatively.

'You should have seen it when we moved in. Foolishly Peter said we would take it as it stood, furniture and all.' She raised her eyes to the ceiling. 'It was dreadful.'

'Well, it's beautiful now.'

'Thank you. Getting organised for May Day?'

'Oh yes, indeed! Flick Charter-Plackett is to be Queen of the May and we've chosen her attendants; now we're practising the dances. I've got a group of mothers in charge of the refreshments, and I've organised the muscle required for bringing the piano onto the Green and carrying out the Maypole. So, all we need now is the weather.'

'I understand there's only been one year when it rained so much they had to hold it in the school, and that was 1902! So, with luck...' Caroline crossed her fingers and laughed.

'Don't you think that's wonderful, this kind of on-going memory?' Kate enthused. 'It gives such stability, such a sense of history. We're all so lucky to be living here, aren't we?'

'We certainly are. You know the village has this superstition that when the royal oak tree dies, the one on the Green' – Kate nodded – 'then the village will die too. They all felt we came pretty close in the recent storm. They considered it was brought on by – well, witchcraft. You've had a narrow escape, Kate. The village can be very vindictive if something doesn't suit.'

There was an uncomfortable pause and Caroline decided to come straight out with it. She'd a right to know.

'My cat.'

'Yes?'

'My cat Mimi.'

'I'm sorry?'

Unexpectedly Caroline's throat was choked with emotion, and she couldn't continue.

Kate said, 'I'm sorry, you were saying . . .?'

'Her collar was found by the fire in Sykes Wood.'

Kate flushed as comprehension dawned. 'I see. I didn't know the cat was yours.'

'What happened? I've a right to know. It was you, wasn't it?'

Kate chose her words with care. 'I was there, yes. She came upon us that night quite by chance. She must have been hunting or something.' Caroline nodded. 'Simone said, and Thelma and Valda agreed with her, "Here's our chance to experiment." I said, "No, we mustn't. It's not right," but they wouldn't listen. Venetia wasn't too sure, and Rhett and Ellie and the weekenders were nervous. "What? Do what?" they said. Simone raised her voice, stretched her arms towards the heavens and said dramatically, "Sacrifice her!"'

Kate wasn't looking at Caroline when she said that; she was staring into the fire, recalling the horror of it all. If she'd looked at Caroline, she wouldn't have continued or, at the very least, would have softened certain aspects of the story, but she felt as though she were in the confessional, and her own need drove her on regardless of Caroline's feelings.

'Simone said—'

Caroline snapped: 'Simone! Always Simone! Didn't you have a mind of your own?'

Kate looked shocked. She didn't answer for a moment and then she said, 'I suppose that's right. At that moment I didn't. But afterwards I did, and protested.'

'When it was too late for my Mimi.'

'I'm sorry, yes. When it was too late.'

'Did she suffer?'

'No – well, I don't think so.'

'You must know whether she suffered!'

'You see, Simone mesmerised her. Spoke to her, hypnotised her, I suppose, so she didn't feel the knife.'

Caroline leapt to her feet. 'The knife! What knife?'

'Simone's.'

'Simone had a knife ready?' Caroline sat down again. 'How . . . how do you know she didn't feel it?'

'Because she didn't fight back.' Kate stared into the fire again, reliving the moment. 'Just lay there motionless, and let herself be sacrificed.'

'Sacrificed? Oh, God! I can't believe I'm talking to a human being. How could you, an intelligent, educated person, allow such a thing to happen? My dear cat, whose only crime was happening upon you at that moment – how could you do it to her?'

'I only watched.'

'Only watched!' Caroline's voice rang with sarcasm. 'Oh well then, that exonerates you, doesn't it?'

Kate shook her head. 'No, it doesn't. I know that now. I'm so sorry.'

'What then?'

In a voice scarcely above a whisper Kate said, 'Then we laid her on the altar as an offering.'

Caroline's voice was dry and throaty as she asked, 'By then, she was properly dead, I hope.'

Kate nodded. The silence between them lengthened while Caroline came to terms with what she'd heard and Kate tried to come to terms with herself.

Peter walked in at that moment. Neither of them had heard his key in the door. He stood just inside the room, looking first at one and then the other, puzzled by the pent-up emotions he could feel.

Kate was the first to notice he was there. She smiled briefly, apologetically at him.

As he put down his sports bag, Peter said, 'Lovely to see you, Kate. I'm just back from playing squash, as you see. I'm going to take a shower and then perhaps—'

'Kate's just leaving.'

'Oh, I'm sorry. I was going to suggest—'

'I said, she's leaving.'

Kate faced Caroline. 'I'm so sorry. If I'd known it was your cat . . .'

'Any cat, any cat at all, not just mine. The guilt is the same. Has it all stopped now with Simone gone?'

'Oh yes.'

'So I should think. Not before time. Such evil. I can't believe it.'

'It has stopped. Definitely. I shall never forgive myself for coming under her influence in such a way. It all stemmed from my experiences in Africa and my grief at losing Jacob. It seemed a comfort at the time; it assuaged my grief a little. But I admit I've been totally wrong.'

'Such evil, in this lovely place. The others were just foolish and misguided and afraid – but you, you *actively* agreed with it all. You knew and understood the thinking behind it. You deserve some kind of punishment for what you've done; what you've encouraged by your lack of protest.'

'I've been punished.'

'Oh – how?'

'I've lost my cat too, in horrific circumstances.'

'No more horrific than my poor Mimi's. Just go – leave my house. Perhaps one day when I feel you are truly repentant I might be able to forgive you, but not right now. Peter's much better than me at that kind of thing.'

Kate left the two of them, took her coat from the chair in the hall and let herself out.

'Whatever you do, *don't* sympathise nor ask me what she's just told me. *Please.*'

'I won't.'

'I need a drink.'

'By the look on your face a brandy might fit the bill.'

Her hands were shaking as she took the glass from him. 'Go and have your shower.'

'I thought I'd delay that for a while, till you look better.'

'I need to be alone.'

He bent over intending to kiss the top of her head, not knowing how else to express his anxiety, but Caroline pulled her head away. 'No! No sympathy, or I shall fold completely.'

When Peter came back downstairs after his shower, she was still sitting where he'd left her. The colour had come back into her face, and the brandy glass was empty. She glanced up at him as he stood before her.

'Sorry for being snappy.'

'That's all right, my darling, I understand.'

'You're too forgiving of me. I wish I could be the same to her.'

'You will one day. You're too generous not to be.'

'It doesn't pay to love too much, does it? Love brings so much heartbreak with it.'

'You mean Mimi?'

'People too, really, not just animals.'

'To get things in proportion, let's thank God it's not one of the children you're grieving for tonight.'

'Oh Peter, what a perfectly dreadful thing to say!' Caroline burst into tears and sobbed as though her heart would break.

Peter knelt down in front of her and took her in his

arms. 'Darling! My darling!' He stroked her hair, while he waited for her tears to subside. 'Please, please don't distress yourself so; I should never have said that. I'm so sorry, so sorry.' He lifted her head from his shoulder and tried to look into her face, but she wouldn't let him. 'Whatever happens, remember it's always, always worth loving to the utmost; nothing less is neither right nor good. You can't hold back on love.'

Caroline's sobs began to lessen. She wiped her eyes. 'I . . .'

'Yes?'

'I'm so sorry. I'm not so much grieving for Mimi as for what Mimi meant to me when I was alone.' She gave a great shuddering sigh. 'Of course, you're quite right. Thank God I'm not grieving for one of the children. That's too frightening even to contemplate. I love them so. And I've caused Beth such pain. I'm so sorry.'

'Not at all. I've realised this parenthood business is something we have to learn as we go along.'

Caroline smiled. 'I suppose so. I'm all tuckered out, as the Australians say. I'll just get a few things ready for tomorrow and then I'm going to bed.'

'Thank you for being such a lovely mother. And wife.'

Caroline dried the last of her tears, and gave him a faint grin. She faked a punch at his jaw. 'Don't let's get all sentimental, for heaven's sake. Life has to go on. But that Kate! I can't forgive her.'

'Neither can she.'

Chapter 26

'So, Gilbert, I wondered if you could possibly bring your Morris dancers that afternoon.'

'May the first?'

'That's right.' Kate moved the receiver to her left ear so she could check her diary. 'It's a Thursday. I know it's short notice, but it suddenly came to me in the night what a highly suitable activity it was for May Day. How about it?'

'The last time I was asked about my Morris dancers, there was a mix-up; two teams turned up and we had an argument. My team's been a bit chary of Turnham Malpas ever since. They were very upset, you see. They'll take some persuading, and of course most of them work.'

'Look, it won't happen here. I don't even *know* another team to invite, I promise. Please — I want to make it a kind of traditional village afternoon. I've got a Punch and Judy man coming and a chap who has a kind of mobile children's roundabout — you know, the old-fashioned kind. I'm desperate to make a success of it. I know that all it's been before is a parade and the crowning and the Maypole dancing and then the tea, but this time I want to make it more worthwhile for people to come. Not to make money or anything – just to provide a thoroughly good afternoon.'

Gilbert didn't answer straight away. He guessed she wanted to make a success of the afternoon to atone for the trouble she'd caused. She'd come within an ace of being on the receiving end of the villagers' wrath; how she'd escaped, he didn't know. Possibly because she was making such a success of the school, *and* because Peter had backed her.

'They'll have already been up before dawn because we always dance at dawn on May Day – perhaps you didn't know that. We go to Bickerby Rocks, the great hill on the other side of the by-pass. It's all very symbolic. Look, leave it with me,' he said, beginning to relent. 'It's short notice, but I'll do my best. I'll let you know by tomorrow night.'

'Thank you, thank you very much indeed. I do appreciate your co-operation.'

Kate replaced the receiver, put her diary back in its place in the top drawer of her desk and gazed out at the bins. She clenched her fist and struck the palm of her left hand. She'd make this May Day a success if she never did another thing. It was ironic that May Day was also an important festival for . . . No, she'd done with all that.

She'd had her talk with Peter. The day after the disastrous evening with Caroline he'd called in when school was finished and everyone except Pat had gone, and they'd sat in her classroom – he on her chair and she perched on a desk with her feet resting on one of the children's chairs. Peter hadn't criticised her, found her guilty, or remonstrated with her. He'd simply sat there and let her ramble on, all the guilt coming out, the fears, the reasons. Her disgust at the turn Simone's activities had taken, her lack of protest. 'That's what I feel so guilty about. If I'd protested louder and more vehemently, all this might have been avoided. It's like Caroline said – by watching and knowing and doing nothing, I was implicated; I can't escape that. But I have put it all behind me and I shan't allow myself to become influenced again, never! I shall make this school so successful they'll be coming from miles around to get their children's names down before they've even been conceived!'

Peter had laughed. 'Good! That's wonderful. You've so much to give – you're a born teacher.'

'Thank you for backing me – I don't deserve such loyalty. I am indebted to you.'

'You're not indebted. My support was freely given. Anything else? I see Pat loitering by the door wanting to get in to clean.'

Kate had slipped off the desk ready to leave and then turned back to say, 'I'd like to have prayers in church again, if that's all right with you, starting this Friday? I couldn't before; my conscience wouldn't let me.'

'But of course. Delighted.'

'Thank you.'

She'd gone straight from school into the church, the first time since she'd arrived in the village. The heavy door had needed all her strength to open it. Inside, the air was chill. She'd chosen a pew at the back just in front of the ancient Templeton tomb with the carved marble knight laid on the top, and sat looking round. There was a scitter-scatter in the aisle and there stood Sykes. His bright eyes looked eagerly at her, his short stumpy tail wagging.

'Hi there, Sykes. What are you doing here?' She could have sworn he'd grinned at her and then he'd leapt up onto the seat beside her and from there up onto the flat smooth surface at the end of the tomb at her shoulder. He'd curled up and settled down to sleep, his back against the knight's ankle and right beside the dog standing by the knight's feet. What a strange little dog, spending his time in church. Perhaps there was more to Sykes than one ever guessed.

She'd relaxed in his companionship and begun looking around at the huge stained-glass window above the altar, the ancient banners rotting away on their poles high up above the pillars, the shining brass on the altar table and the flowers below the pulpit. It was all so beautiful, so peaceful and . . . The door had opened and Muriel had come in.

'Good afternoon, Lady Templeton.'

'Why, good afternoon, Kate. I hope you don't mind but I've got very late with my brass polishing this week. It's my week, you see. Will I trouble you if I polish while you meditate?'

'Can I help?'

'That would be wonderful. I need to be quick because we're going out to dinner tonight, and I always take ages to get ready. I do so like to do Ralph credit and I hate to be late. Of course I never *am*. Ralph tells me I couldn't be late if I set out to be – it isn't in my nature. I always worry I shall be though. Have done all my life. Silly, isn't it? I'll just get the cloths out. They're all clean, as I gave them a good wash last week.' Sorting through the wooden box which housed her polishing materials, Muriel had taken out a couple of well-washed cloths and a tin of brass polish and said, 'Now, I usually start with the big cross.'

'I'll climb up and do that, shall I?'

'How lovely! I always use one of the altar chairs to stand on. Spread this cloth over it first before you climb up, it seems irreverent to stand on the tapestry seat without a cover. Here's your Brasso and this one's the putting-on cloth. I'll make a start on the lectern.'

Together they had rubbed and polished and buffed until all the brasswork gleamed. When they'd finished they sat together in the front pew to admire their handiwork.

'It all looks so beautiful,' Muriel sighed. 'You know, we have some wonderful old silver things for the altar on high days and holy days. They're kept locked away in the safe when they're not in use; they're too valuable to be on display every day. But I'd miss cleaning the brass if the silver was out all the time. So satisfying, isn't it, when it's all shining?'

'It is. It looks lovely.'

'I'm always reminded of that penniless acrobat who in desperation went to seek shelter in a monastery. I can't remember where I heard the story, maybe it was in a sermon? The monks fed him and gave him a bed and he stayed for a few days. When he knew it was time to move on he didn't know how to thank God for their loving care. He'd no money to give, he couldn't sing like they did, he hadn't the first idea about how to pray, but he could turn cartwheels and things. So he did. Right in front of the altar. He gave the performance of his life. It was the only thing he could do, you see, to thank God. I'm sure God must have smiled on him, don't you think? So, I keep hoping He smiles on me for doing the polishing, for I haven't much more to offer than that. I haven't skills like you have, for teaching and such. I'm not terribly clever, you see. Whereas you, you've so much to offer. There, I'll be off.' Muriel had stood up and looked down at her. 'Thank you for your help, my dear. I'm glad you've got things sorted out. We all of us need to be at peace with ourselves.' Muriel had kissed her cheek and left with her polishing box under her arm.

Kate had felt very humbled. She'd sat a while longer after Muriel had left, pondering on how foolish she had been. She'd been within an ace of being killed in her desperation to rescue Cat, but Peter had grabbed her arm and forcibly dragged her to the door: the other women had been too intent on saving their own skins to bother about her and Cat – so much for the sisterhood. A bond wrought by fear wasn't the strongest, after all. All that was left of all that business was Simone's remains, laid to rest in the churchyard. She knew Peter had had a struggle with his conscience about that, but in the end he'd agreed. She'd no one but herself to blame for being taken in by Simone. She'd wept silent tears for Jacob, for Simone, and for Simone's children.

She'd been to see them. Though they'd cried when they saw her because she reminded them of their mother, she could see how much better they were all looking. She was sure Dickon had grown; he'd certainly put on weight. Florentina was wearing a delightful outfit and her hair was well-washed and brushed and tied in bunches with matching ribbons. She'd even smiled a little. Hansel and Valentine were bright-eyed and energetic as all little boys should be. But Opal! The biggest change was in her. She'd blossomed from a thin, listless sort of baby with enormous dark eyes in a pale luminous face, to being bouncy and giggly and quite adorable.

Their foster-mother was a large, comfortable woman who obviously enjoyed having them. When Kate had thanked her, she'd laughed. 'Don't be silly, I'm loving it. Couldn't believe my ears when they rang me and said "It's an emergency, we've got five for you!" We've only just started fostering, you see. The kiddies have transformed our lives. In fact, my hubby and I have talked about asking to adopt them all. We've got this big house and garden going to waste. It's hard work, mind, 'cos they've got problems, as you can imagine – tantrums and bad temper and the like, and the four older ones need training in more ways than one. Sometimes when I go to bed, I am so tired I feel like sending them all back! But I'm hoping good food, and a routine and love, most of all love, will solve everything. It'll all come right, given time.'

'I'm sure it will. I'll keep in touch.'

'I'd be glad if you would. You'll be like family you see, for them.'

'Of course.'

And she would keep in touch. She owed them that; it was the least she could do. No, that wasn't absolutely true. She *wanted* to see them again. She couldn't take them on herself; the school meant too much to her for that. She'd be no good as a mother anyway. But she'd remember their birthdays and take them out.

Well, she'd been given her chance to start afresh and that was what she would do. School was her first priority now. She still had the opportunity to develop it along the lines she wanted; that at least hadn't been taken from her.

Her reverie was brought to a halt by the sight of Brian creeping round to the recycling bin. He lifted the lid and began throwing handfuls of the paper up into the air, scattering it to the four winds, gleefully watching it spiralling away. She rapped briskly on the window. He looked up startled, grinned, and reluctantly began collecting what he could and putting it back into the bin.

The bell rang for afternoon school. She rubbed her hands together in anticipation.

After school Kate went into the Store. Another decision she'd taken that day was that she'd stop being a vegan; she'd be a vegetarian instead. There was a limit to the number of hair-shirts she could tolerate and being a vegan was, she'd realised, one too many.

Jimbo was nowhere to be seen; only Bel Tutt and Linda were there.

Linda called across, 'Hello, Ms Pascoe. Nice day!'

'It certainly is. How are you, Linda? Someone was saying you hadn't been well.'

Linda blushed. 'Well, no, I haven't but I'm much better at the moment.'

'Stomach upset, they said.'

'That's right.' Linda leaned as close to the post office grille as she could get and whispered, 'Well, actually, it wasn't really a stomach upset. I'm expecting.'

'No! Are you pleased?'

She blushed even redder. 'Oh yes. And Alan's thrilled to bits.'

'I am glad. Congratulations!'

'Thanks.' She was about to launch herself on the story of her pregnancy when they heard Jimbo's voice booming out from his office at the back.

'Mother! This I do not believe!' There was a silence and then they heard him say, 'Very well. Of course I'm not saying I don't want . . .' The rest they missed as he had lowered his voice, then they heard the slam of the receiver and he stormed through into the Store. He'd left his boater somewhere, his bow tie was askew and as he marched thunderously up and down between the shelves muttering to himself, he constantly ran a hand over his bald head.

Linda kept her head down and busied herself with her accounts. Bel Tutt, to escape his wrath, plodded away into the storeroom for further supplies for her shelf-filling. Jimbo almost ran Kate down by the ice-cream freezer.

'So sorry.' He went to raise his boater and found to his amazement it wasn't on his head. 'I do beg your pardon. Running the customers over isn't quite the thing, is it? So sorry.'

'Is there something the matter, Jimbo? You seem very agitated.'

He seemed surprised. 'Do I?' He considered this for a moment. 'Well, I am. Very. What Harriet is going to say I do not know. May God have mercy on my soul because I'm going to need it.'

'Is it something I can help you with?'

He gazed distractedly at her and then said, 'Would that you could! Linda, I'm going home. I could be back in ten minutes, on the other hand if I'm not, you'd better order flowers; sprays preferably, I don't like wreaths.'

He rushed out of the Store and Kate watched him dash down Stocks Row. Suddenly his footsteps slowed and he stopped, undecided. He turned back, changed his mind, and walked slowly in the direction of home.

Kate said, 'I wonder what on earth is the matter.'

'Well, he did say "Mother", didn't he?'

'Yes, he did.'

'See – his mother's a right you-know-what. "Old cow" comes to mind. Been to stay a few times, she has. Mrs Charter-Plackett can't bear her. They have stand-up rows. Trouble brewing, by the sound of it.'

Kate laughed. 'Well, well, I've never seen Jimbo so upset. Didn't think anything could ruffle *him*.'

'No? You should have seen him when . . .' But Linda had a customer who was in a hurry and wouldn't wait. What was the matter with everyone today? They usually liked a gossip. It was always so much more interesting if the customers lingered a while. Sometimes it took her an hour to tell Alan all the news she'd garnered.

Kate took home her luxury ice cream, and her cheese and her eggs and all the things she'd denied herself for so long, put them away in the fridge and the cupboards and then sat at the kitchen table and ate a whole tub of pecan and toffee ice cream and felt sick. But somehow, released.

Chapter 27

'Mummy? Mummy?'

Jimbo snapped. 'Be quiet, Flick, please.'

'Daddy!'

'I mean it. Just go away and watch TV or something, but don't bother Mummy right now.' Jimbo stood looking out of the window. Harriet sat on the sofa. In reality, the actual distance between them was small but it felt like a million miles. When Jimbo had broken the news about his mother, Harriet had stared at him in disbelief.

'I shan't. Just tell her I shan't.'

'I know, but she's already sold her own.'

'I don't care. As far as I am concerned, she can sleep in a cardboard box in a shop doorway in the Strand. She can be a bag lady. That's right – a bag lady. Serve her right.'

'Now, Harriet.'

'And don't look so reproachfully at me. You don't want her either.'

'I never said that!'

'You didn't need to. Well, I shan't sell Mother's house to her. Definitely not. My mother wouldn't rest easy *ever*, with her in the house.'

'That is ridiculous.'

'No, it's not. Ring her – no, I'll ring her. I'll tell her she's not buying my mother's house. It *is* mine so I can choose who buys it.'

'Now, Harriet.'

'"Now, Harriet" nothing! Watch my lips: I shall say this only once. *Your mother is not living in my mother's house. I won't sell it to her.*'

'Now, Harriet.'

'If you say that once more . . .'

'All right, all right. But she is an old lady and getting very frail.'

'Frail – your mother? God, that's a laugh! Frail – huh!'

'Now, Harriet!'

'Right, that's it. You're not listening to what I'm saying. Sitting on the fence you are and waiting to see which way to jump. Well, I'm not having it.' She got up from the sofa and went to get her coat from the hall cupboard. 'The meal's all ready in the oven. I'll leave you to it.'

'Harriet, please! I haven't agreed anything, you know.'

'No, but you soon will. She'll steamroller you like she always does.'

'She doesn't!'

Harriet looked sadly at him. 'Jimbo, she does. It's not fair. I was so looking forward to Flick being May Queen. Now I shan't enjoy one minute of it, thinking about her coming to live here. It's all ruined. Ruined!' Her eyes brimmed with tears and threatened to spill over onto her cheeks. She shrugged on her coat, picked up her handbag and stormed out of the front door. Flick and Fran were crying and so too, almost, was Jimbo.

He heard the car rev up, watched her drive away, and sent up a silent prayer for her safety. Jimbo scooped up Fran and took hold of Flick's hand. 'We'll get the boys their drink and biscuits out, come on.' He looked down at Flick and her grief-stricken face broke his heart. For her sake he had to stop his voice shaking when he reassured her. 'Don't worry, she'll be back. Mummy's just a bit cross, that's all. She'll have to come back, 'cos she hasn't got her toothbrush with her.'

Flick smiled through her tears and squeezed Jimbo's hand. 'Of course, she'll have to come back. She's so particular about her teeth, isn't she?'

Jimbo discovered Harriet cleaning her teeth when he went to their bathroom. He had been sitting in Fergus' bedroom talking with him man to man about women and the problems they could cause men.

'When all's said and done, Dad, are they worth all the trouble?'

'Definitely. Oh yes. Can't manage without 'em. Bless their hearts.'

'Well, with the problems you've got with Gran and now with Mum.'

'Ah, well. There you are.'

Fergus settled down to sleep and asked as Jimbo was switching off the light, 'She will be back, won't she?'

'Of course.'

Jimbo stood in the bathroom doorway enjoying the sight of Harriet bent over the washbasin. As she rinsed her mouth for the last time she brought up her head and saw him in the mirror. They looked at each other for a moment and he broke the silence.

'You're back.'

'I am.'

'The best I can say is that she can't buy your mother's house, but if she really wants to come and live here, she can buy another house when one becomes empty. How about that?'

'I'll think about it.'

'Thank you.' He paused. 'Where've you been – if I can ask, that is.'

'At the rectory with Caroline.'

'All this time?'

'A lot of it.'

'I see.'

'Do you?' Harriet turned to face him as she spoke.

'I try.'

'I'm going to give the children a goodnight kiss.' Harriet tucked Fran in more tightly and smoothed Flick's hair away from her face and, in the half-light, saw the sleepy smile on her face as she felt her mother's kiss. She took some books off Finlay's bed and straightened his duvet for him, and kissed Fergus who gave her a hug and said, 'Glad you're back, Mum. It's Dad who's been really upset.' Then she too went to bed.

When Jimbo emerged from the bathroom she was sitting up making a list. 'This is my list for Thursday.'

'What's happening on Thursday?'

'May Day.'

'Of course. I'm thrilled Flick's going to be Queen. Who's doing the crowning bit?'

'Muriel.'

'Oh great! It's a lovely thing for Flick and she'll do it superbly. Just like her mother, everything she does, she does well.'

'Jimbo! Flattery will get you nowhere with me.'

'It's true! I shall record the whole event on the old camcorder.'

'Oh, of course! What a good idea. Mother would have gloried in her being Queen. Oh, I do miss her.'

'Of course you do. We all do.' He sat silent on the edge of the bed for a while and then said, 'She was a pearl of great price.'

'She adored you.'

'Did she? I didn't know.'

'I'm sure she'd have married you if you'd have had her.'

Jimbo laughed. 'No! I'm glad I married her daughter.'

'So am I.'

'Forgiven?'

'Almost. But I must let it be known now this minute and then I shall never refer to it again, that I do not get on with your mother. Never have done, never will. But I do appreciate that she isn't getting any younger and needs family about her, but I can't, I *won't* sell her my mother's house. In any case, it's far too big for someone your mother's age.'

'Thank you. I'll warn her off, right? I can't brook her interference either. She's keeping out of the Store, which I know she'd love to reorganise for me, and she's to be kept out of our family affairs. I won't have the boys upset by her constant criticism. And she's not having a key to our house like your mother did, that's definite. Mother did suggest she took over the mail-order now we've no longer got Sadie, but Mrs Jones is doing such a good job, way beyond anything I'd expected, that there's no way I'm putting Mother in charge. So that's the agreement.'

'Right, it's a deal. Oh Jimbo, why didn't you have brothers and sisters, then they could have taken their turn?'

'Having me nearly killed her, she says. Couldn't believe childbirth could be so appalling and so *uncivilised*. So that was that. My father was extremely disappointed.'

Harriet rolled her eyes. 'Some men do have a lot to put up with, don't they?'

Jimbo turned off his bedside light and sighed. 'Indeed

they do. Look at me for instance. Slaving from dawn to dusk. Money to find for two sons at Prince Henry's, and soon even more for a daughter at Lady Wortley's *and* she's being May Queen so there's the dress to pay for, an incredibly pretty small daughter to feed and clothe,' he paused, 'and sadly, truth to tell, the biggest fly in the ointment is the wife. I can see there's going to be no end to my troubles . . . ever.' In the darkness at his side of the bed he grinned, thumped his pillow and laid down. Harriet kicked him.

'Ow!! That hurt.'

'I'm glad.'

There was a silence while Jimbo rubbed his leg. 'The children were very upset.'

'I'm sorry. I was just so angry and you didn't seem to be listening.'

'I was and I am. I'm torn, you see.'

'I know. But if I can be assured you're on my side, then that's all right.'

'I am.'

'Good. I'll finish this list and then . . .'

'Right.'

Harriet wasn't the only one with a list. Kate had one, too. Thursday was proving a hectic day. She'd worked all week with the children – cajoling, inspiring, organising. There wasn't a stone left unturned. Hetty Hardaker had to admit that for organisation Kate couldn't be bettered. 'I thought Mr Palmer had everything at his fingertips, but you . . .'

'Thanks, Hetty. Thanks for all your help, too. Without you we couldn't have managed.'

Hetty flushed with pleasure. 'I'm sorry I was so awkward to begin with. But some of it was justified, wasn't it?'

Kate smiled. 'Yes, it was. But I think now we've come to an understanding.'

'You've changed since you came. All the witchcraft business, it wasn't right. It felt so lovely going into church on Friday for prayers. You have to admit Peter is good with children.'

'He is. Very good.'

'Now, back to basics. Margaret wants to know how she will know when to commence playing the piano when she's out on the Green and can't see for all the parents. We could do with a couple of mobile phones.' They walked away together discussing the whys and wherefores. With only two hours to go there was still a lot to do.

Mercifully the sun had decided to shine. Occasionally a cloud came over but it remained dry which was as well because the piano, and the maypole, and the children's chairs awaiting the parents and friends were already out on the grass. Someone, somewhere must be smiling on them, Kate thought.

Mr Fitch had given permission for a couple of his estate-workers who were parents to give a hand, and as Kate and Hetty went back into the hall they were heaving the large wooden boxes which, fixed together, would create a dais for the Queen and her attendants to sit on for the crowning and where Flick would sit to preside over the dancing.

'I've got a gorgeous bright red Indian cloth for covering the dais – I'll bring it out in a moment. The Queen's chair is here, look, already decorated.'

'Thanks, Ms Pascoe, we'll just get these sorted first. All right, Bill. Your end first.' They staggered out with two of the boxes, down the narrow passage to the main door. Kate watched them squeeze out and as they left, in came Greenwood Stubbs. He touched his cap to Kate and said, 'Mr Fitch has asked me to bring you some plants to decorate the platform for the Queen.'

'Oh, Mr Stubbs, how kind! Why, they're magnificent.'

'This is just two of them – there's a vanload outside. Barry Jones has brought them down for me. Come out and tell me where to put them all.'

'A vanload? This I don't believe.'

She rushed outside and was stunned by how beautiful they looked.

'How's that then?' Barry laughed at her delight. 'Brilliant, eh?'

'Yes – brilliant!'

'We've to put them all out for you and then we'll collect them at the end. Except you've to choose the one you like best and keep it. It's a present from Mr Fitch. He's coming, he says, if that's all right.'

'Of course it is. Right – they need to be banked round the dais when Bill and Ben have put it together.'

Barry gave a mock salute. 'As you say, Ms Pascoe. Where's the Queen? Just need a glimpse of her, can't stay to watch.'

'She's inside already dressed. Go and take a look.'

He found Flick seated on Ms Pascoe's chair, the skirt of her white dress spread carefully out so as not to crease it. On her head she had a small circlet of fresh flowers, her long plaits had been undone and her hair was hanging down her back shining and bright. Her eyes were alive with pleasure.

'Why, Flick! You look gorgeous, absolutely terrific! Has Pat seen yer yet?'

Flick was blushing. Barry always made her feel like that. 'Thank you, Barry. No, she hasn't.'

'I'll tell her to come and take a look. Best May Queen in years.' He bowed like some eighteenth-century courtier, gave a flourishing wave at the door and disappeared.

Harriet, too, couldn't believe how pretty Flick looked. It was Fran who had the beauty in their family but today, somehow, it was Flick's turn. Flick waggled her white satin pumps in the air and said, 'Aren't they just beautiful, Mummy? I could be a bridesmaid in these, couldn't I?'

'You could. Fran – no, don't pull them off.'

'Let her. You try one on, Fran.' Fran did so. Flick always let her have her own way with everything.

The classroom was full of mothers dressing the attendants, changing the Maypole dancers into their outfits, teachers rushing in and out with messages, Pat collecting the last of the home-made refreshments everyone had volunteered, children getting underfoot, teachers disciplining the wayward ones.

The temperature and the tempers began to rise. With only half an hour to go, Kate was beginning to fray. 'Yes, that's right, they all sit on the left. No, not the Maypole dancers. They stay with me – right! OK?'

The questions were unending, the children excited, the parents almost beyond control and there sat Flick enjoying every minute of her reign.

In the midst of it all, Muriel arrived. 'Should I be here or out there?'

'Lady Templeton! There you are. We've borrowed chairs from the church hall and you and Sir Ralph are to sit on the front row of them in the middle. There are names on the seats. There's a quarter of an hour to go.'

'I must be in your way. I'll leave you to it, you're obviously busy. And the crown?'

'Ah! Sebastian Prior has the crown. He'll present it to you on a velvet cushion at the appropriate moment.'

'I've prepared a short speech – just a couple of lines.'

'Lovely!'

'Oh Flick, my dear. How pretty you look!' Muriel's eyes filled with tears. She bent down and kissed her on either cheek. 'You make a wonderful May Queen!'

Muriel smiled at Harriet, and Harriet smiled back.

Gilbert came in then. 'Ms Pascoe, we're here!'

Kate turned to look at him – a transformed Gilbert. A Gilbert with a blackened face and a bowler hat covered with bright feathers and badges, and a black jacket to which he'd fastened gaily-coloured strips of material. On his feet were boots, and on his ankles bells which jingled at every step he took. 'As promised!'

'Wonderful! I could give you a kiss!'

'Past experience tells me you'll have a black face if you do! Just reporting in. We're sitting on the grown-ups' chairs awaiting our turn. Is that all right?'

'Of course – here's the programme of events. Keep that. Flick will call upon you to perform.'

'At your service, Your Majesty!' Gilbert grinned at Flick and left.

Seated alongside Muriel and Ralph and in front of the Morris dancers were Mr Fitch and Louise.

Gilbert had given her one of his special smiles when he'd come to take his place. Mr Fitch, arms folded, leant towards her and whispered out of the corner of his mouth, 'When are you going to marry that man?'

Louise blushed. 'Shortly.'

'Good. Not before time, from what I hear.'

Louise blushed even redder. The cheek of the man. Really! And she thought no one but her mother knew. You couldn't do a thing in this village.

On the other side of Mr Fitch sat Muriel. She'd been waiting for her chance and now it had come. While Ralph went to help Margaret Booth readjust the piano stool and devise a method of keeping her music from blowing away while she played, Muriel took the bull by the horns.

'Mr Fitch.'

'Craddock please, Muriel.'

'Craddock then. You know I've beeen very disappointed with you of late.'

He looked startled. 'Disappointed, with me? What about?'

'About lacking understanding.'

'If I've been tactless about something, please put me right.'

'Sometimes one does more good, you know, by *not* doing something than by doing it.'

'You're speaking in riddles, Muriel. I don't understand.' He followed her gaze and realised she was looking at Ralph.

'It's about cricket. The whole village are grateful for what you've done with the pavilion and the equipment, believe me they are, but they don't like . . .'

'Yes?'

'They don't like you trying to lord it over them.'

Mr Fitch began to boil. Lord it over them? Not him! Ralph did that – he was an expert at it. He himself did nothing but good. *Nothing but good.*

Muriel, staring into the distance, said, 'It's tradition, you see, that's what counts. The village likes to keep its traditions. Like today. Like Stocks Day and the Village Show.' She turned towards him and smiled at him in such a genuinely kindly way that he felt uncomfortable, and knew she was going to get him to do something he didn't want to. 'And the cricket team comes under the same heading, you see,' she went on gently. 'They want things to remain as they were. There's a place for tradition and a place for progress, we need them both. So for your sake, *not* Ralph's, you need to let him be president of the cricket club.'

The village green was bustling with life. Mothers and the dads who could spare the time from work were squatting on the school chairs; the throne for the Queen was ready; the flowers arranged around the dais giving it glorious colour; the Punch and Judy man was waiting his turn beside his red-and-white striped booth; the horses on the merry-go-round were poised to spring into action. Now, round the corner of the Village Store trotted a procession of the playgroup children coming to take their places, led by Beth and Alex walking hand-in-hand. The Maypole was waiting, the dancers self-conscious in their costumes sitting around its foot. Muriel watched Ralph talking to some of the parents on his way back to his seat, and she thought how much she loved him. Her love for him gave her courage.

'Well, Craddock?'

'You've a very persuasive way with you, Muriel Templeton. Very persuasive. But I don't see what I shall gain if I step down.'

'You won't gain anything visible or tangible, but you will march to the same drum as them if you do.'

'March to the same drum?'

'Think about it.' The piano burst into life. 'Oh, they're about to begin, and I've forgotten to look at my speech, and here comes Ralph. Oh dear, and now I can't find my speech – where did I put it?' Mr Fitch bent down and picked up a piece of paper from under Muriel's chair.

'This it?'

'Oh, thank you.'

There came a breathless hush as Muriel waited for one of the attendants to remove Flick's circlet of flowers. Then she held the crown high above Flick's head and said in ringing tones, 'On this wonderful gloriously happy day, I have the great honour to crown Felicity Jane Charter-Plackett Queen of the May. Long may she reign! Long live Queen Felicity!!'

Peter stood up and called for three cheers for the Queen. *Hip Hip Hurray! Hip Hip Hurray! Hip Hip Hurray!!*

Queen Felicity stood up, her crown, plain gold-coloured metal with ten points around the top, each with a large pearl attached, its red velvet edge nicely placed along the top of her forehead, and said in a loud clear voice: 'I thank you all for coming to my crowning today. I hope you will all enjoy yourselves. My subjects will now perform the traditional Maypole dancing, for your delight.'

The crowd sat down again, ready to be entertained. Margaret Booth at the piano performed miracles and the dancers were inspired. Their final dance, the 'Spider's Web' was the most complicated, and when they finished the intricate weaving and unravelling of the ribbons, the crowd got to its feet as one and clapped and cheered.

'Brilliant!'

'Wonderful!'

'Well done!'

They watched the Punch and Judy Show, jeering and hissing and clapping at all the right moments, and when Flick announced the Morris Dancers there was a cheer of delight. Chairs were moved to make a bigger space in front of the Queen. Gilbert played a lively tune on his melodeon and the dancing began.

Kate was beside herself. She was standing at the back watching everyone. It was all going perfectly splendidly. She couldn't have asked for a more worthwhile and rewarding afternoon. Gilbert was giving it all he'd got, playing with gusto while his dancers nimbly entertained the crowds. It seemed impossible that in his working life Gilbert was a serious academic. At this moment, he was a medieval man celebrating the First of May like villagers had been doing for centuries. The crowd began clapping and an impromptu group near Kate got up from their chairs and began dancing too. She laughed. What fun! Someone dragged hold of her hand and pulled her in and made her dance. She didn't know what was expected of her but she joined in just the same. It didn't seem to matter. Nothing did except total happiness.

When the applause for the Morris dancers had died down, Queen Felicity announced from her throne that tea was being served and the merry-go-round would begin shortly.

There was no need for Kate to help with the refreshments for Pat had got that under her control. There was obviously more to Pat than she had realised and Kate felt quite disappointed that Pat would be leaving the school when she got married. Apparently she was going to work for Jimbo in his catering business. Well, she would be well qualified for that, judging by this afternoon. Then Kate felt a small hand slip into hers. She looked down and saw it was Beth's.

'Hello, Beth, isn't this lovely?'

'Yes. I'd like to be Queen when I'm big.'

'Would you?'

'Can I wear a crown like Flick's?'

'Of course. I'll remember.'

Beth looked up at her and smiled. 'I like playgroup at your school.'

'I'm glad.'

'It's nice.' She looked up again. '*You're* nice.'

'Thank you. And so are you.'

'I like you next best after my mummy.'

'That's only right. Your mummy comes first. Here she is – look.'

Caroline was walking towards them, hand-in-hand with Alex. 'Oh there you are, Beth! I've been looking for you. Do you want squash or tea?'

'Squash, please. Mummy, Miss Pascoe says I can be Queen when I'm big. Isn't she nice?'

Caroline looked at Kate, and Kate looked at her.

It was Caroline who smiled first. 'Wonderful afternoon, Kate. I've had a lovely time. You must feel delighted with yourself.'

'Good, I'm glad you've enjoyed it. Thank you.'

'Come along then and we'll get you your squash.' Caroline walked away with the two children leaving Kate feeling grateful that things had thawed a little between the two of them.

'Kate!' It was Harriet bringing her a cup of tea. 'I've come to say thank you for giving Flick such a wonderful afternoon. She's loved it.'

'Oh! Tea – just what I need! Thank *you* for having such a smashing daughter. She's done well, really well. I'm proud of her. She'll be in her element at Lady Wortley's, I'm sure.'

'You don't mind any more then?'

'No. Why shouldn't she have the chance?'

'Thanks. I didn't want to remain at loggerheads about it. After all, I've got Fran coming along!'

'I expect I shall be here still. This place gets into your bones, doesn't it?'

'It certainly does. I'm glad you've come here – the school did need a shake-up, though I won't have a bad word said about Mr Palmer'.

'Certainly not.'

'Hold it, you two, keep talking!' It was Jimbo with his camcorder. 'I've filmed just about everyone else so I

mustn't miss the chief organiser of the event, must I?'
He filmed busily whilst Kate and Harriet chatted.

Kate interrupted him. 'There's Hetty signalling.
Must go. Sorry, Jimbo!' She dashed away.

'All right, darling, you can take a break.'

Jimbo switched off the camcorder and stayed to talk.
'Wasn't Flick lovely? I'm so proud of her.'

'So am I. I almost cried.'

'Hope the thought of Mother coming hasn't ruined
the day for you?'

'No, but I'm not looking forward to it.'

'Perhaps she's run out of steam a bit now she's older.'

'I doubt it, Jimbo.'

He shifted the camcorder to his other hand and put
an arm round Harriet's shoulder. 'I shan't let her upset
you, honestly I won't. She's an old dragon and we shall
have some tempestuous times while she settles in, but I
shall keep her under control if I die in the attempt!'
Flick came walking sedately towards them, remembering to hold her head carefully because of her crown.
'Here she comes, Queen for a day.'

'Mummy, do you think it wouldn't be queenly to
take my crown off? I can't do a thing when I'm wearing
it.'

'Take it off, and go and enjoy yourself. Even queens
are allowed a bit of fun sometimes. Here, give it to me.'

Flick gave Harriet her posy of flowers too and ran off
to queue for a ride on the merry-go-round.

Ralph was having a cup of tea. He'd lost Muriel somewhere; no doubt she was helping in one capacity or
another. What a lovely afternoon he'd had. And the
summer only just begun. What fun life could be. He
spotted Mr Fitch threading his way across the green
towards him. Oh no, not old Fitch today.

'Afternoon, Craddock,' he said affably. 'Surprised to see you here. Thought this wouldn't be quite your scene.

'I provided the flowers for the dais, Ralph, so I had to come to make sure they looked good. Got to keep up standards, you know.' Mr Fitch cleared his throat. 'I've been thinking.'

'Yes?'

'This cricket business . . . I've been wondering if perhaps I've made a mistake. The way I see it, you and I each have our own role to play. I play the benefactor, you do the paternal bit. So I've given it my earnest consideration and the long and the short of it is, I really think it would be best if you were president of the club.'

'I see.'

'Tradition and all that, you know. All part and parcel of village life. Best if you're president. People will like that. Afternoons like this make one realise how important tradition is.'

'Well, I must say, Craddock, that's very generous of you. I shan't refuse. Tradition is it, that made you stand down?'

'That's right.'

Ralph followed the other man's gaze, which was focused on Muriel standing behind the huge teapot she'd borrowed from the church kitchen. 'I do appreciate your gesture,' he said, then added mischievously, 'I'm glad you came to your decision all by yourself.'

Mr Fitch looked hard at him. 'Oh yes, it was my decision, all right. I make all my own decisions – *after* I've weighed up the evidence.'

'Of course, just like me.' Ralph raised his cup in salutation to Muriel, and in acknowledgement of the smile she was giving him. 'Thanks anyway.'

'My pleasure. It doesn't affect the name over the pavilion though – that stays.'

'Naturally. Your generosity has to be acknowledged. I wouldn't want it any other way. All the arrangements for Saturday are well in hand. Opening ceremony at two forty-five. Game commences at three. Jimbo's doing the food for the inaugural match like we arranged.'

Mr Fitch said, 'Send me the bill.'

'Well, that's even more generous of you. We shall be in debt to you for years.'

Mr Fitch ignored Ralph's gratitude and nodding his head in Muriel's direction, he grunted, 'That wife of yours. Was she in the Diplomatic Service too?'

'No, she just has her own way of achieving her objectives.'

'A perfect lady, Ralph. Someone to be treasured. You're a very lucky man'.

'Indeed I am. We were childhood sweethearts and then got separated and met up again quite by chance. Well, maybe it wasn't chance. Perhaps it was meant to be.'

'Childhood sweethearts, eh? I wish, how I wish that Sadie . . .'

Ralph glanced at him and then looked away. Didn't want to embarrass the chap, don't you know. 'I'm sorry, so very sorry. Mrs Beauchamp was much loved.' His voice was gruff.

'She was. Different as cheese from chalk, your Muriel and her, but each quite splendid in their own way.' This time they both raised their cups to Muriel and she blushed bright red.

It was five o'clock by the time everything had been cleared up and the last of the children shooed off home. The Green had returned to its usual quiet self. Jimmy's geese, having at last got their grazing ground back again, were busily marching up and down re-establishing their ownership. Barry Jones' van was heading off to the Big House filled with the plants Mr Fitch had provided. In her hand Kate had the one she had chosen. In her other hand was a bag of cakes Pat had given her. 'Surplus to requirements, so you'd better take them. You've done a great job, Ms Pascoe. Best May Day we've had in years and I've seen my share, I can tell you! I'm glad you've come to Turnham Malpas, and I'm sorry to be leaving the school, but I can't turn down this offer of Mr Charter-Plackett's. It's too good to be true. Bel Tutt will do a good job, I know. Sleep well – I'm sure you will after the day you've had!'

Kate crossed the school playground and slotted her key in the door. She heard a mewing sound, it was Beano and Dandy greeting her return. They stood on her toes, chewed her sandals, jumped up to catch at her skirt with their claws.

'Now you two, in you go. I want a cup of tea. I know, yes I know, you want feeding too.

That night before she went to bed, Kate sat by the open bedroom window in her nightgown, a peach silky affair, and looked out. The sky was still quite bright with small clouds sailing lazily across it. She could just see the new houses Sir Ralph had built, and the trees behind them. Tomorrow after school she'd put on her boots and go for a long walk by the beck. Blow her cobwebs away. She'd been here only four months and yet the place had wound itself round her heart. Their cheers at the end of the afternoon were something she didn't deserve. Truth to tell, she'd nearly brought the village to its knees, and retrieved it only just in time. They seemed to have overlooked that; how generous-hearted they must be. On Saturday she was taking the three older children of Simone's out for the day. She was looking forward to that. In fact, there was a lot to look forward to. Cricket teas. Computers. New children next term. Beano and Dandy. Church. The youth club she intended starting – a debt she had to repay if only for Rhett's sake.

The sun was slowly going down and the village was becoming rosy in the fading light. She could hear the laughter in The Royal Oak. What fun they must be having; a visit there from time to time would be a good idea. She needed other relationships besides those with her children. She drew the curtains and climbed into bed. The awkward corner by the eaves was just the right place for Mr Fitch's plant; after she'd turned out the light the white of the petals glowed in the half-darkness. As Kate closed her eyes, the scent of the flowers reached her and she smiled. She remembered an embroidered picture her grandmother had hanging over her bed. There was a little thatched cottage on it, with a tiny country garden in front, and embroidered underneath were the words: *Home is where the heart is*. As a child she'd never understood it, but now she did.

Puppies Online

Puffin Patrol

Jennifer Gray & Amanda Swift

with illustrations by **Steven Lenton**

Quercus

For Archie
J.G.

For Carol, Gus and Harry
A.S.

For my nephew, Zak
S.L.

First published in Great Britain in 2015 by

Quercus Publishing Ltd
Carmelite House
50 Victoria Embankment
London EC4Y 0DZ

An Hachette UK company

A CIP catalogue reference for this book is available
from the British Library

ISBN 978 1 84866 520 0
EBOOK ISBN 978 1 84866 828 7

1 3 5 7 9 10 8 6 4 2

Printed and bound in Great Britain by Clays Ltd, St Ives plc.

Contents

1
Welcome Back!

On a sunny day in spring, Einstein, a
little brown dachshund puppy, sat on
the back seat of his owner's little car.
The car was stuck in a traffic jam.
Einstein looked up their location on
his owner's tablet computer. '*Traffic
jam*,' he read. I can see the evidence
of that, he thought, looking out of the
window at the long line of cars ahead

and behind. He scratched his ear. But what I want to know is what's *caused* this traffic jam.

Not far behind Einstein's car, a big, fluffy, grey and white Old English sheepdog named Puzzle was peering out of the front window of his owner's smart grey saloon. Perhaps there's been in incident on the road ahead, he thought. Maybe a puppy's been kidnapped?

A little way behind that, a black and white, medium-sized springer

spaniel called Bounce leaned out of
the window of her owner's muddy
white jeep and sniffed the salty sea air.
I hope we get there soon, she thought.
So that I can get out and run around
and have fun!

All three puppies were on their
way to spend their holidays at Sandcliff
Lighthouse Kennels. They had been
there once before and had such an
exciting and fun holiday together.
They couldn't wait to return!

The long line of traffic crawled through the seaside village, along the road by the beach. Eventually the cars containing the three puppies squeezed through the traffic jam, climbed the narrow track up the hillside and pulled up outside the lighthouse.

The puppies jumped out. They were surprised to hear the sound of barking. New kennels had been put up in the garden! Inside the kennels were all sorts of other dogs that the puppies had never seen before.

The puppies greeted each other warmly. Puzzle gave Einstein and

Bounce a lick on the nose. Bounce leaped and barked. And Einstein held out his paw for the other two to shake.

'What's going on?' asked Puzzle.
'I thought it was going to be just us
three staying here again this time.'

'You thought, but you didn't
know,' said Einstein. 'You had no
evidence that it would be just us three
here again this time.'

Puzzle shook his shaggy head in
disbelief. 'I see you're still droning on
like a scientist,' he said. 'I thought you
might be a bit more fun this holiday.'

'Don't worry about that,' said
Bounce, doing little jumps over
Einstein as if Einstein were a cone in
a dog-training session, 'because *I'm*

even more fun than I was last time.
I've learned to juggle *and* I can
balance a ball on my nose.'

'What's the use of that?' asked
Einstein.

'You never know,' said Bounce.
'One day I might join a seaside
circus.'

Just then a girl of about nine
came out of the lighthouse. She wore
a T-shirt, shorts and sandals, and
she was smiling. The three puppies
immediately raced up to her.

'Jackie!' they cried, but of course
all she heard was barking.

'Hello, puppies!' said Jackie, hugging them all at once. 'How lovely it is to see you again!'

Just then Jackie's grandad Trevor, the ex-lighthouse keeper and current owner of the kennels, came out to say hello.

'Welcome, welcome,' he said, shaking the owners' hands and giving the puppies a pat. 'Sorry if you got held up in traffic. The beach has been closed this morning, for some reason. I don't know why.'

'Come and meet the other dogs, puppies,' said Jackie. 'Grandad built some new kennels. He only finished them last week and we're full already!'

'I hope none of them is sharing our bedroom,' said Puzzle. 'I'm not happy sleeping next to someone I don't know. They might bite me in the night.'

'I don't mind sharing our room, but it won't leave much space to play,' said Bounce.

'Let's wait and see what happens,' said Einstein.

They didn't have to wait long, because Jackie called them again to follow her.

'Heel!' she said. The puppies immediately did as they were asked.

Jackie looked impressed. 'Wow!' she said. 'You've really grown up in the last few months.' She led the way to the lighthouse. 'You three are in your old room. We didn't think it was fair for you to have to share, so the other dogs are all in the new kennels. We've made it really nice for them, with comfy baskets and toys, just like you've got.'

Einstein, Puzzle and Bounce raced up the stairs to their bedroom on the second floor of the lighthouse. Then they slid straight back down on the helter-skelter slide that ran around the inside wall. They did this a few times before they decided to stop and unearth all the toys in the box in their bedroom. Once Jackie was sure they were settled she went down to the kitchen to help make the tea.

'Ah, it's good to be back,' said
Einstein, trying out his soft round basket.

'We've got some new toys!' said
Bounce, still digging through the toy
basket. 'Wow! Little plastic balls! I can
use these to practise my juggling.'

'Never mind juggling, let's check
out the den.' Puzzle was staring at
the wooden stairs that led from the
bedroom to the old control room of
the lighthouse. On their last holiday
the puppies had used the control room
as a den. It was a secret meeting place
where they could make plans and go
on the computer.

'I wonder if there's a criminal hiding up there,' said Puzzle.

Einstein sighed. 'Are you still on about criminals? We looked last time, remember, and there wasn't.'

'I know, but one might have moved in since we left,' said Puzzle. 'You have to understand the criminal mind.'

'And you have to understand that I'm trying to have a nap.'

'I'm too excited to sleep,' said Bounce, bouncing up the wooden stairs. 'Come on, you two! Let's go up to the den and make some plans for our holiday.'

Puzzle and Einstein followed
Bounce. When she reached the top of
the stairs she carefully pushed open the
trapdoor to the control room.

'Don't forget to ask for the
password!' Puzzle called up.

'OK,' said Bounce. 'What's the password, Puzzle?'

'I can't remember,' said Puzzle.

'It's "pow-cat",' said Bounce.

'No it's not,' said Einstein.

'I remember now,' said Puzzle. 'It's "cat-pow".'

'It's not that either,' said Einstein. 'It's "cowpat". Now can we just stop talking and get up there?'

Bounce climbed up into the control room, followed by Puzzle. Then they both helped Einstein up because his legs were too short to climb up on his own.

'Wow! I'd forgotten how good the view is from here,' said Bounce, jumping up on to the swivel chair and looking out of the big round windows at the sparkling sea.

'Ah! It's good to be back,' said Einstein, checking out the computer and all the rest of the machinery.

'Right! How are we going to solve the crime?' said Puzzle, grabbing the binoculars.

'There hasn't been a crime,' said Einstein.

'Well, what are we going to do then?' said Puzzle.

'Let's go for a swim,' Bounce suggested.

'I can't swim, remember?' Einstein said.

'All right then, we'll teach you,' Puzzle said to him.

'Good idea!' said Bounce. 'And once you've got the hang of swimming I can teach you to juggle.'

'I see two problems with that plan,' said Einstein. 'Problem number one: I don't want my collar to get wet.' Einstein had a very special collar with a camera hidden in it and the camera would break if it got wet. 'Problem number two: I'm scared of the sea.'

'I can solve problem number one,' said Puzzle. 'You can take your collar-cam off!'

'And I can solve problem number two,' said Bounce. 'We'll teach you in the paddling pool!'

'But I don't even know which stroke to do!' said Einstein, sounding a bit panicky.

'That's easy,' said Bounce. 'Doggy-paddle!'

2
No Puffins

Einstein dipped a toe in the paddling pool. 'It's freezing! I'm not getting in there!'

'You are if I push you,' Puzzle said, edging towards him and giving him a shove.

'Stop it!' Einstein bounced off the side of the paddling pool.

'Honestly, it's fun! Look!' Bounce
dived in.

SPLASH!

Drops of water showered over
Puzzle and Einstein.

'I think I'll join you!' Puzzle
panted. He took a run up.

'Wait until I take my collar
off, can't you!' Einstein cried. Very
carefully he slipped his collar-cam
over his head and hid it under a bush.

SPLOOSH! Puzzle landed in the
water.

This time a deluge of cold water
engulfed Einstein.

'You might as well get in now,'
Bounce said. 'You're wet through
anyway.'

Einstein sighed. 'All right.' He
clambered over the side of the
paddling pool. Some of the air had
gone out of it when Puzzle had
landed. It sagged and wobbled like an
old beanbag.

'Hurry up!' Bounce said.

'I'm trying!' Einstein slipped and slithered. Eventually he did a sort of somersault and landed on his bottom in the water.

'This is how you do doggy-paddle,' Bounce said. She circled her front paws, making a delicate splash.

Einstein copied her. 'I think I'm getting the hang of it!' he said.

'Only because you're sitting down,' Puzzle objected. 'Try it with your back paws off the ground.'

'I can't.' Einstein stood up. 'The water's too shallow.'

There were only about ten centimetres of water left in the paddling pool. It came up to Einstein's tummy.

'How did that happen?' Puzzle asked. 'I'll bet a criminal sneaked up and stole the water when we weren't looking.'

Einstein shook his head. Water dripped off his ears. 'There's a perfectly logical explanation. When *you* jumped in, the water was pushed out. It's called the Archimedes' principle.'

'Arky who?'

'Never mind.'

'There you are, puppies!' The puppies looked round. It was Jackie! She was with her friend Bradley. 'We thought you might like to take a trip over to the island in the boat.'

The island! The puppies glanced at one another. The island was where Mike Dodger lived. *Why would Jackie want to go there?* Mike Dodger was the local villain. He didn't like the puppies, or Jackie and Bradley for that matter. Last time the puppies stayed at the lighthouse they had stopped Mike from stealing some valuable treasure. Mike had ended up in a lot of trouble.

Einstein let out a curious yip.

Jackie seemed to understand. 'Don't worry, we won't go anywhere near Mike's house. We want to see the puffins. Grandad says they come every year at the same time to nest on the island.'

'Hooray!' Bounce leaped out of

the paddling pool. 'I've always wanted to see a puffin! What is a puffin by the way?'

'It's a seabird with a colourful beak,' Einstein told her. 'And how do you know you want to see one if you don't know what it is?'

'I just do!' Bounce said. 'I want to see everything. I love it here so much.'

The three puppies clambered out of the paddling pool. Einstein collected his collar-cam and slipped it back on.

'Let's go,' said Bradley. He threw his backpack over his shoulders. 'I've brought some biscuits in case we get hungry.'

'We'll have to take the boat,' said Jackie. 'The tide's covering the causeway.'

The causeway was a path from the mainland to the island but at high tide it was covered by water.

The children led the way along the cliff path towards the beach where the boat was pulled up on to the sand.

The puppies trotted after them.

'You do realize what this means, don't you?' Puzzle said.

'What?' Bounce chased about, pretending to catch rabbits.

'We can look for clues.'

'What sort of clues?' puffed Einstein. His legs were so short he was struggling to keep up.

'Clues about what Mike Dodger's up to.'

'We don't know he's up to anything,' Einstein said.

'That's why we have to look for clues!'

'That's not logical.'

'Yes it is.'

'No it isn't.'

'Stop arguing,' Bounce said. 'Come and chase rabbits instead. It's way more fun.'

Puzzle charged after her but Einstein didn't have the puff. Luckily Jackie noticed he had dropped behind. She picked him up and gave him a kiss on the nose.

'Silly Einstein,' she said. 'If you didn't spend so much time barking, you wouldn't get so tired.'

Einstein snuggled into her. He couldn't argue with that!

* * *

'Are you sure this is the place?' Bradley asked.

The boat bobbed about in the water.

'I think so,' Jackie said.

'But there aren't any puffins,' Bradley said.

The puppies scanned the island

carefully. The boat was in a safe spot near the beach. Away to their right was Mike's house. To their left the land rose up from the sea in a grassy headland.

'They should be over there,' Jackie said, pointing towards the headland.

'Maybe we should take a closer look,' Bradley suggested.

'OK.'

He and Jackie jumped out and pulled the boat on to the sand. The puppies followed – quietly this time. They didn't want to alert Mike Dodger. And they sensed that something was wrong.

The little group set off towards the headland.

'Grandad said the puffins make their nests in burrows,' Jackie said. 'That's why they like it here. I don't understand where they've gone.'

She flopped down on to the grass

with Bradley. They unpacked the
backpack. Bradley had brought
two lots of biscuits: some chocolate
digestives for him and Jackie and some
dog biscuits in the shape of bones for
the puppies.

'I'm starving!' Puzzle went and sat
beside the children. He gave Jackie a
pleading look with his big eyes and laid
his chin on her knee.

'You can have one in a minute,
Puzzle,' Jackie laughed.

'Why don't you take some photos?'
Bradley suggested to her. 'So that we
can show your grandad.'

Jackie took her mobile phone out of the backpack. She held it up and took some snaps of the deserted hillside.

'Where do you think the puffins have gone?' Bounce whispered to Einstein.

Einstein sniffed about. There were lots of old puffin burrows but they were all empty. 'Search me. Something must have frightened them away,' he said.

'I told you Mike Dodger was up to something,' Puzzle said without looking round. He was still concentrating firmly on the biscuits.

'We don't definitely know it's because of Mike—' Einstein began.

'We don't definitely know it isn't,' Puzzle shot back.

'Here we are.' Jackie opened the packet of dog biscuits.

'CA-HA-HA! CA-HA-HA! CA-HA-HA!' A horrible cawing came from somewhere above them.

'What's that noise?' Bounce whispered.

The puppies looked up. So did the children.

'Look out!' shouted Bradley. 'It's a seagull!'

An enormous grey and white bird hurtled towards them out of the sky. It snatched the packet of dog biscuits out of Jackie's hand and flew off.

'Give them back!' Bounce set off in pursuit but the seagull flew on to a rock where she couldn't reach it.

'CA-HA-HA! CA-HA-HA! CA-HA-HA!' it cawed, tearing into the biscuit packet with its sharp beak.

'Are you all right?' Bradley asked Jackie.

'I think so!' Jackie smiled bravely. 'And anyway I'm not going to let that horrible bird spoil our fun.' She carefully unwrapped the cellophane on the digestives. 'Just this once, you can have one of these instead!' She gave one each to the puppies.

The puppies wolfed the biscuits down.

'Now come here,' Jackie said. 'I'll take a selfie.'

'What's that?' asked Einstein.

'I know,' said Bounce. 'It's when you take a photo of yourself on a phone. My owner does it all the time so she can show me the exciting places she's been to.' Bounce's owner was a stuntwoman. She travelled all over the world.

'Oh, OK,' Einstein said. He straightened his collar.

The two children knelt down with

the three puppies in front of them.
Everyone crowded into the picture.

'Smile!' said Jackie. She pressed the
button. 'Let's do another one with the
puppies on our laps,' she said.

They did that too.

'Now let's get one of the puppies
on their own!'

'This is fun!' Einstein barked.

Very soon the puppies were having
such a lovely time making silly faces
for the photos that they
forgot all about
the annoying
seagull.

3
Poo Alert!

'Look!' said Jackie. 'No puffins.'

The next morning Jackie was showing Trevor the photos she'd taken of the empty hillside. They were sitting outside the lighthouse on deckchairs while all the dogs played in the garden.

'Nopuffins!' said Bounce. 'Let me see!'

She rushed over to Jackie and rested her head on Jackie's arm so that she could see the photos. Einstein and Puzzle followed their bouncy friend.

'I can't see them,' said Bounce.

'That's because they're not there,' said Puzzle.

'But Jackie said there were "nopuffins". I want to see if they look different from puffins.'

Einstein sighed. 'There's no such thing as a "nopuffin". Jackie just means there *AREN'T ANY PUFFINS*. No offence, Bounce, but sometimes you are quite silly.'

Bounce turned away from Jackie and hung her head. Einstein could see that he had made her feel sad. He tried to cheer her up.

'But you're good at lots of things,' he said to her.

'Like what?' asked Bounce.

'Like . . . swimming!' said Einstein. 'Could you give me another lesson?'

'Of course I could!' said Bounce. She jumped up and rushed over to the paddling pool. Einstein followed her.

'I'll stay here and listen for clues,' said Puzzle. 'I'm good at that.' And he sat very still with his head cocked to